Pan Study Aids

Accounts and Book-keeping

R. Warson

Pan Books London and Sydney
in association with **Heinemann Educational Books**

First published 1981 by Pan Books Ltd,
Cavaye Place, London SW10 9PG
in association with Heinemann Educational Books Ltd
ISBN 0 330 26116 9

Printed and bound in Great Britain by
Richard Clay (The Chaucer Press) Ltd, Bungay, Suffolk

Pan Study Aids
Titles published in this series
Accounts and Book-keeping
Biology
Chemistry
Commerce
Economics
Effective Study Skills
English Language
French
Geography 1 *Physical and Human*
Geography 2 *British Isles, Western Europe, North America*
History 1 *British*
History 2 *European*
Human Biology
Maths
Physics

Brodies Notes on English Literature
This long established series published in Pan Study Aids now contains more than 150 titles. Each volume covers one of the major works of English literature regularly set for examinations.

Contents

Acknowledgements

The publishers are grateful to the following exam boards, whose addresses are listed on page 7, for permission to reproduce questions from examination papers:

Associated Examination Board, Joint Matriculation Board, University of London School Examinations Department, Royal Society of Arts Examinations Board.

To the student

This Study Aid is not intended to be a complete accounting text up to GCE O level; primarily it is designed to be used for revision purposes by those who, having covered the basis of their particular syllabus, are preparing for a public examination.

Time and time again students do not do themselves justice in the examination because of inadequate guidance in examination techniques and insufficient practice in answering suitable examination-style questions on the many topics that make up the syllabus. A glance at any examination paper shows that on any one topic (e.g. depreciation) there is no set way in which the problem is put. Particularly at O level, questions are often quite lengthy and it is sometimes difficult to interpret and understand them. Again, any one question may require knowledge of several areas of the syllabus; thus a final accounts problem is likely to need an understanding of depreciation, bad debts, expense adjustments, direct and indirect charges. This Study Aid gives the student the opportunity to meet the many and varied problems set by examiners, and shows how they can best be tackled. It is intended for those taking a GCE O level or equivalent examination of any of the boards, the Elementary Stage of the London Chamber of Commerce, Stage I of the Royal Society of Arts and similar commercial examining bodies as well as Elementary and Intermediate stages of Pitman's Examination Institute. It more than adequately covers the Business Education Council General level option module in book-keeping (which is rather below Stage I), and the Certificate in Secondary Education syllabus of all the regional bodies. It will also prove extremely useful for BEC National students on their compulsory core module 'Numeracy and accounting' and also for RSA Stage II candidates.

A comparison of various examinations may assist readers – the following assessment reflects both the range of topics in the syllabus as well as the marking standard. The list is in order of levels of difficulty, beginning with the lowest (CSE has been excluded as its awards are graded).

1 Pitman I; BEC General
2 London Chamber of Commerce Elementary, and Royal Society of Arts I
3 Pitman II
4 GCE O } about the same standard
5 RSA II and LCC Inter. }
6 GCE A – note that there is a very big gap between O and A and therefore only those who obtain a good pass grade in GCE O (an A or a B) should consider commencing studies for (6).

Note also that though examinations may be called 'Book-keeping', 'Book-keeping and accounts', 'Principles of accounts' or 'Accounting', nowadays they all test 'principles' – the days when one could achieve success by learning rules-of-thumb are long since gone. So you, the student, need to understand the principle involved; then you must know how to apply it – just as you may know the principles of car driving but need considerable practice before you can be called a driver. Remember that in accounting, the topics are interdependent, which means that, having mastered one topic, you will need its understanding for a later one. 'I hear and I forget, I see and I remember, *I do and I understand*' should be your motto. It is constant practice that is required.

Many students may well have dealt with the whole of a syllabus either in the classroom, on a correspondence course, or by private study, but may still fail because of insufficient guidance and assistance in the techniques of answering questions. This need not be the students' fault: they may have missed classes, have been taught badly, or have suffered from timetable dislocations. It would be quite wrong, therefore, to assume that all readers have had a thorough grounding in the subject to their examination level, and so the first chapter deals fairly briefly, but adequately, with some basic book-keeping principles and procedures; it is vital that these are understood before proceeding to Chapter 2.

The exam boards

The addresses given below are those from which copies of syllabuses and past examination papers may be ordered. The abbreviations (AEB, etc.) are those used in this book to identify actual questions.

Associated Examining Board (AEB)
Wellington House
Aldershot, Hants GU11 1BQ

University of Cambridge Local Examinations Syndicate (CAM)
Syndicate Buildings
17 Harvey Road
Cambridge CB1 2EU

Joint Matriculation Board (JMB)
(Agent) John Sherratt and Son Ltd
78 Park Road, Altrincham
Cheshire WA14 5QQ

London Chamber of Commerce and Industry (LCC)
Commercial Education Scheme
Marlowe House
Station Road
Sidcup, Kent DA15 7BJ

University of London School Examinations Department (LOND)
66–72 Gower Street
London WC1E 6EE

Oxford Delegacy of Local Examinations (OX)
Ewert Place
Summertown
Oxford OX2 7BZ

Northern Counties Technical Examinations Council (NCTEC)
5 Grosvenor Villas
Grosvenor Road
Newcastle upon Tyne NE2 2RU

Northern Ireland Schools Examination Council (NI)
Examinations Office
Beechill House
Beechill Road
Belfast BT8 4RS

North West Regional Advisory Council For Further Education (NWRAC)
Town Hall
Walkden Road, Worsley
Manchester M28 4QE

The Royal Society of Arts Examinations Board (RSA)
Murray Road
Orpington
Kent BR5 3RB

Southern Universities Joint Board (SUJB)
Cotham Road
Bristol BS6 6DD

Welsh Joint Education Committee (WEL)
245 Western Avenue
Cardiff CF5 2YX

Examination technique

This section is to help you make sure you do yourself justice in the examination, so that if you have worked conscientiously, and with understanding, you will pass by a comfortable margin. Experience has shown that, generally speaking, students do somewhat worse 'on the day' compared with their performance outside the examination hall, e.g. a 'mock' or trial test. So it is dangerous to be complacent; aim high, do not be content with a mere pass. The minimum percentage mark necessary for success may vary slightly from one examination to another, but it is safe to assume that around fifty per cent is the magic figure. (You will find in this book advice on marking schemes given at various points.)

Before the examination

1 Study the examining body's regulations yourself and make sure your entry form is submitted in time. Though college tutors do assist in providing necessary information, it is your responsibility not theirs.
2 Obtain a copy of the current year's syllabus. Libraries normally carry these but if not you can obtain regulations and the syllabus direct from the examining body; they expect 'cash with order', so if you do not know the exact sum send a crossed cheque (leaving the amount blank) marked 'NOT OVER £1' – even with current inflation that sum should suffice! Syllabus changes are announced at least a year in advance, and most bodies indicate changes clearly (e.g. by a black vertical line in the margins where appropriate).
3 Also obtain up to six recent question papers – the regulations will tell you how to purchase them, or alternatively adopt the technique in point 2 allowing 30p per paper. Note however that objective test questions are usually not sold. (See notes on p. 205 about the new-style AEB examination, from June 1982.)

4 Your examination admission slip should arrive several weeks before the date concerned – make sure you know where you have to go and how to get there.
5 Aim to arrive thirty minutes before the scheduled time – take adequate personal stationery (pens, pencils, ruler, eraser). Liquid paper-correction fluid (as used in typing) is very useful for corrections; if calculators are allowed see that you have a spare battery.

Tackling the question paper

1 Read the instructions carefully. Usually the total possible marks per question are indicated – if there is no choice and marks are not shown, do not assume that there will be the same allocation for each.
2 Work out roughly how much time you can spend per question, based on the marks indicated, and allow at least ten minutes at the beginning for reading through the questions and, say, twenty minutes at the end in case you overrun your time – if you do not need them, then you have earned a bonus period for checking.

   Example: 3 hours overall, therefore 150 minutes' work to be planned: Section A: 2 questions at 26 marks = 52; Section B: 3 questions at 16 marks = 48. So provisionally plan to spend about 75 minutes on each section, i.e. Section A about 35 minutes each question; Section B about 25 minutes each question. Time each question but do not panic if you overrun slightly; however, do not spend too long trying to get a correct solution. This can happen on the type of question (e.g. final accounts – see Chapter 6) where you may not know definitely you are right but where normally you will realize if you are wrong. It does no harm to add a note for the examiner, e.g. 'Balance sheet totals do not agree, unable to find errors.'

   In the Joint Matriculation Board examination, Section A consists of short questions (all compulsory) and carries twenty per cent of the total marks and you are *advised* by the JMB to spend not more than half an hour on it.
3 In which order should your chosen questions be tackled? There is a strong case for commencing with the question(s) on which you feel you can earn good marks in the time available. This will increase your confidence. Many students like to answer a final accounts question first – if there is one. One

advantage of this is that often it is not too difficult to earn the minimum pass mark even if you cannot deal satisfactorily with every point. However, look carefully at Chapter 6, where some pitfalls in final accounts are referred to.

4 Sometimes you feel you have insufficient time to make the necessary changes in your answer to correct an error you may have made. In these circumstances, make it quite clear by writing a note (or drawing arrows) to show the effect of the correction; an expense item which you debited to profit & loss a/c instead of trading a/c (say, carriage on purchases): '£160 carriage on purchases should be a trading a/c item. Reduce GP by £160.'

5 You may feel there is an ambiguity in a question or that insufficient information is provided. Deal with the former by a note: 'I have assumed that . . .' Regarding the latter, it is possible that you have to make certain deductions to arrive at the correct decision. For example, 'carriage/duty on imports' can only refer to purchases (for you cannot import your sales!) so it will be a trading a/c item.

6 The answer book is likely to have eight sheets including ordinary ruled A4 paper, ledger ruling and two-column cash or journal ruling. *You* make the decision how to make the best use of the answer book. Unless instructed otherwise, give the whole of an answer consecutively on one sort of paper, even if this means that a written answer to a part of a question is on book-keeping paper. For example, part (a) may ask you to explain why some businesses make a provision for bad debts and part (b) may involve writing up the various ledger accounts from given data. The answer to the whole question can be given on ledger ruling. If part of an answer has to be in another part of the answer book then indicate this clearly on both pages involved (additionally write a note: '5(c) – see page 7').

7 Work neatly, writing figures clearly and keeping them aligned vertically – this aids addition/subtraction. Remember that the examiner needs to be able to follow what you have done. It is unnecessary to write in '00' representing 'no pence' – use a dash in the pence column. The £ sign is also unnecessary as a prefix to each sum of money entered into an account. Try to fit the figures into the space available and enter the decimal place quite boldly when you are not using the account columns, e.g. £68.54.

8 Some help with arithmetic: As well as basic addition, subtraction, multiplication and division, you are likely to have to do percentage calculations (which of course are only combined multiplications and divisions). Note the following points:

(a) Keep 'derived' figures in pencil until you are reasonably sure they are correct. Alternatively use correcting fluid. This is particularly important in situations where an error will have a 'snowball' effect – so if gross profit is wrong, net profit and balance sheet will be incorrect.

(b) Check calculations by another method. Thus in the following example add from the 7 upwards then confirm your total by working downwards from the 8. Often it is helpful to insert a subtotal as shown – even though textbooks rarely do this. So the steps are:

1 find subtotal, i.e. 940,
2 add credit side 1,015,
3 enter 1,015 on debit side,
4 1,015−940 = 75,
5 check 940+75 = 1,015

258	750
21	265
654	
7	
940	
75	
1,015	1,015

Similarly, double-check multiplications by divisions, e.g. (i) 819÷9 = 91, so (ii) 9×91 = 819.

(c) Percentages. Generally in examinations the only percentages used are those capable of easy simplification, so: $12\frac{1}{2}\% = \frac{1}{8}$, $25\% = \frac{1}{4}$, $33\frac{1}{3}\% = \frac{1}{3}$, $50\% = \frac{1}{2}$, $66\frac{2}{3}\% = \frac{2}{3}$. Sometimes a percentage calculation can be broken down into two easy steps: 15% of £380 is 10% of £380 = £38 *plus* 5% of £380 = £19 (i.e. half) = £57

Remember that if a power of 10 is involved it is only necessary to move the decimal point: 1% of £695 = $\frac{1}{100}$ of £695 = £6.95. Always do a mental approximation to prevent ridiculous answers: 21% is just over $^1/_5$. 72% is a little less than ¾.

9 Arithmetic workings. Show the steps taken to arrive at the answer to a calculation. In the JMB examination two pages are marked 'for rough work'. On other papers allocate a section of the page (e.g. the bottom few lines) for workings and do not cross it out unless it is incorrect. However, no examiner would require you to show steps that are reasonable to do mentally. So to calculate 12½% (which is ⅛) you are *not* required to show the following: 12½% of 687 = $^{12\frac{1}{2}}/_{100} \times 687 = {}^{25}/_{200} \times 687$, etc.

10 Each examination syllabus has its own objectives, and subject matter may differ slightly between boards. However all book-keeping and accounting examinations are intended to test these main objectives:
(a) Knowledge of methods of accounting, terms in use, concepts (i.e. basic principles), and conventions (recognized practices, e.g. a current liability is regarded generally as due to be settled within a year).
(b) Comprehension (i.e. the ability to understand and interpret accounting information and to recognize errors).
(c) Application – using your knowledge and understanding to deal with a given situation.
(d) Evaluation – comparing items of information and assessing information from records and documents; for example, commenting on the year's financial results from the final accounts and making a comparison with a previous year.
(e) Presentation – ability to present data in a clear, concise and neat manner and to write clearly about accounting topics.

11 The new-style AEB examination (reproduced on p. 206). The AEB are introducing a new style examination for the academic year 1981–2, and although this Study Aid has taken this into account candidates sitting in 1981 are assured that the types of question that will be set then are fully covered.

Objective testing

The new AEB exam includes an 'objective test' with fifty items in it. There will be two types of question:

1 **Multiple-choice** There will be thirty-five of these. In each case there is a 'stem' followed by four alternative options. The correct or best of the options has to be chosen; this one is called the 'key', the remaining three are called 'distractors'.

2 **Multiple-completion** There will be fifteen of these. Here one or more of the three alternatives given is/are correct. The instructions given you are as follows: **A** if 1, 2 and 3 are all correct, **B** if 1 and 2 only are correct, **C** if 1 only is correct, **D** if 3 only is correct.

Experience of examiners, including the author, has shown that students do not always do themselves justice with objective tests. Remember that the 'distractors' have been carefully selected by experts and have been pretested with students; each one is intended to 'trap' a proportion of examinees – so beware. Often with multiple-choice questions several of the responses may be correct in certain sets of circumstances but only one will be generally correct. For example:

Bank receipts and payments are
A *entered in a 3-column cash book*
B *entered in a bank cash book*
C *normally entered in either a 3-column cash book or a bank cash book.*

A or **B** – could be correct in some firms but not necessarily in all. **C** – is the best option, because normally firms would use one of these books.

Because objective test questions are such a useful way of judging progress on a course, and because they enable a much wider range of topics in a syllabus to be tested quickly and easily, a considerable number of this type of question are given in this Study Aid. In addition to the AEB specimen ones, others have been included. Note that as well as a choice of three or four options (as with the AEB) there is no reason why five choices should not be provided.

Each question will be preceded by the initials *MC*, e.g. *MC3*. *Answers* to these questions are given at the end of each chapter.

1 Some basic principles and procedures

A business or other organization would find it quite impossible to operate efficiently without written records, kept in an orderly fashion, which could be easily referred to. This chapter deals with the basic financial records (**accounts**) that a business needs to keep, why and how they may be kept, and the essential principles involved. It is vital that you work through this chapter thoroughly before proceeding.

What is profit?

Businesses exist to make profit. Consider a business which in a given period spends £1,000 on buying goods for resale and receives £1,300 in the same period from customers to whom it sells the goods. It has apparently made a profit of £300. In selling the goods, however, the business will have to meet certain expenses, e.g. rent, wages, heating and lighting, delivery charges. If these amount to £90 then the real profit will be £210.

Practice work

Complete the following table – the first and eighth examples have been worked out (note that losses are placed in brackets).

Purchases of goods	*Sales*	*Expenses*	*Gross profit or loss*	*Net profit or loss*
3,700	4,700	100	1,000	900
2,000	2,900	300		
3,900	4,850	640		
2,100		160	300	
	6,700	260	1,200	
	4,400		800	560
3,870	4,850			580
1,900	2,200	360	300	(60)
2,300	2,000			(175)
	2,650	410	(850)	
6,136		498	(852)	

Summary
If income from sales exceeds cost of purchases there is a *gross profit.*

If income from sales is less than cost of purchases there is a *gross loss.*

If gross profit exceeds expenses there is a *net profit.*

If gross profit is less than expenses there is a *net loss.*

What is expenditure?

To the layman, 'expenses' means all money spent. However, from the accountant's point of view expenditure can be divided into three groups:

1 **Purchases**, i.e. goods for resale (or materials for manufacture and resale). It is important to only use the term 'purchases' in this connection.
2 **Overheads**, or running expenses. These are the normal everyday expenses incurred by a business which enable it to function. Examples are salaries and wages, rent, heating and lighting, insurance premiums, printing and stationery, repairs to equipment. Most of these items are payments for 'services' as distinct from tangible (physical) items.
3 Major items which **increase the value of a business**, e.g. machinery, office equipment, delivery vans. These possessions, unlike the ones in 1, are not bought primarily for resale (though they may be sold second hand, possibly in part exchange).

1 and **2** are both called **revenue expenditure**, and at this stage only items in **1** and **2** will be included in our expenses figure in calculating profit. In general terms they are 'used up' in any particular accounting period. Thus in the year to 31 March 19–1, £2,000 may be paid for rent, in return for which premises are used for that period.

Items in **3** will normally be in use for a number of years, so it is reasonable to spread the cost of, say, machinery which is expected to last ten years over that period in the books (see Chapter 4).

What is capital?

Imagine that a couple are trying to calculate their **assets** (items or possesions of value) and **liabilities** (amounts owing to others). A statement of their affairs (i.e. their balance sheet) at 31 March 19–1 might look like this:

Statement of affairs of Mr and Mrs B at 31 March 19–1

Assets		£
Motor vehicle		2,000
Furniture		1,600
Household equipment		250
Clothes, etc.		300
Cash		150
		£4,300
Liabilities		
Owing to HP company	1,100	
Telephone and electricity bills owing	100	
		1,200
Net assets		£3,100

Net assets, therefore, means total assets less total liabilities. It is their capital or net worth. Remember not to think of capital as just cash.

The accounting equation is capital equals assets *less* liabilities (C = A–L); thus: (C) £3,100 = (A) £4,300 – (L) £1,200; and therefore: (C) £3,100 + (L) £1,200 = (A) £4,300.

Practice work

Complete the following table (where possible):

Assets	*Liabilities*	*Capital*
£	£	£
30,000	20,000	
31,650	9,250	
41,600		38,350
19,735		19,735
	2,710	8,840
9,000		

You will have realized why you cannot carry out the last calculation – there are two missing figures.

Effect of transactions on the balance sheet

Above we illustrated a balance sheet of a married couple. Consider a simple business. How will each of its transactions affect the balance sheet (which is just a financial 'picture' of the business at any given moment)? The following shows the result of each transaction (imagine that no books of account are kept).

Transaction 1 The owner pays £15,000 into a business bank account:

Capital	£15,000	Bank	£15,000

Note that this is the only time when the capital will be all in cash.

Transaction 2 He buys goods for resale (i.e. purchases) paying £900:

Capital	£15,000	Goods (Stock)	£900
		Bank	14,100
			£15,000

Transaction 3 He buys a small van paying £3,500:

Capital	£15,000	Vehicle	£3,500
		Stock	900
		Bank	£10,600
			£15,000

Transaction 4 He sells goods that cost him £600 for £800:

Capital	£15,000	Vehicle	£3,500
+ Profit	200	Stock (i.e. 900–600)	300
	£15,200	Bank	11,400
			£15,200

Note that for the first time the capital has increased.

Transaction 5 He paid various expenses £150:

Capital		£15,000	Vehicle	£3,500
Profit	200		Stock	£300
less			Bank	£11,250
Expenses	150	50		
		£15,050		£15,050

Note that capital is reduced because cash at bank has reduced without any equivalent asset being acquired.

Transaction 6 He sold the remaining goods *on credit* for £460 to G. Jones (now called his **debtor**):

		£		£
Capital		15,000	Vehicle	3,500
+ Profit no. 4	200		Debtor – G. Jones	460
Profit no. 6	160		Bank	11,250
	360			
less				
Expenses	150	210		
		£15,210		£15,210

Note that the debtor is treated as an asset – the sum owing is legally due. (If you had £15 but a colleague owed you £5 you would regard your net worth as £20.)

Check:

	£
Total purchases	900
Total sales (800+460)	1,260
Gross profit	360
less Expenses	150
Net profit (= increase in capital)	£210

Transaction 7 is now introduced so that another basic transaction can be shown. We have now bought for cash and on credit, paid expenses in cash, and sold goods for cash and on credit. (The profits calculation was taken after no. 6 to avoid dealing with unsold stock at this stage – see Chapter 2.)

Transaction 7 He purchased £1,000 goods *on credit* from A. Allen:

	£		£
Capital	15,000	Vehicle	3,500
Net profit	210	Stock	1,000
		Debtor	460
		Bank	11,250
			16,210
		less Creditor	1,000
	£15,210	Net assets or net worth	£15,210

Refer back to the formula C = A – L.

If you thoroughly understand the above principles you will be able to reason out many problems (in particular you will be helped in 'single-entry' and other computational exercises).

Practice work

On 31 December 19–1 a small business had a total capital of £18,560. State the effect on capital of each of the following transactions, thus calculating the final capital figure:

(a) Purchases value £970 bought on credit from L. Williams (**creditor**)*. Refer back to the case of Mr and Mrs B.*

(b) Bought various items of office furniture paying by cheque £395.

(c) A debtor who owed £165 (which is of course included in the capital at 31 December 19–1) paid the whole sum.

(d) Paid various expense items £85.

The ledger

It would be impossible to try to record all the transactions of a business by amending a balance sheet. Thus accounting records are kept classifying information in various ways. The key to the accounting system is the ledger (there are likely to be a number of these), which contains many separate accounts each referring to one particular 'classification' of information – asset or liability, income or expenditure. At the end of a given period, summaries of this information can be gathered together to produce the firm's financial results. And at any moment of time information can be read from the accounts.

Principle of double-entry

Each transaction has a two-way effect – there is an exchange element in each transaction. Basically, the particular account *receives* or *gives*. Traditionally (and for no other reason) in standard accounting books we enter the incoming item on the left-hand side (or in the left hand column) and the outgoing item on the right-hand side (or column). Left-hand entries are called debits, right-hand entries are called credits – but do not try to apply the normal English dictionary definitions to these purely technical accounting terms. Thus:

Transaction 2 The business *received* goods for resale, *gave* cash.

Transaction 3 The business *received* a vehicle, *gave* cash.

Transaction 5 The business *received* 'services'; *gave* cash (possibly postal charges, advertising or car insurance).

Transaction 7 The business *received* goods for resale; A. Allen *gave* value (for which he will be paid later).

NB Both sides of each transaction are dealt with at the time it occurs; at this point in time the business records that it *owes* money to Allen. When it pays (and only then) it will show the payment to Allen. Little trouble occurs in practice in making entries – those involving cash receipts and payments are the easiest to deal with (thus as cash received is a left-hand or debit entry, the other one must be a credit).

Summary

The seven transactions above clearly illustrate (a) the 'double' effect on the business of each transaction, and (b) that capital increases when a profit is made and reduces when expenses are paid or if a loss is made:

1: needs a special explanation – see below.
2, 3, 7: no alteration in capital because:
  2: asset stock +£900; asset cash –£900,
  3: asset vehicle +£3,500; asset cash –£3,500,
  7: asset stock +£1,000; liability creditor +£1,000.
4, 5, 6: alter capital because:
  4: asset stock –£600; asset cash +£800; capital +£200,
  5: asset cash –£150; capital –£150,
  6: asset stock –£300; asset debtor +£460; capital +£160.

(Net effect of 4, 5, 6 is combined net profit, or capital increase, of £210.)

Capital account

A special mention is needed of the capital account. The business is a separate entity from its owner. This is called the 'business entity concept'. So when the owner pays in capital to his business, a capital a/c is opened to show that the owner has *given* – the business cash a/c *receives* value. The capital a/c can be regarded as the owner's personal account – he is a 'creditor' of the business (though in event of the business closing down, outside creditors must be given priority). At the end of any accounting period the net profit is added to the capital account, similarly any net loss is deducted. Money withdrawn for his personal use is deducted (see drawings, Chapter 7).

The following example, with the notes of explanation, will help you to understand double-entry principles, how to balance accounts economically. Transactions 1–7 are given as well as several others not dealt with earlier. Note that the old-fashioned prefixes 'to' and 'by' are not used – they have no particular meaning.

Capital a/c

		4 Jan. Bank a/c (**1**)	£5,000

Bank a/c

	£		£
4 Jan. Capital a/c (**1**)	5,000	6 Jan. Purchases a/c (**2**)	900
7 Jan. Sales a/c (**4**)	800	6 Jan. Vans a/c (**3**)	3,500
17 Jan. G. Jones a/c (**9**)	460	9 Jan. Expenses a/c (**5**)	150
		14 Jan. Expenses a/c (**8**)	67
		15 Jan. A. Allen a/c (**10**)	750
			5,367 (**a**)
		16 Jan. Balance c/d	893 (**c**^{1})
(**b**^{1})	£6,260		£6,260 (**b**^{2})
17 Jan. Balance b/d	893(**c**^{2})		

Purchases a/c

	£		
6 Jan. Bank a/c (**2**)	900		
11Jan. A. Allen a/c (**7**)	1,000		
	1,900		

Sales a/c

			£
		7 Jan. Bank a/c (**4**)	800
		9 Jan. G. Jones a/c (**6**)	460
		16 Jan. G. Jones a/c (**11**)	835
			2,095

Vans a/c

6 Jan. Bank a/c (**3**)	£3,500		

Expenses a/c

	£		
9 Jan. Bank a/c (**5**)	150		
14 Jan. Bank a/c (**8**)	67		
	217		

G. Jones a/c

	£		£
9 Jan. Sales a/c (**6**)	460	17 Jan. Bank (**9**)	460
16 Jan. Sales a/c (**11**)	835		

A. Allen a/c

	£		£
16 Jan. Bank a/c (**10**)	750	11 Jan. Purchases a/c (**7**)	1,000
16 Jan. Balance c/d	250		
	£1,000		£1,000
		17 Jan. Balance b/d	250

Notes

1 The entries are 'paired' numerically to assist you.
2 The other account involved is shown against each entry.
3 Purchases and sales a/c can be thought of as:
goods a/c – debit goods 'in', credit goods 'out'.
4 Balancing of accounts means calculating the difference between the total debits and total credits in any account. Generally but not necessarily this would be done monthly (though with a mechanized system the balance is extracted automatically – refer to any bank statement). Where there are items on one side only there is no point in making unnecessary entries. In the above accounts only the bank account and A. Allen's a/c need the balancing entries. Textbooks rarely show a subtotal (£5,367) but it is helpful. The letters **a**, $\mathbf{b}^1$, $\mathbf{b}^2$, $\mathbf{c}^1$, $\mathbf{c}^2$, indicate the order of the balancing operation. It is important to double check, i.e. $\mathbf{b}^2$–**a** = £893; **a**+$\mathbf{c}^1$ = £6,260.
5 Students frequently are confused over the terms debit/credit balance: bank a/c has a *debit* balance because the total of the *debits* exceed that of the *credits*; A. Allen's a/c has a *credit* balance because the *credit* exceeds the *debit*.
6 Accounts can be divided into: **personal** – showing amounts owing *by* debtors (G. Jones) or *to* creditors (A. Allen); **impersonal** – (i) **real**, i.e. actual possessions (cash, vans); (ii) **nominal**, in effect all accounts that are neither **personal** nor **real** (the majority of these will be expenditure accounts but some will be income a/cs, e.g. rent received).
7 **Debit** balances on a (i) **real** a/c – represents total value of the particular asset; (ii) **personal** a/c – represents amount owing *by* the *debtor* (Jones); (iii) **nominal** – a/c represents the total expenditure or charge (in practice there would be separate a/cs for the various categories of expenditure, e.g. rent, rates, salaries, motor vehicles expenses).
Credit balances on a (i) **real** a/c – normally this means an accounting error must have been made, e.g. you cannot pay out more

cash than you have in the account; (ii) **personal** a/c – represents money owing *to* the *creditor* (Allen); (iii) **nominal** a/c – normally this will not occur in an expense a/c unless an adjustment is involved (see Chapter 5). In an income a/c (e.g. sales, commission, rent or interest received) it represents the total income.

Summary

1 A debit balance is either expenditure or an asset. A credit balance is either a gain (income) or a liability. It can be argued that there should be two debit columns and two credit columns.
2 Transferring of balances to trading and profit and loss a/cs is dealt with later.

Ledger subdivision

In the above example very few ledger accounts were employed. In practice there might well be hundreds, if not thousands (the majority being personal accounts). It is convenient to subdivide the ledger, a common arrangement being:

Sales ledger, containing the personal accounts of all debtors (customers).

Purchase (or **bought) ledger,** containing the personal accounts of all creditors (suppliers).

General ledger, which may be subdivided into: **nominal ledger** – all income and expenditure accounts – and **private ledger** – accounts of a confidential nature (e.g. directors' salaries, partners' capital and drawings accounts).

Many organizations use mechanized or semi-mechanized accounting methods. The basic accounting principles are the same but the accounting rulings will vary. Again, whatever the method employed, the layout of accounts and documents will differ considerably from office to office. With many systems a ledger account is likely to resemble the one below (it contains the two transactions already illustrated plus one additional one).

A/c no. 1/7545 A. Allen *Folio ref. PL12*

Date	*Details*	*Reference*	*Folio*	*Debit*	*Credit*	*Balance*
				£	£	£
11 Jan.	Purchases	75296			1,000.00	1,000.00
16 Jan.	Cheque	165278		750.00		250.00
24 Jan.	Purchases	75352			154.65	404.65

NB Extra information is often included in ledger accounts. Here references 75296 and 75352 represent the supplier's invoice numbers, and 165278 is the firm's cheque number.

Books of original entry (or subsidiary books)

In small organizations it may be practicable to make entries directly into the ledger accounts from the appropriate documents (as we did above). Generally it is more convenient to use a system of subsidiary books (particularly for purchases and sales on credit). The original entry from the document is made in a subsidiary book and then at fixed intervals (possibly weekly or monthly) totals only are entered in purchases or sales ledgers a/cs. However, entries in the personal a/c (in sales and purchase ledgers) must be made in every instance – because it is essential to have up-to-date information about debtors and creditors. (Cash sales are not involved, as they do not require personal a/cs.) The system is illustrated below in respect of a week's credit sales transactions. Invoices covering consignments to customers are sent and accounting entries are made from the copy invoices.

Sales day book *SB16*

Date	Customer	Invoice no.	Folio	Amount
				£
16 March	Crest & Wave	625	SL17	89.35
16 March	High & Low	626	SL38	120.00
18 March	Able Baker & Co.	627	SL45	55.93
19 March	Crest & Wave	628	SL17	325.72
20 March	High & Low	629	SL38	22.22
				£613.22
				(Gl5)

Sales ledger *Crest & Wave a/c* *SL 17*

16 March	Sales	SB16	89.35			
19 March	Sales	SB16	325.72			

High & Low a/c *SL38*

			£			
16 March	Sales	SB16	120.00			
20 March	Sales	SB16	22.22			

Able Baker & Co. a/c *SL45*

18 March	Sales	SB16	£55.93			

General ledger *Sales a/c* *GL5*

				20 March	Total for week SB16	£613.22

Notes

1 Purchases on credit are dealt with similarly, i.e. individual entries in purchase day book, individual credit entries in the personal accounts of suppliers, and the total purchases debited to purchases a/c.
2 Remember that the day book is not an account but only a memorandum book.
3 'Sundries' is often used instead of 'total for . . .'
4 Double-entry in the ledger is still maintained – there are five individual debits totalling £613.22.
5 The folio cross-reference system should be clear from the example; the SL customer account numbers are not consecutive because there are many other customers to whom there have been no sales this week.
6 If and when payment is made by customers, the amounts will be entered in the cash book and credited to the individual.

Trade or quantity discount

Some suppliers (particularly in 'trade') use the discount method of charging – the quotation, price list or catalogue shows a gross price, and a percentage discount is allowed to the buyer. This may vary, e.g. a buyer of a very large quantity may receive a greater percentage discount, or alternatively a similar incentive may be given on slow-moving sales lines. However, the buyer is being charged a net amount, and only this need show in the books. Similarly, the details of the sale are on the invoice and need not be repeated in the books.

So the full details of invoice no. 626 for £120 to High & Low might have been:

6 'Peerless' type-C steam-dry electric irons	
@ £25 each =	£150.00
less 20% trade discount	30.00
	£120.00

(VAT is dealt with in Chapter 10).

Returns and allowances

Occasionally the amounts invoiced in credit transactions are incorrect. This can happen for a number of reasons: arithmetic error, incorrect discount, shortages, returns of faulty or incorrect goods, or goods invoiced but not sent. The correction may require (a) a reduction in the charge or (b) an increase in the charge.

Many firms nowadays prefer wholly to cancel the original invoice charge and issue a replacement invoice. Some still prefer to issue:

(a) a credit note, reducing the charge by a stated sum; or (b) a debit note, increasing the charge by a stated sum.

This method is the one in general use by examining bodies. You will find these adjustments referred to in questions as: returns inwards or sales returns; returns outward or purchase returns.

Therefore:

Net sales = total sales less sales returns.
Net purchases = total purchases less purchase returns.

Take care to deduct any trade discount – so if two electric irons were rejected by High & Low, the credit would be for £40 (two at £20), not £50.

Assume that credit notes are issued as follows:

28 March	C/n 16	High & Low	£40.00
31 March	C/n 17	Able Baker & Co.	£11.30

then entries would be:

Returns inwards and allowances day book *RB3*

Date	*Customer*	*C/n no.*	*Folio*	*Amount*
				£
28 March	High & Low	16	SL38	40.00
31 March	Able Baker & Co.	17	SL45	11.30
				£51.30
				(Gl8)

Sales ledger

(The two personal accounts are shown again, brought up to date – there is no adjustment on Crest & Wave, of course.)

High & Low a/c SL38

			£				£
16 March	Sales	SB16	120.00	28 March	Returns	RB3	40.00
20 March	Sales	SB16	22.22				

Able Baker & Co. a/c *SL45*

			£				£
18 March	Sales	SB16	55.93	31 March	Returns	RB3	11.30

General ledger a/c

Total returns for the period is posted to the debit side of returns inwards account, thus giving net sales of £561.92 (£613.22 *less* £51.30).

Returns inwards and allowances a/c *GL8*

31 March	Total for week	RB3	£51.30	

Note

Returns outwards are dealt with similarly. Individual entries are made in the returns outwards day book, suppliers are debited individually (because they were credited when the original purchase invoices were entered), and total returns credited to returns outwards (because total purchases were debited originally to purchases a/c).

Cash and bank transactions

The majority of business transactions are settled by payment through the banking system. In general, even if there are cash receipts (e.g. in retailing), it is better accounting practice to bank this in full and then withdraw cash from the bank if it is needed (e.g. for petty cash payments or for wages). Most textbook authors still illustrate a combined cash and bank book, and some examining bodies expect students to be able to answer questions involving this layout. Example of a three-column cash book (the discount columns are dealt with later).

Cash and bank *CB7*

	Discount allowed	Cash	Bank		Discount received	Cash	Bank
		£					£
1 Jan. Balance b/f		30.30	500.65	4 Jan. ABC & Co.			69.30
2 Jan. Cash sales		140.72		5 Jan. Rent			85.65
4 Jan. Cash sales		212.62		5 Jan. Casual labour		10.00	
5 Jan. G. Jones			75.00	5 Jan. Cash sales banked		353.34	
5 Jan. A. Smith			16.64				
						363.34	154.95
5 Jan. Cash sales banked			353.34	5 Jan. Balances c/d		20.30	790.68
		£383.64	£945.63			£383.64	£945.63
6 Jan. Balances b/d		20.30	790.68				

(Folio referencing, having been explained, is now mainly dropped.)

Notes

1 On 1 Jan. there was cash-in-hand of £30.30 and a current account bank balance of £500.65.
2 A cheque was sent to ABC & Co.
3 On 2 and 4 Jan. there were receipts from sales in cash and this total sum (£353.34) was banked on 5 Jan. – there is an entry each side (*contra* entry) because cash was reduced and bank increased.
4 Rent was paid by cheque.

5 Casual labour was paid in cash.
6 Cheques were received and banked from Jones and Smith.
7 The balancing is carried out as already explained, thus
8 On 6 Jan. there was cash in hand of £20.30 and a balance at the bank of £790.68.

The bank cash book

In practice, only a small minority of businesses use the above method. A majority keep a bank cash book, which deals with banking transactions only, and if there are payments in cash these are dealt with through a petty cash account (see Chapter 9). Cash receipts, as already explained, will be banked as received daily, therefore no 'cash' entry is needed. A major advantage is that the total deposited on any paying-in slip is shown.

Bank cash book

Date		Details	Bank		Details	Bank
			£			£
1 Feb.	Balance b/d		270.50	3 Feb. Advertising		35.64
3 Feb.	R. Watson	85.00		4 Feb. Petty cash		25.00
	Anthony & Co.	25.40				60.64
	Sinbad & Son	10.07		5 Feb. Balance c/d		553.96
	Cash sales	68.05	188.52			
5 Feb.	Cash sales	130.50				
	Jones & Sons	25.08	155.58			
			£614.60			£614.60
6 Feb.	Balance b/d		553.96			

Notes

1 A cheque for advertising was paid out on 3 Feb.
2 A cheque was cashed for £25 on 4 Feb. so that petty cash would be available.
3 On 3 Feb. a total of £188.52 was deposited, details as shown.
4 On 5 Feb. a total of £155.58 was deposited, details as shown.
5 The amount in hand on 5 Feb. was £553.96.
6 The discount columns already shown (but not used) on p. 28 have been omitted above. They will now be dealt with.

Cash discounts

To encourage prompt payment, suppliers may offer a small percentage discount if payment is made within a certain period. The buyer makes his own commercial decision between saving some money and having the use of his funds for a longer period. Because of this the cash discount is not deducted by the seller on the invoice; it is up to the buyer to make the necessary reduction if he so chooses.

We use the terms: **discount allowed** (by the seller) – he receives *less* than the invoiced sum; thus it is a loss or expense to him; **discount received** (by the buyer) – he pays *less*, thus it is a gain to him. The principle can be illustrated without showing the entries in the subsidiary books.

Books of Atkins & Co.

Sales a/c

		10 Jan. Jones Bros (**a**)	£250

Jones Bros a/c

	£		£
10 Jan. Sales (**a**)	250	20 Jan. Bank (**b**[1])	245
		Discount (**b**[2])	5
	£250		£250

Bank

20 Jan. Jones Bros (**b**[1])	£245		

Discount allowed a/c

20 Jan. Jones Bros (**b**[2])	£5		

Notes

(**a**) Goods sold on credit by Atkins & Co. and invoiced to Jones Bros.

(**b**[1]) & (**b**[2]) Assuming a cash discount of 2% (2p in the £) for payment within 14 days is offered, then (**b**[1]) shows the actual amount received and (**b**[2]) introduces the discount.

The net effect is that the personal account of Jones is now settled.

In the buyer's books the reverse process takes place:

Purchases:	Dr £250	
Atkins	Dr £245	Cr £250
	Dr £5	
Cash		Cr £245
Discount received		Cr £5

Using the discount columns in the cash book

There are likely to be many discounted items. It is therefore convenient to use a system whereby, although individual discounts are recorded in the personal accounts, totals only for a given period are entered in the two discount accounts in the ledger. More and more in accounting you will find a similar practice in use. It has already been employed with sales/purchases day books. Detailed information is entered in a subsidiary book (not itself part of the ledger double entry) and summary totals in a ledger account.

In the following example, the sale to Jones on 10 Jan. dealt with above is included, plus two more sales on credit:

1 To Smith & Smythe on 13 Jan. £160 – 1% cash discount if paid by 27 Jan.
2 To Jones Bros on 21 Jan £280 – 2% cash discount if paid by 31 Jan.

In both cases cheques are received on 26 Jan.

The sales day book entries and the total sales entry for the period in the sales account are omitted – there is no change here. Fictitious entries are made for 15–18 Jan. in the bank cash book to enable account balancing to be shown.

Jones Bros

	£		£
10 Jan. Sales	250.00	20 Jan. Bank	245.00
21 Jan. Sales	280.00	Discount	5.00
		26 Jan. Bank	274.40
		Discount	5.60
	£530.00		£530.00

Smith & Smythe a/c

	£		£
13 Jan. Sales	160.00	26 Jan. Bank	158.40
		Discount	1.60
	£160.00		£160.00

Discount allowed a/c

31 Jan. Total for Jan.	£12.20		

Bank cash book

Date	*Disc. All.*	*Details*	*Bank*		*Disc. rec.*	*Details*	*Bank*
			£				£
15 Jan.		Balance b/d (say)	354.20	18 Jan. (say)		Rent	150.00
20 Jan.	5.00	Jones Bros	245.00	31 Jan.		Balance c/d	882.00
26 Jan.	1.60	Smith & Smythe	158.40				
	5.60	Jones Bros	274.40				
	£12.20		£1,032.00				£1,032.00
1 Feb.		Balance b/d	£882.00				

Notes

1 Double-entry principle is preserved; three individual credits in the personal accounts equal the debit total in discount allowed a/c.
2 Naturally the example could have been carried out with the three-column cash book.
3 The discount column is used *for convenience*. It is *not* a debit in the bank cash a/c (a debit in this type of account represents 'value inwards' and we certainly have *not* received the three sums listed!).
4 Discount received is the reverse process. As an exercise, show how Jones Bros would show these two buying transactions in their books.

Practice work

Some topics have been dealt with only in a very elementary way so far; therefore questions which include them are not suggested till later.

Wherever AEB–S is given as the source of the question, it has been taken from Part I of the specimen paper for the new syllabus; however, all students need to know how to deal with the topics dealt with. In some cases (e.g. question *3*) notes are given to assist you.

Answer the following multiple-choice questions:

MC1 Which one of the following accounts would be found in the sales ledger?
A *Sales*
B *Returns inwards*
C *E. Owen, a customer*
D *H. Kean, a supplier.* (AEB–S)

MC2 A trader purchased goods from a supplier at a cost of £1,000. The terms stated on the invoice are trade discount 10% and cash discount 5% for payment within 7 days.

If the trader pays within the 7 days period he will send the supplier a cheque for
A *£850*
B *£855*
C *£900*
D *£950.* (AEB–S)

MC3 Which one of the following is a 'nominal' account?
A *Carriage outwards account*
B *Machinery account*

C *J. Smith's account*
D *Drawings account.*
(*NB* Carriage outwards = transport costs on sales).
(AEB–S)

MC4 *A credit note received from a supplier would be recorded in*
A *the cash book*
B *the sales day book*
C *the returns inwards book*
D *the returns outwards book.*

The following are multiple-completion questions.

MC5 *A credit balance on Abraham's account in your purchases ledger means that*
1 *the amount shown is owed to you by Abraham*
2 *Abraham has sent you an invoice for that amount*
3 *Abraham is owed that amount by you.*

MC6 *In a retailer's books, which of the following entries could correctly record the purchase from a trading stamp organization of stamps for issue to customers?*
1 *Credit cash account – debit advertising account*
2 *Credit cash account – debit trading stamps account*
3 *Credit cash account – debit customer's account.* (AEB–S)

MC7 *In which of the following circumstances would it be appropriate for a supplier to issue a credit note? When he discovers that*
1 *a recent invoice to his customer had a total which was overstated*
2 *an item was omitted from a recent invoice sent to his customer*
3 *a recent invoice to his customer had been lost in the post.* (AEB–S)

(Answers to multiple-choice and multiple-completion questions are given at the end of each chapter.)

1 (a) A professional man banks all his business receipts daily and pays all expenditure over £5 by cheque. You are asked to prepare a bank cash book from the following:

		£
(i) Cash at bank on 3 Jan. 19–1		472
(ii) Business cheque book counterfoils:		
3 Jan.	A. Clay	24
	R. Blick (£40 *less* cash discount £1)	39
4 Jan.	L. Baker	120
	D. Jay (£320 *less* cash discount £8)	312
5 Jan.	Vehicle insurance	60
	Cash (wages £480, petty cash £20)	500

(iii) Paying-in book counterfoils:		*Total paid in*
3 Jan.	Cash sales £140; cheques from M. Spiers £80, W. Payne £585 – in full settlement of £600 owed by him	805
4 Jan.	Cash sales £230; cash from E. Toms, a debtor, £5	235
5 Jan.	Cash sales £300; cheque from J. Evans £117 – in settlement of debt of £120	417

Rule off and (a) balance the cash book at the close of business on 5 January 19–1.
(b) Write up the discount accounts in the general ledger. (RSA I)

2 G. Kingston's ledger

A. Wilkinson's a/c

	£		£
1 Jan. Balance b/d	790.20	12 Jan. Containers	22.00
3 Jan. Sales	200.50	15 Jan. Cheque	705.30
3 Jan. Returnable Containers	25.00	15 Jan. Discount	5.50
		22 Jan. C/note (overcharge)	79.40
		31 Jan. Balance c/d	203.50
	£1,015.70		£1,015.70
1 Feb. Balance b/d	203.50		

The above is the personal account of A. Wilkinson in the books of G. Kingston. You are asked to:

(a) Explain (without using book-keeping terms) the meanings of the entries dated 1, 3, 3, 12, 15, 22, and 31 January. Your answer should include possible explanations for (i) the discrepancy between the two amounts for containers, (ii) the difference between the balance due 1 Jan. and the total payment and discount on 15 Jan.

(b) State whether in A. Wilkinson's books *the balance of £203.50 would show as a debtor or a creditor.*

(c) Show the entry in A. Wilkinson's account that G. Kingston would make on 12 Feb. if, by agreement, an extra allowance of £50 in respect of faulty goods had been given. (*RSA I*)

NB In *(a) (ii)*, the £25.00 charged to Wilkinson, in addition to the £200.50 charged for the actual goods, obviously covers a *number* of containers . . . Calculate the difference between the 1 Jan. and 15 Jan. amounts – that should give you the clue you need.

Without using book-keeping terms' means no terms like debit, balance, carried down.

Answers to multiple-choice questions:

MC1 **C**; *MC2* **B**; *MC3* **A**; *MC4* **D**; *MC5* **3**; *MC6* **1/2**; *MC7* **1**.

2 Profits and stock

Chapter 1 concentrated on revision work on an introduction to book-keeping. This was done to make sure that you as the student have understood thoroughly some very important basic points. The revision dealt with the principles of double-entry and the way in which this is applied in keeping accounting records – each transaction being recorded twice – in the appropriate ledger accounts. You must be able to make the necessary entries involved in recording straightforward transactions (and must be able to interpret them) before proceeding with this and subsequent chapters.

To remind you of an essential principle: **purchases** means goods bought for resale, or materials and components bought for manufacture and resale (the latter are dealt with in Chapter 17, manufacturing accounts). Examiners find that this technical definition of purchases is not always understood, and thus both 'fixed assets' as well as normal revenue expenditure on overheads appear, wrongly, as charges reducing gross profit.

Treatment of unsold stock

In this chapter the following basic matters are covered:

(a) definition of 'unsold stock';
(b) methods of valuing unsold stock;
(c) arithmetical calculation of gross profit – emphasizing that profit is taken into account in the accounting period in which goods are actually sold;
(d) the actual book-keeping work needed to produce the trading account;
(e) the effects on the financial results caused by undervaluing or overvaluing stock.

A definition of 'unsold stock'

A part of an examination question at Elementary level might be:

Explain clearly what is meant by 'unsold stock'.

It is important to give a full answer; one which merely states that unsold stock is 'goods awaiting sale' is not sufficient. Remember that many businesses are manufacturers. A suitable answer would be: 'Unsold stock means either: (1) goods for resale – for example, in wholesaling; or (2) materials/component parts bought for manufacture and resale.'

Stock valuation and its effect on profits

Consider this question:

(*a*) *In arriving at his gross profit, a trader only takes into account the goods he has actually sold in the accounting period in question.*

(*b*) *A trader normally values his unsold stock at the purchase price because profit must not be anticipated.*

Explain these statements using the following information to illustrate your answer:

A small firm commences business in January dealing in second-hand cars. During this month four cars are purchased and cars A, C, and D are sold (leaving car B unsold at 31 Jan.).

January	*A*	*B*	*C*	*D*	*Total*
Purchases	£600	£800	£500	£450	£2,350
Sales	£720	—	£610	£600	£1,930

Notes

Total sales in this example are less than total purchases, but it would be misleading to say there has been a loss on trading activities. To make a fair comparison between purchases and sales, only the goods actually sold are taken into account.

In normal circumstances the trader will value the unsold stock at the price he paid for the goods; this is because, although he expects to make a profit when they are in fact sold, profit must not be anticipated. Therefore, in this example, only cars *A*, *C*, and *D* are included in the January calculations.

January results are:

	£	
Purchases	2,350	
less Unsold stock 31 Jan.	800	
	1,550	– i.e. cost (to firm) of cars sold (*A, C, D*).
Sales *A, C, D*	£1,930	– £380 gross profit on *A, C, D*.

Check:

	£	
Profit on *A*	120	
C	110	
D	150	380

The same firm has the following transactions in February:

	E	*B*	*F*
Purchases	660	—	710
Sales	640	875	—

Find the profit for this month.

Notes

Remember to take the purchase price of car *B* into account as it was not included in the January calculation. You will of course be aware that stock unsold at the end of one period (in this case January) is called 'closing stock'; it is referred to as the 'opening stock' of the next period (February). February results are:

	£	
Opening stock *B*	800	
Purchases *EF*	1,370+	
Goods available for sale	2,170	
less Unsold stock Feb 28	710	
Cost of cars sold (*EB*)	1,460	
Sales *EB*	£1,515 – 55	gross profit on *EB*.

Check:
Profit on *B* 75
Loss on *E* 20 – 55

Example

Under what circumstances would a trader value his unsold stock at a lower sum than cost price?

Occasionally a lower valuation than cost or purchase price might be considered desirable. For example, supposing that as a result of general price reductions the business could replace the goods at a lower price than the one originally paid. A case where this happened a few years ago may be of interest – a very large clothing manufacturing organization incurred heavy losses because, in order to safeguard their supplies of raw materials, they had made large advance purchases of Australian wool – the world price of which then dropped considerably.

Again, it may be that a business expects that it will not be able to sell goods it has purchased at a profit. This could be because of substandard quality, or possibly a competitor has introduced a better alternative at a lower price. In the case of clothing items, unsold goods may have to be reduced in price considerably because of changes in fashion.

In Chapter 16 there will be further work on stock valuation – several methods called 'FIFO' (first in, first out) and 'LIFO' (last in, first out) will be dealt with; they are often employed where the same articles are purchased over a period at a variety of prices. Both GCE 'O' and Stage II examination papers sometimes contain questions on this subject.

Practice work

If you can complete successfully the following table for the months shown (referring to the same car trader) then you have understood the points dealt with above. Set out your calculations as illustrated in the February results:

	Opening stock	*Purchases*	*Closing stock*	*Goods available for sale*	*Sales*	*Gross profits*
March	710	3,000	630	3,080	3,490	
April		3,400	590		3,860	
May		2,900	1,020		2,810	
June			660	3,330	4,000	

Notes

June may look tricky. The following will help:

Opening stock	*
+ Purchases	?
Available for sale	*

* represents known information

One missing figure can always be calculated (think of 8 + ? = 29).

The trading account

The book-keeping entries required

The principle of allowing for unsold stock has been dealt with. Now it is necessary to revise the book entries needed to achieve the end result. Even though you may be quite happy about this topic it is really important in accounting to have ample practice – provided the principles are understood first. You need to be able to make entries accurately, reasonably quickly, and neatly. Too many people forget that information is recorded so that it can be available to others as well. Remember to keep totals and balances in pencil until you are certain that no mistakes have been made.

An examination question of the following type is unlikely to appear in GCE 'O' or RSA II but it is a possibility in Stage I, also at CSE level or the Business Education Council General level.

A new business makes the following purchases during January – its first month of trading:

Cash purchases – weeks ending 7 Jan. £350; 14 Jan. £310; 21 Jan. £420; 28 Jan. £400
Credit purchases – from Ofco Ltd 18 Jan. £230; Equipment Supplies 23 Jan. £290; Ofco Ltd 29 Jan. £410.

At the end of January, stock unsold was valued at £1,350 (its cost price).

Total cash sales in the month were £1,540 (there were no credit sales).

You are required to write up the appropriate accounts in the nominal ledger and then produce a trading account, thus arriving at gross profit.

Notes

Now a stock account is introduced for the first time; this is used purely to record unsold stock at the end of an accounting period; purchases and sales are never entered in it. The first of the two summary accounts (the trading a/c) is opened and this will show the gross profit. Later you will find that certain expense accounts (direct expenses) are charged against gross profit.

Purchases a/c

		£			
7 Jan. Cash		350	31 Jan.	(transferred to Trading a/c	2,410 **(d)**
14 Jan. Cash		310			
19 Jan. Ofco Ltd		230			
21 Jan. Cash		420			
23 Jan. Equipment Supplies		290			
28 Jan. Cash		400			
29 Jan. Ofco Ltd		410			
	(a)	£2,410			£2,410

Sales a/c

31 Jan. transferred to Trading a/c	**(c)**	£1,540	31 Jan.	Total	£1,540 **(b)**

Stock a/c

31 Jan. Trading a/c	(e)	£1,350		

Trading a/c month of January

31 Jan. Purchases	(d)	2,410	31 Jan.	Sales	1,540 (c)
less Unsold stock	(e)	1,350			
Cost of sales		1,060			
Gross profit c/d to P&L	(f)	480			
		£1,540			£1,540

(**a**) (**b**) Purchases and sales transactions entered.
(**c**) Total sales transferred to trading a/c.
(**d**) Total purchases transferred to trading a/c.
(**e**) Unsold stock now deducted from total purchases in trading a/c and *entered in a stock a/c*. At first sight this might appear to be two debit entries, but of course the one in the trading a/c is a *deduction*. The stock a/c is an *asset* a/c (Chapter 1).
(**f**) P&L a/c is profit & loss a/c (see later in this chapter).

The alternative way of showing unsold stock

The method shown above is now accepted as good accounting practice, as it shows the cost of the goods disposed of in the month. However, some older-style textbooks may still enter unsold stock as a credit item – possibly some of you may have learned this way in your classes. Whilst the same gross profit is obtained, the cost of sales can only be calculated by carrying out a subtraction calculation. It is strongly recommended that the modern-style trading account always be used – examiners will expect this.

Older trading account layout (not recommended)

	£		£
31 Jan. Purchases	2,410	31 Jan. Sales	1,540
Gross profit c/d	480	31 Jan. Closing stock	1,350
	£2,890		£2,890

Example

The following information relates the the month of February for the same business. Totals only are given and purchase returns (returns outward) and sales returns (returns inwards) are introduced, also two typical 'direct' expense accounts – more of these are dealt with in the next chapter in connection with wages and salaries.

Prepare stock and trading accounts for the month:

Opening stock, 1 Feb. £1,350 (this was of course the 'closing' figure 31 Jan.); purchases £3,165; purchase returns £265; sales £3,560; sales returns £120; carriage inwards £115; import duties £90; unsold stock 28 Feb.: £1,665.

Notes

Only the stock a/c and the trading a/c are asked for – you should have had no trouble with the four routine accounts for recording buying/selling/returns transactions if these had been required.

Carriage inwards (i.e. carriage on purchases) and import duties have to be included in the trading a/c because they are both direct charges – part of the costs of getting the goods into the premises. If the seller was delivering them free of charge, he would have added this sum to the selling price he quoted; and the import duties increase the real cost to the purchaser.

Notice the logical and orderly layout of the trading a/c – get used to the technique of insetting amounts particularly where there are deductions as well as additions and also where a subtotal is useful and informative.

Stock a/c

31 Jan. Trading a/c	£1,350	1 Feb. Trading a/c	£1,350 (**a**)
28 Feb. Trading a/c	£1,665		

Trading a/c (month of February)

	£			£
1 Feb. Stock a/c (**a**)		1,350	28 Feb. Sales	3,560
28 Feb. Purchases	3,165		*less* Returns In	120
less Returns	265			
	2,900			
Carr in	115			
Duty	90	3,105		
		4,455		
less Closing stock		1,665		
Cost of sales		2,790		
Gross profit c/d to P&L a/c		650		
		£3,440		£3,440

This 'clears' the stock a/c at the beginning of the month and the debit entry in trading a/c enables opening stock to be counted in the cost of sales for February.

Practice work

This relates to the same business.
March Total cash purchases £2,430, total cash sales £3,960, unsold stock 31 March £1,055.

Prepare purchases, sales, stock, and trading a/cs for March. Remember that your trading a/c must commence with the unsold stock 28 Feb.

Effect of over- or understating unsold stock

This topic is common in examinations. Consider the combined results for January and February in above examples.

	£
Total purchases (2,410 + 3,105)	5,515
less Unsold stock 28 Feb	1,665
	3,850
Total sales (1,540 + 3,440)	4,980
Gross profit Jan. and Feb.	1,130
Check:	
Jan.	480
Feb.	650
	£1,130

Assume that the stock at the end of January (which does not have to be taken into account in a combined calculation as above) had in error been overvalued by £100; that is, a true assessment would have been £1,250 instead of the £1,350 actually used in the January results.

The corrected results for January would have been:

		£	
Purchases	2,410		
less Unsold stock 31 Jan.	1,250		
		1,160	
Sales		1,540	
Gross profit		380	– £100 *less* than originally.

Correction for February		
Opening stock 1 Feb.	1,250	
Purchases	3,105	
	4,355	
less Closing stock 28 Feb.	1,665	
	2,690	
Sales	3,440	
Gross profit	£750	– £100 *more* than originally.

This illustrates practically that an overvaluation *increases* profit in the accounting period in which made, and *reduces* profit in the following period by the same amount. Similarly, an undervaluation *decreases* profit in the accounting period in which it is made, and *increases* profit in the following period.

Despite this, it is important to make the stock calculation as accurate as possible, otherwise an incorrect picture of the profits in any one period is given. Imagine there had been a serious undervaluation to the extent of £500 at 31 January, unsold stock having been taken as £750 instead of £1,250. Then results would have been recorded as:

Jan Loss	20	(480 *less* 500) instead of profit	480
Feb Profit	1,150	(650 *plus* 500) instead of profit	650
	1,130	– Total profits –	1,130

This would be very misleading.

There may be several reasons for incorrect valuations; examples are: (1) quantity errors (miscounts or omissions); (2) unit price errors (wrong price per item); (3) calculation mistakes (quantity and price being correct).

Practice work

In each of the following instances, the original stock valuation was later found to be inaccurate, the amended figure is given in the last column. In each case, calculate the gross profit based on the original incorrect figure, and then show the effect when the correct figure is used:

	Purchases	Sales	Original closing stock	Adjusted closing stock
	£	£	£	£
Firm *A* April	19,650	28,545	5,210	4,210
May	21,735	30,643	7,160	7,360
Firm *B* April	6,410	9,350	1,050	1,350
May	7,950	12,672	2,130	2,310

Notes

In the case of both firms, assume they are new businesses; thus there is no opening stock on 1 April.

The examiner will wish to see a concise tabulated answer showing how your final results are arrived at. Though the question does not ask for trading a/cs to be written up, this is probably the best way to handle the question – certainly for firm *A*; you may then be able to produce firm *B*'s figures with just an arithmetical calculation. Remember, it is essential to state the period involved in each case. Recheck your arithmetic each time, by complimentary methods, e.g. 2,500 + 1,450 = 3,950 ∴ 3,950 – 1,450 = 2,500.

Rate of stock turnover

A business should hold adequate but not excessive quantities of stock. Different classes of goods may sell at varying rates, i.e. the time the stock of any particular item remains unsold would differ. Businesses consider it important to know this 'rate of turnover' because unsold goods are not earning money – capital is 'tied up' in this way for an appreciable period. In general terms, the more expensive durable goods will have a lower rate of turnover than everyday 'convenience' goods (e.g. foodstuffs). So a business not only needs to know its gross profit, but how long it took to earn that profit.

Calculation of rate of turnover

Supposing a second-hand car dealer maintains an average stock of 10 cars, and during a particular year he sold 60 cars, then his rate of turnover (as far as quantity is concerned) was 6, i.e. 60 ÷ 10. Each car on average remained in stock for 2 months, i.e. 12 months ÷ 6.

The businessman needs to know his rate of turnover in terms of value (with modern computerized methods it is quite possible to know the rate for individual items).

The calculation is:

$$\frac{\text{Cost of goods sold}}{\text{Average stock}}$$

You should know that 'cost of goods sold' means the amount the goods sold (in the period) actually cost the business. Refer back to the trading a/c on p. 41 – cost of sales was £2,790.

A common error is to take sales instead of cost of sales – sales includes a profit element which needs to be deducted. Profit percentage is indicated in one of two ways:

1 *Mark-up* – profit is calculated as a percentage of cost price, e.g. goods cost £100, sold for £125, mark-up is 25%, i.e. (25/100) × 100.
2 *Margin* – profit is calculated as a percentage of selling price; so in the same example, margin is 20%, i.e. (25/125) × 100.

Example

(a) On 1 April 19–1, stock unsold was £25,000; purchases in the year to 31 March 19–2 were £110,000. Sales during the year amounted to £150,000, gross profit margin being maintained at a standard rate of 30%.

Calculate closing stock at 31 March 19–2 and then rate of turnover.

Sales = £150,000; margin (30% on SP) = £45,000.

Therefore cost of sales = £105,000.

Trading a/c

Stock 1 April 19–1	25,000	
Purchases	110,000 +	
	135,000	
less Stock 31 March	? –	
Cost of sales	£105,000	

Therefore closing stock = £135,000 – £105,000 = £30,000.

Average stock = $\frac{25,000 + 30,000}{2}$ = £27,500.

Rate of turnover = $\frac{\text{cost of sales}}{\text{average stock}} = \frac{105,000}{27,500}$ = 3.8 Approx.

i.e. Goods are in stock for an average of about 14 weeks before sale (52 ÷ 3.8).

(b) Supposing the calculation is re-done assuming this time a 'mark-up' of 30% (i.e. 30% profit on cost price). The cost of sales calculation is more difficult: cost of sales ? – profit 30% of ? = sales £150,000. The technique is to assume a cost of sales of £100, then profit would be £30 and sales would thus be £130. So cost of sales is 100/130 of sales:

100/130 × 150,000 = 11,540 (to nearest £10).

The rest of the calculation follows the same lines as the previous one.

Practice work

Complete the following table, (a) has been done for you.

	1 *CP*	2 *% profit on CP 'mark-up'*	3 *% profit on SP 'margin'*	4 *Actual profit*	5 *SP*
	£	£	£	£	£
(a)	100	50%	33 ⅓%	50	150
(b)	120			30	
(c)	150	33 ⅓%			
(d)			10%		250
(e)	200		33 ⅓%		

Note

Calculate in this order: *(c)* 4,5,3, *(d)* 4,1,2, *(e)* 5,4,2 – method for finding 5 is – assume SP of £100, then CP is 66 2/3 (which simplifies to SP3 CP2 – so SP = 3/2 × CP, etc.

Questions involving stock calculations are fairly common in examinations. Sometimes these are in narration form and the values needed may be given indirectly, i.e. a calculation will be required from information provided. This emphasizes the point already made – understanding is essential, few marks can be earned by learning 'parrot' fashion'.

1 (a) Define rate of stock turnover.

(b) P. Chinon had recently been informed by his accountant that his rate of stock turnover was too low. For the last accounting year it had been calculated as ½. Gross profit on sales was 25% and sales for the year were £40,000. The accountant advised him to double his sales and to increase his rate of stock turnover to 3 for the coming year. On the assumption that this is possible:

(i) Calculate his average stock level for the past year and the coming year.

(ii) State what financial effect the changed stock level will have on the business. (AEB)

Notes

Current year

1 Sales = £40,000. Therefore gross profit = £10,000 (i.e. 25%). Cost of sales is £30,000. Rate of turnover = cost of sales ÷ average stock = ½. Therefore 30,000 ÷ ? = ½. Average stock = £60,000.

? is used instead of the algebraic term *x* Cross multiply to solve.

Another example to help: assume 250 ÷? = ²/₃; twice an 'unknown' = 750. Therefore ? = 375.

Following year

Sales will be £80,000. Gross profit will be £20,000. Cost of sales will be £60,000. Rate of t/o 60,000 ÷ ? = 3. Average stock level will be £20,000.

2 Unsold stock represents capital 'tied up' not earning interest. Thus £40,000 of capital (£60,000 – £20,000) is 'released' for other purposes. Assuming a deposit interest rate of 10% (much higher at time of writing) this represents a gain of £4,000 p.a.

(This question was allocated 10 marks. Likely allocation would have been *(a)* 2/3 *(b)* 6/4 *(ii)* 2/3.

It is important to bear in mind total allocation when answering – only short (but explicit) answers would have been required for *(a)* and *(b)* *(ii)*).

Practice work

2 *(a)* *(i) What is meant by the term 'turnover'? (ii) What is meant by the term 'rate of turnover'?*

(b) J. Bromley's trading account for the year ended 31 March 19–1 is as follows:

	£		£
Stock 1 January	7,000	Sales	200,000
Purchases	190,000		
	197,000		
Stock 31 December	9,000		
	188,000		
Gross profit	12,000		
	200,000		200,000

(i) What is Bromley's turnover?

(ii) What is Bromley's rate of turnover?

(iii) Calculate the gross profit as a percentage of sales.

(iv) Calculate the gross profit as a percentage of cost.
(v) If sales and profit margins remain unchanged, by how much must average stocks be reduced so that rate of turnover is increased to 25 times a year?

(C)	£		£
January	7,000	July	7,000
February	6,000	August	7,000
March	6,000	September	7,000
April	5,000	October	7,000
May	6,000	November	8,000
June	6,000	December	9,000

The figures above show stock figures month by month. Calculate the rate of turnover using the abcve figures, and explain why the answer is different from that to (b) (ii) above. (LOND.)

Notes

(b) (ii) Cost of sales is £188,000.
(iii) Eliminate the noughts, thus it is 12:200 which you can do mentally.
(iv) 'Cost' is of course 'cost of sales'.
(v) 'cost of sales' will also remain unchanged. Use the formula already given.

(c) There will be varying buying/selling patterns, so rate of turnover from twelve valuations will differ from one taken from two only. A more accurate t/o rate is arrived at from monthly figures.

3 *A fire at the warehouse of Steady Trading Co. on the night of 31 March 19–1 destroyed part of the stock and the stock records. From the following particulars prepare a trading account for the three months ending 31 March 19–1 to show the estimated value of stock destroyed.*

	£
Stock at cost 1 Jan. 19–1	8,500
Purchases from 1 Jan. to 31 March	17,400
Sales from 1 Jan. to 31 March	20,200
Stock salvaged was valued at	3,500

Steady Trading Co.'s usual gross profit is 25% selling price. (RSA I)

Notes

What would stock have been if no fire had taken place? Prepare a trading account – you are given every figure but one, so that can be calculated. Complete the account in this order: opening stock, purchases, gross profit, cost of sales.

The difference between your calculation and £3,500 is the figure you need.

MC1 The following information was available for a business in a particular year.

Rate of turnover	5
Cost of goods sold	£30,000
Sales	£40,000
Closing stock	£ 5,000

By making appropriate use of the information, state which of the following was the opening stock for the business.

A *£ 6,000*
B *£ 7,000*
C *£ 8,000*
D *£11,000.* (AEB–S)

Answer to multiple-choice question:
MC1 **B**

3 Profit and loss; the balance sheet

In the previous chapter the only expenditure items dealt with were some of those that are charged against gross profit (e.g. carriage inwards, customs duties on imported goods). With the exception of these, which are included in the trading account because they are really part of the cost of purchases, the remaining expense items are deducted from gross profit in the profit and loss account. Thus this will show the net (or actual) profit; remember though that this will not all be shown as extra cash. As seen in Chapter 1, net profit increases the owner's capital (or net worth) of a business, but this increase is spread over the assets and liabilities. Later (Chapter 18), 'flow of funds' is dealt with – 'where have all the profits gone, they are not reflected in the cash position?'

Calculation of net profit

Profit and loss account

The total of each nominal expenditure account not chargeable in the trading a/c is transferred to the profit and loss a/c (another summary a/c). The effect of this is to *close* the revenue expenditure accounts because the totals involved are being counted against profits for the period. (See later in this chapter for more on the important distinction between capital and revenue expenditure). Totals of revenue income accounts are also transferred – these increase income.

Example

Gross profit for the year to 31 December 19–1 of John Browning: £15,445. Revenue expenditure: rent £3,700; salaries £6,535; vehicle expenses £984; office expenses £1,065. Additional income: discount received £125; interest receivable £530.

Two transfers to profit and loss are illustrated here:

Rent a/c

19–1		£			£
15 Jan.	Bank	850	31 Dec.	(transferred to) P&L a/c	3,700 **(a)**
18 April	Bank	950			
18 July	Bank	950			
21 Oct.	Bank	950			
		£3,700			£3,700

19–2, (etc)

Discount received a/c

	£		£
31 Dec. (transferred to) P&L a/c	125	**(a)** 31 Mar. 19–1 Total for quarter	30
		30 June " " "	29
		30 Sept. " " "	40
		31 Dec. " " "	26
	£125		£125

Profit & loss a/c for year to 31 December 19–1

	£			£	
Rent	3,700	**(a)**	Gross profit	15,445	
Salaries (say)	6,535		Discount received	125	**(b)**
Vehicle expenses	984		Interest receivable	530	
Office expenses	1,065				
	12,284	**(c)**			
Net profit to capital a/c	3,816	**(d)**			
	£16,100			£16,100	

Notes

(a) The double-entry for the rent transfer.

(b) The double-entry for the discount transfer. Individual 'discount receivable' items have been shown in the special column in the cash book and totals posted quarterly to the ledger a/c. Discount allowed (not shown) would be an expense item.

(c) Subtotal is helpful.

(d) See first paragraph of this chapter. You will now see that the combined trading and profit and loss a/cs are really just a device to save unnecessary detail in the capital a/c – because the £3,816 is the amalgamation of all the income and expenditure items in the accounting period and each item either increases or decreases capital.

Wages and salaries

A special note is needed about payments to employees (called either wages or salaries); commercial practice has been to refer to cash paid to staff on hourly or weekly rates – particularly if non-office personnel – as wages. Salaries has been taken to refer to payments at monthly or longer intervals – many of which, though not all, would have been office/administrative staff.

For simplicity in accounting examinations, in the absence of contrary instructions, treat wages as being chargeable in the trading account because it is regarded as a prime and basic expense directly affecting the cost of goods to be sold. Salaries are debited to profit and loss account because they are more of an 'overhead' expense – not varying directly with production costs (e.g. wages paid to 'production line' employees are likely to increase more or less *proportionately* as production increases; the accounts office manager's salary will not).

In Chapter 17, concerning manufacturing accounts, this subject will be dealt with in greater detail. If wages and salaries totals are shown separately charge wages to trading, salaries to profit and loss.

Sometimes an instruction will be given, e.g. wages and salaries £9,654 – $^2/_3$ to trading, balance to profit and loss.

Drawings by owner

This refers to cash (or goods) withdrawn by the owner for his *personal* use – in effect, the equivalent of salary. However, one cannot be both an employee and an employer, so there is a different procedure in the books.

Drawings reduce the owner's capital – he is anticipating profit. It is necessary to show the net profit made before owner's drawings are deducted.

Therefore, instead of debiting salaries (income tax and national insurance problems would also arise if this happened) a separate drawings account is opened, and at the end of the accounting period the total is transferred to the capital account, thus reducing it. An example is shown in the next paragraph.

The balance sheet

Assume in the case of John Browning (in the example on p. 50) the following additional balances remain in the books after the trading

and profit and loss a/cs have been dealt with.

Capital 1 Jan. 19–1 (i.e. total assets *less* total liabilities)	£13,184
Drawings by owner during 19–1: £500 every three months	
Unsold stock 31 Dec. 19–1	£5,700
Equipment and furniture	£3,165
Motor vehicle	£2,100
Cash at bank	£3,721
Owing by debtors	£1,672
Owing to creditors	£1,358

(*NB* We have already calculated net profit as £3,816.)

Notes

Drawings and net profit would appear as follows:

Capital a/c

19–1		£	19–1		£
31 Dec.	Drawings	2,000 (**a**)	1 Jan.	Balance b/d	13,184
31 Dec.	Balance c/d	15,000	31 Dec.	P&L a/c (net profit)	3,816
		£17,000			£17,000
			19–2		
			1 Jan	Balance b/d	15,000

Drawings a/c

19–1		£	19–1		£
31 Mar.	Bank	500	31 Dec.	Capital	2,000 (**a**)
30 June	Bank	500			
30 Sep.	Bank	500			
31 Dec.	Bank	500			
		£2,000			£2,000

(a) Shows transfer of total drawings.

There are no balances for purchases, sales, stock at 1 Jan. and the various expense accounts because these have already been closed by transfer to trading account (not shown above) and the profit and loss a/c (given above).

The remaining balances represent assets or liabilities, and these are listed in the balance sheet at 31 December 19–1. They are not transferred by double-entry because the asset/liability accounts are not being closed – they 'continue' in existence.

Balance sheet layout

Traditionally in the United Kingdom balance sheets have been shown with the capital and liabilities on the left-hand side and the assets on the right-hand side (refer to Chapter 1 – the accounting equation: C + L = A). This is illustrated below but is **not** recommended nowadays.

Balance sheet at 31 December 19–1

	£				£
Capital 1 Jan. 19–1	13,184		*Fixed assets* **(c)**		
add Net profit for 19–1	3,816		Equipment & furniture	3,165	
	17,000		Motor vehicle	2,100	
less Drawings in 19–1	2,000				5,265
Capital 31 Dec 19–1 **(a)**	15,000	**(b)**			
Current liabilities			*Current assets* **(d)**		
Creditors	1,358	**(e)**	Stock	5,700	
			Debtors	1,672	
			Cash at bank	3,721	11,093
	£16,358				£16,358

Notes

(a) There is no need to write the date in but it helps at this stage.

(b) Note that net profit and drawings are shown separately, this being more informative than merely showing closing capital only. The amount by which net profit exceeds drawings is called profits *retained* or *ploughed back*.

(c) **Fixed assets** – those comparatively permanent or semi-permanent assets bought for use in the business which are not normally intended for resale or conversion into cash; other examples are premises (if owned), plant and machinery. Note that minor items are not included (staplers, office scales, etc. would be treated as ordinary expense items).

(d) **Current (or circulating) assets** – these are the ones which in the ordinary course of trading change in value. Thus goods are bought and cash is paid, goods are sold and either cash is received or debtors increase. Debtors pay so cash increases and so on.

(e) **Current liabilities** – normally these refer to bills which will have to be paid within a year.

Recommended layout 1 (C = A − L)

Balance sheet at 31 December 19–1

	£			£
Capital 1 Jan. 19–1	13,184	*Fixed assets*		
add Net profit for 19–1	3,816	Equipment & furniture	3,165	
		Motor vehicles	2,100	
	17,000			
				5,265
less Drawings	2,000	*Current assets*		
		Stock	5,700	
		Debtors	1,672	
		Cash at bank	3,721	
			11,093	
		less		
		Current liabilities		
		Creditors	1,358	9,735
	£15,000			£15,000

Notes

This is more informative than the older-style layout because **working capital** (current assets *less* current liabilities) is shown within the balance sheet as one value (£9,735). Working capital is a vitally important figure for consideration in trying to assess the financial state of a business.

Recommended layout 2

In recent years, many businesses have adopted the vertical style. The only change is that the left-hand side in layout 1 is now shown underneath (full details have been omitted).

Balance sheet at 31 December 19–1

	£
Fixed assets	
(etc.)	5,265
Current assets	
(etc.)	
less *Current liabilities*	
(etc.)	9,735
	£15,000

represented by:

Capital	13,184
add Net profit	3,816
	17,000
less Drawings	2,000
	£15,000

It is suggested that layout 1 is adopted by students.

Summary

1 Each transaction is entered in the two relevant accounts (though often 'totals' only via a subsidiary book).
2 At the end of the accounting period, the balance on each account is calculated (in fact they will then be listed in a trial balance which is discussed in the next chapter).
3 Some of these balances (the income and expenditure ones) are used in the trading a/c and the profit & loss a/c.
4 The remaining balances, being assets and liabilities, are entered into the balance sheet.

Capital expenditure and revenue expenditure

This has already been referred to – in the present chapter and Chapter 1.

Capital expenditure is concerned with the purchase of the fixed assets. As the useful life of these is spread over a period of some years, they are helping to earn income for that period, and it would be wrong to charge the whole cost of any particular fixed asset against the year of purchase. (See Chapter 4 on depreciation.) Note that improvements or additions to an asset are capital expenditure.

Revenue expenditure refers to the general day-to-day or running expenses of the business (e.g. rent, vehicle expenses, salaries). The expenditure has no benefit for the future – it is generally used up during the period concerned (some adjustments may have to be made but these are dealt with later, Chapter 5). All revenue expenditure accounts will be taken into account in arriving at the profit for the period. Note that repairs and redecoration are revenue expenditure because basically they restore the asset to its original state.

Care is necessary in deciding if an item is capital or revenue – the type of business and the purpose for which the expenditure is incurred must be considered. For example, a car purchased for use by a representative is capital expenditure, but a car bought by a car dealer for resale is not. Similarly, you must distinguish between typewriters for office use and those for resale.

Effect of an error

1 Charging capital expenditure as revenue expenditure (e.g. the typewriters for office use) will fail to increase the value of office equipment under fixed assets. If counted as revenue expenditure, the effect will therefore be: fixed assets – too low; net profit – too low.

2 Charging revenue expenditure as capital expenditure (e.g. treating typewriters bought for resale as capital expenditure) would mean: office equipment value – too high; purchases – too low; thus profit too high.

Important points which have caught out many students:

1 Costs incurred in fixing machinery into position (e.g. concreting) are treated as part of the cost of the asset.

2 A firm uses its own staff to carry out, say, the erection of a building for use as a store. If their pay has been debited to salaries and wages a/c, the proportion that applies to this job should be transferred to the premises a/c. Otherwise, premises a/c will be too low and the revenue expenditure a/c too high, thus making net profit too low.

A worked example

Students often have difficulty with problems involving *working capital*. A fully worked question may help.

Effective layout of the answer is important. The basic rule is: are cash, debtors, stock, or creditors affected? If so, then working capital will also be, *unless* an increase and a decrease offset each other as in 2 below.

Draw up a statement showing the effect (if any) of the following transactions on a firm's working capital:

		£
1	Sales for month (all on credit: cost of goods sold amounted to £22,575)	27,982
2	Cash received from debtors	25,228
3	Cash discount allowed to debtors	672
4	Debtors' account written off as bad debts	103
5	Proceeds of sale of old machinery	385
6	Partners drawings.	300

Answers
Effect on working capital

		Increase	Decrease
1 Sales (stock –22,575; debtor +27,982)		£5,407	
2 Cash received from debtors		NO EFFECT	
3 Discount allowed to debtors			£672
4 Bad debts			103
5 Sale of machinery (fixed asset)		385	
6 Partners' drawings			300
		5,792	1,075
		1,075	
	Net increase	£4,717	

Practice Work

1 *(a) Distinguish between 'revenue' expenditure and 'capital' expenditure.*
(b) Indicate, by placing either the letter R or C against each of the following items, which of them would be revenue items and which would be capital items in a wholesale bakery.
(i) Purchase of new motor van
(ii) Purchase of replacement engine for existing motor van
(iii) Cost of altering interior of new van to increase carrying capacity
(iv) Cost of motor taxation licence for new van
(v) Cost of motor taxation licence for existing van
(vi) Cost of painting firm's name on new van
(vii) Repair and maintenance of existing van. (JMB)

Notes
(i) Is the van for sale?
(ii) (iii) (vi) (vii) Apply the test – is it an improvement/addition to an asset or is it repair, redecoration or replacement to put the asset broadly back into its original state?

2 *(a) What do you understand by the term 'working capital'?*
(b) State, with reasons, whether or not the following transactions would increase or decrease the working capital of a business:
(i) Machinery no longer required is sold.
(ii) £1,000 is paid for a van.
(iii) £400 is received from a trade debtor. (RSA I)

3 *(a) On 31 December 19–1 S. Turner had the following assets and liabilities:*
Motor vehicles £1,830; furniture and fittings £585; trade deb-

tors £1,980; stock £2,240; cash in hand and balance at bank £670; trade creditors £2,560; expense creditors £45. Loan (15 years) from J. K. Loans Ltd £1,000.

Draw up Turner's balance sheet in such a way as to show within the balance sheet the:

(i) total of fixed assets;
(ii) total of current assets;
(iii) total of current liabilities;
(iv) working capital. (LOND)

Notes

Note the words underlined. Use recommended layout 1. The long-term loan is not a current liability – it is providing you with funds for a long period to use to acquire assets for running the business. So show this on the left-hand side, i.e.

Capital	?
Loan	1,000

You will know ? after you have completed the right-hand side.

Trade creditors – refers to sums owing to suppliers of goods, etc.

Expense creditors – refers to sums owing for services (e.g. rent, telephone).

4 The following is a pro-forma balance sheet of F. Lang, as at 1 December 19–1:

	£		£
Capital	80,000	Fixed assets:	
Profit (to date)	5,000	Premises	50,000
		Fixtures and fittings	6,000
		Current assets:	
		Stock	
			18,000
		Bank	11,000
	£85,000		£85,000

During the month 1 December to 31 December, F. Lang had the following business transactions:

1 Bought stock costing £2,000 from Wholesale Goods Ltd on credit.
2 Took £2,000 from bank, for own use.
3 Sold goods costing £3,000 for £6,000 on credit and is still unpaid for these sales.
4 Cash sales of goods costing £10,000 for £15,000.
5 Bought delivery van on credit from Newmotor Company Ltd, valued £4,000.

(i) Show the balance sheet as at 31 December 19–1. All calculations must be clearly shown. (RSA I)

Notes

You may prefer to open rough ledger a/cs and write in the double-entry (no need to put in any details other than the amounts).

Each transaction must keep the balance sheet in agreement.

1 Increases stock, introduces creditors.
2 'Own use' – drawings.
3 & *4* Both produce a profit. In each case adjust the appropriate balances first then increase profit.
5 A new fixed asset.

Suggest layout 1 is used.

MC1 The correct heading for an annual balance sheet is
- **A** *Balance sheet as at 31 December*
- **B** *Balance sheet for year ending 31 December*
- **C** *Balance sheet for period ending 31 December*
- **D** *Balance sheet for year as at 31 December.* (AEB–S)

MC2 Which one of the following would increase the working capital of a sports shop?
- **A** *The purchase on credit of rugby balls*
- **B** *The receipt of cash from a debtor*
- **C** *The sale for cash of the delivery van*
- **D** *Payment by cheque to a creditor.* (AEB–S)

MC3 Which one of the following items would be classified as capital expenditure?
- **A** *Withdrawals of cash by the owner for his own use*
- **B** *Redecoration of existing premises*
- **C** *Breakdown-lorry purchased by a garage for its own use*
- **D** *Several cars for resale, purchased by a motor dealer.* (AEB–S)

1 The following is a multiple-completion question.

MC4 Which of the following items would appear as current assets in a balance sheet?
1. *Closing stock*
2. *Cash at bank*
3. *Trade debtors.* (AEB–S)

Answers to multiple-choice questions

MC1 **A**; *MC2* **C**; *MC3* **C**; *MC4* **All**.

4 Accounting adjustments at year end – 1

Bad debts and provision for bad debts

Actual bad debts

Chapter 1 showed that sales on credit are recorded in the books as income when the goods are invoiced. Therefore they are included in the trading account and count towards gross profit; it is the balance sheet which shows that certain amounts owing remain unpaid. Occasionally debtors are unable to pay even when given an extended period to clear their debts, and sometimes the firm concerned is forced to close down; this means that the unfortunate creditor will receive either no payment at all or a part payment in settlement. Sometimes payment is not received because the buyer maintains he is not liable for the debt.

The seller's financial management personnel will decide at which stage to eliminate the debt in whole or in part from the books.

Example

ABC are unable to meet their obligations which includes £250 payable to XYZ covering various sales during 19–1. On 16 March 19–2 the accountant of XYZ decides to write off (cancel) the amount in full. Show the necessary entries in the books of XYZ.

ABC a/c

19–1		£	19–1		£
25 July	Sales	126	31 Dec.	Balance c/d	250
19 Aug.	Sales	72			
26 Aug.	Sales	52			
		£250			250
19–2					
1 Jan.	Balance b/d	250	16 March	Bad debts	£250

Bad debts a/c

16 March	ABC	250			

Notes

The £250 was taken into account at 31 December 19–1 in calculating profit for the year. It is too late to alter 19–1 profit figures, so the £250 will be treated as an expense in the 19–2 accounts and the amount eliminated from debtors. Naturally XYZ's credit controller will have refused to give further credit from the moment he realized the financial problems of ABC – this would have been months before the final 'write-off' (probably September).

1 The £250 has been changed from something of value (i.e. owing by a debtor) to an expense item.
2 Other bad debts written off during 19–2 will receive similar treatment, and the total of bad debts a/c transferred to profit and loss a/c at 31 December 19–2.

Bad debts recovered

Occasionally part or the whole of the amount written off may be paid after all. This can arise if the liquidator (the accountant appointed to wind up the firm's business affairs) obtains further funds (say, from the unexpected sale of an asset). Supposing on 17 August he was able to make a payment of £50 to XYZ. There is now *no* personal account for ABC – the easiest way to deal with this is Dr bank; Cr bad debts. Thus the total bad debts for 19–2 will be £50 less than if this sum had not been recovered.

Alternatively open a bad debts recovered a/c and credit it – at end of 19–2 transfer the amount(s) involved to the credit (income) side of profit and loss a/c.

Provision for bad debts

In the above example the sales transactions occurred in 19–1, so 19–1 earned the 'profit'. This proved non-existent, and 19–2 suffered the 'loss'. Many firms prefer to write off an estimated amount each year to cover possible bad debts (i.e. doubtful ones). This of course is 'guesswork' to some extent. In certain types of business, where there is a great deal of credit, the firm will have a reasonably good idea from past experience of the proportion of bad debts likely to be incurred. For example, Barclaycard (one of the major credit-card companies in the UK) find that they lose about one-half per cent total debtors each year. Hire purchase finance companies may well lose around one per cent (in this type of business there are likely to be large numbers of quite small amounts owing; the company will not spend too much time 'chasing' them).

Do not confuse the following: **bad debts** means an *actual* loss; **provision for bad debts** means an *expected* loss.

Example (part 1)

PQ & Co. have total debtors at 31 December 19–1 of £25,000, and they decide to adopt the policy of trying each year to write off an amount to cover their likely bad debts. From experience they feel this is likely to be 1 per cent of total debtors.

It is not possible to write off actual debtors in advance, so an account called provision for bad debts is opened. In practice there will be many personal accounts, but for this exercise assume there are only three:

Debtor no. 1

19–1 31 Dec.	Balance b/d	£6,600	

Debtor no. 2

19–1 31 Dec.	Balance b/d	£18,100	

Debtor no. 3

19–1 31 Dec.	Balance b/d	£300	

Provision for bad debts (PBD)

	19–1 31 Dec.	P&L a/c	£250

Profit & loss a/c (extract)

19–1 30 Dec.	PBD	£250	

Balance sheet at 31 December 19–1 (extract)

	£	
Debtors	25,000	
less PBD	250	£24,750

Note

We have reduced our net profits by £250 and debtors by the same sum.

Example (part 2)

During 19–2 assume that the only actual bad debt is debtor no. 3, who is only able to pay £200 off his debt; balance of £100 has to be written off. We have thus overestimated our likely bad debts for 19–2 by £150 – if it had been possible to look into a crystal ball our PBD would have been £100 only – however, the overestimate is compensated for at the end of 19–2.

Assume that total debtors at 31 December 19–2 amounted to £27,600 – PBD to again be calculated at 1 per cent. Therefore the total provision now needs to be £276 – as there already is a balance of £250 in the account only £26 needs to be provided at 31 Dec.

Debtor no. 3 a/c

19–1		£	19–1		£
31 Dec.	Balance b/d	300	17 April	Bank	200
				Bad debts	100
		£300			£300

Bad debts 19–2 a/c

19–2			19–2		
17 April	Debtor no. 3	£100	31 Dec.	P&L	£100

PBD 19–2

			1 Jan.	Balance b/d	250
			31 Dec.	P&L	26
					£276

Profit & loss a/c (extract)

19–2		£			£
31 Dec.	Bad debts	100			
31 Dec.	PBD	26			

Balance sheet at 31 December 19–2 (extract)

	Debtors	£27,600
	less PBD	276
		£26,324

Proof: combined bad debts and PBD charge in 19–2 is £126 PBD 1 Jan. 19–2 £250 *less* actual bad debts in 19–2 £100 is:

	150
Provision now	£276

Practice work

1 (a) *What is the difference between 'bad debts' and 'provision for doubtful debts'?*

(b) *State* two *reasons for creating a 'provision for doubtful debts'.*

(c) *R. Browning keeps his books on the financial year January to December. The figures below show his debtors at the end of the years indicated.*

		£
January to December	19–1	8,000
	19–2	6,000
	19–3	9,000
	19–4	9,000

He decided to create a provision for doubtful debts of 5% of debtors in December 19– and to maintain it at that percentage.
Write up the provision for doubtful debts account for the years ended 31 December 19–1 to 31 December 19–4. (LOND)
To help you, part of the question is answered below.

(c) *Provision for bad debts a/c*

19–2	£	19–1	£
31 Dec. P&L	100	31 Dec. P&L a/c	400
Balance c/d	300		
	£400		400
		19–3	
		1 Jan. P&L a/c	£300

Notes

1 At 31 December 19–2 there is an overprovision. Thus by the entry Dr – PBD with £100 and Cr – P&L this is adjusted.
2 Though the question does not request the balance sheet extract to be compiled, this is shown below as at 31 December 19–2.

Balance sheet as at 31 December 19–2 (extract)

Debtors	6,000	
less PBD	300	£5,700

2 The table below shows the figure for debtors appearing in a trader's books on 31 December of each year from 19–1 to 19–4. The provision for doubtful debts is to be 1% of debtors from 31 December 19–1. Complete the table indicating the amount to be debited or credited to the profit and loss account for the year ended on each 31 December, and the amount for the final figure of debtors to appear in the balance sheet on each date. (RSA I)

Date: 31 Dec.	*Total debtors*	*Profit and loss*	*Dr/Cr*	*Final figure for balance sheet*
	£	£		£
19–1	*7,000*			
19–2	*8,000*			
19–3	*6,000*			
19–4	*7,000*			

To assist, part of the question is answered below:

	Debtors	*P&L*	*Dr/Cr*	*Final B/S figure*
	£	£		£
19–1	7,000	70	Dr	6,930
19–2	8,000	10	Dr	7,920

Check:
Total debited to P&L (£70 + £10) equals 1% of £8,000.
Final balance sheet figure 31 December 19–2 £8,000 – £80 = £7,920.
Be careful with 19–3 – total debtors has *decreased*.

3 *L. Rimmer prepared his final accounts at 31 December 19–1. On 1 January there was a balance of £127 on his provision for bad debts account.*

During 19–1 debts amounting to £102 were written off as bad debts.

On 31 December 19–1 debtors' balances totalled £3,607, and on that date Rimmer decided to write off a further £32 as bad debts and to make a provision for bad and doubtful debts of 4% on the total of the remaining debtors.

Make the necessary entries relating to bad debts and provision for bad debts in Rimmer's ledger accounts (including the profit and loss account) for the year 19–1 and show the item 'debtors' as it would appear in his balance sheet as at 31 December 19–1.

Balance the accounts shown (except the profit and loss account). (AEB)

Notes

1 Start with the existing PBD at 1 January 19–1 – credit balance £127.
2 Write off £102 bad debts (you have *no* entries to make in debtors' accounts) *plus* the additional £32 making a total charge to P&L a/c of £134.
3 At 31 December 19–1 the PBD has to be adjusted to 4% of (£3,607 – £32), i.e. £143 – this is the part of the question likely to trip examinees; as the £32 has become an *actual* bad debt it must be written off before the 4% calculation is made. As there is an existing balance in PBD of £127 entry will be Dr P&L £16; Cr PBD £16.
4 Debtors will therefore show in balance sheet as £3,575 less £143.

Provision for discount on debtors

If a business allows cash discount fairly regularly, it may decide to provide for this at the end of the financial period. The principle is similar to the one used for bad debts provision.

Example

XYZ normally allow 3% cash discount for prompt settlement and find that, in practice, about two-thirds of the total amount of discount that could be claimed is, in fact, deducted. XYZ had total debtors of £18,600 at 31 December 19–1 and decided to make a 2% discount on debtors' provision ($^2/_3$ of 3%). Calculation is made to the nearest £10.

Provision for discount on debtors a/c

	19–1 31 Dec.	P&L	£370

The profit and loss a/c is accordingly debited with £370. At the end of 19–2 the provision account is adjusted (as with PBD), e.g.

1 Assume it is to be 2% of £21,650. New provision will be £430, so entry is Dr P&L; Cr provision a/c £60.
2 If however provision had to be *reduced* the following year to say, £400, then – *Dr* provision a/c; *Cr* P&L £30.
3 Remember that if there is a bad debts provision, this should be deducted from debtors before the discount provision is calculated – obviously cash discount does not arise here.

Depreciation of fixed assets

Chapter 1 pointed out that because fixed assets were held on a long-term basis their initial cost was not charged against profits in the year of purchase; the original cost was 'spread' over the period of the expected life of the asset. Basically, each year a fixed asset (say a machine on a production line) helps to earn income, but at the same time 'wears out' to some extent. Therefore, it is reasonable to charge a proportion of its cost against profits in each accounting period. In addition to depreciation caused by normal wear-and-tear, other causes are:

1 Obsolescence – possibly because of a new process of production, e.g. transistors instead of radio valves, plant and machinery, though not worn out, may have to be replaced.
2 Inadequacy – a particular asset may become too small because of business expansion, e.g. larger delivery vehicles may be needed).
3 Depletion – some assets are of a 'wasting' character, e.g. resources like mines and oil wells.
4 Running out of time – this particularly applies to leases, e.g. a factory may be leased for a period of twenty-one years for a fixed sum.

Methods of calculating depreciation provision

Generally, there must be an element of guesswork in trying to assess the useful life of an asset and its likely value on disposal at a given date. All that can be done is to try and charge the cost of the asset as fairly as possible over its useful life. In the end an adjustment has to be made to correct the guesswork. Thus, if a motor vehicle cost £4,500 in 1980 and is sold for £2,900 in 1983, then the capital cost of the vehicle to the business is £1,600, and this is all that can be charged against profit. Note that, under certain circumstances, certain additional tax concessions are granted, but that is outside the scope of this text. The two common methods in use are:

1 Straight line or equal instalment

This is being used increasingly and is regarded by accountants as the most suitable one in most sets of circumstances. Each year an equal amount is charged as depreciation.

$$\frac{\text{Original cost} - \text{estimated 'scrap' or residue value}}{\text{Expected life in years}} = \text{Annual depreciation provision}$$

e.g. $$\frac{\text{Plant cost £92,000} - \text{£8,000}}{\text{12 years}} = \text{£7,000 annual charge}$$

Note that the 'scrap' or residual value is likely to be ignored if it is expected to be a comparatively small sum.

2 Reducing balance

A fixed percentage is applied to the *balance* remaining at the end of each account period. Therefore the actual amount charged will be high at first and reduce year by year.

An involved formula has to be applied to arrive at the percentage (but in an examination question it would be given); it has to be several times greater than the percentage used in the example below (method (1)).

Using 40% over 4 years on an asset which cost £25,000:

		£
Cost		25,000
Year 1	Depreciation provision 40%	10,000
	Balance (or 'book value')	15,000
Year 2	40% of £15,000	6,000
	Balance	9,000
Year 3	40% of £9,000	3,600

	Balance	5,400
Year 4	40% of £5,400	2,160
	Balance	£3,240

It will take 10 years to reduce the balance to about £150 – *nil* is never reached.

Using method (1) a 10% annual charge (£2,500 a year) would write the asset off in 10 years.

Method (2) is being used less and less, though small firms may prefer it as it is the way the Inland Revenue calculate the depreciation allowance for taxation purposes. Many accountants, however, maintain that this alone does not justify the use of this system.

Recording of depreciation provisions

The method which is recommended (and which is compulsory under the Companies Acts) is to maintain a separate account for the depreciation provision. Illustrated below are the entries needed for the first two years of the example given under method (1) (in fact the same book-keeping entries in principle will be made, irrespective of the method in use).

Plant and machinery a/c

19–1				
1 Jan. Bank	£92,000			

Provision for depreciation plant and machinery a/c

			£
		19–1	
		31 Dec. P&L a/c	7,000
		19–2	
		31 Dec. P&L a/c	7,000
			£14,000

Profit and loss a/c

19–1			
31 Dec. Depreciation	£7,000		
19–2			
31 Dec. Depreciation	£7,000		

Balance sheets

as at 31 December 19–1	P&M (at cost)	£92,000	£85,000
(extracts)	*less* Depreciation to date	7,000	
as at 31 December 19–2	P&M (at cost)	92,000	
	less Depreciation to date	14,000	78,000

Notes

1 Asset a/c remains at original cost.
2 In the balance sheet the *accumulated* depreciation is always shown. Thus the following year entry will be £92,000 less £21,000.
3 In this example, the first day of the year was conveniently chosen for the purchase of the plant! In an examination, if dates are shown for purchase of assets, calculate in months (i.e. x/12) unless instructed otherwise.

Asset disposal

Many assets are likely to be sold (or part-exchanged) before the end of their expected life. Two examples follow.

Example 1

In the case used above, there is little problem, as there is only one piece of equipment. Credit the asset a/c with sale proceeds (assume this to be £73,500) and transfer total on provision account to the asset a/c.

Plant and machinery a/c

19–1		£	19–3		£
1 Jan.	Bank	92,000	12 Mar.	Bank	73,500
				Depreciation provision w/b	14,000
				P&L	4,500
		£92,000			£92,000

Notes

1 Do not waste time calculating depreciation to 12 March.
2 The loss on sale is charged to P&L a/c. The capital cost to the firm was £18,500 (£92,000 *less* £73,500) – charged over 3 years (£7,000 + £7000 + £4,500).

Example 2

In practice, in a fixed asset account there would be a number of items, or groups of items, purchased at different dates, e.g. a lorries a/c might show many purchases and disposals. A subsidiary book (in this case a vehicles register) might be needed to show full details of purchases, annual depreciation (which need not be at the same percentage rate for different classes of vehicle), and disposals. An asset disposals a/c will be needed:

Vehicle *A* purchased 7 April 19–1	£12,000.
Vehicle *B* purchased 9 Jan. 19–2	£14,000.

Depreciation (calculated in whole months) 25% p.a. on original cost.

Vehicle C purchased for £16,000 10 Mar. 19–3.
Vehicle A given in part exchange for £7,050.

Lorries a/c

		£			£
19–1			19–3		
7 April	Bank	12,000	10 Mar.	Lorry disposals	12,000
19–2					
9 Jan.	Bank	14,000	10 Mar.	Balance c/d	14,000
		26,000			£26,000
19–3					
10 Mar.	Balance b/d	14,000			
10 Mar.	AZ Garage	16,000			
		£30,000			

Depreciation provision a/c

		£				£
19–3			19–1			
10 Mar.	Lorries Disposal	5,250	31 Dec.	P&L **(a)**		2,250
	Balance c/d	3,500	19–2			
			31 Dec.	P&L		
				(a) 3,000		
				(b) 3,500		6,500
		£8,750				8,750
			19–3			
			10 Mar.	Balance b/d		3,500
			31 Dec.	P&L **(b)**	3,500	
				(c)	3,333	6,833
						£10,333

Lorry disposals a/c

		£			£
19–3			19–3		
10 Mar.	Lorries	12,000	10 Mar.	Depreciation provision	5,250
10 Mar.	P&L	300	10 Mar.	AZ Garage	7,050
		£12,300			£12,300

AZ Garage a/c

19–3			19–3		
10 Mar.	Lorry Disposals	£7050	10 Mar.	Lorries	£16,000

Notes

1 Depreciation workings:
19–1 ¾ of 25% of £12,000 (**a**)
19–2 { 25% of £12,000 (**a**)
25% of £14,000 (**b**)
19–3 { Full year (**b**)
10 months (**c**) ⁵⁄₆ of 25% of £16,000 = £3,333.

2 Transfer of total depreciation of (**a**) £2,250 + £3,000.

3 Profit on sale of (**a**) proceeds £7,050 *less* £6,750.

4 AZ Garage is owed £8,950.

5 Lorries account has been balanced on 10 March to assist understanding.

6 In practice these entries would be journalized (see Chapter 7).

7 Only one disposals a/c would be needed, however many lorries were owned.

8 Balance sheet extract as at 31 December 19–3 will thus be (in full):

	£	
Lorries at cost	26,000	
less Disposals	12,000	
	14,000	
add Additions	16,000	
	30,000	
less Depreciation to date	10,333	£19,667

Appreciation of fixed assets

Normally no accounting action would be taken if fixed assets increase in value (for explanations, see Chapter 18).

Practice work

4 On 31 December 19–7 the following accounts appeared in the books of Smallbrook (Engineers) Ltd. The financial year runs from 1 June to 31 May every year.

Machinery and plant:

19–1		£
1 Jan	Bank	500,000

Provision for depreciation:

19–7		£
31 May	Balance b/d	300,000

On 31 December 19–7 half the machinery and plant was sold for £150,000 cash. New machinery was purchased for cash on 15 February 19–8 for £700,000. At the end of the financial year all

machinery is depreciated by 10% of cost. No charge is made for parts of a year.

Write up the two accounts in Smallbrook (Engineers) Ltd ledger, and show how the asset would appear in the balance sheet on 31 May 19–8. (You may use a separate disposal account if you wish.) (LOND)

Notes

1 Note the financial year end (not everyone uses 31 December or 31 March).

2 Use a disposals a/c – transfer half the asset and half the depreciation provision as follows:

Plant and machinery disposals a/c

19–7		19–7	
31 Dec. P&M	£250,000	31 Dec. Depreciation provision	£150,000
		31 Dec. Cash	£150,000

There is thus a substantial profit on sale; transfer this to P&L account thus closing the above.

3 *Then* enter the new plant followed by the balance sheet extract – noting that depreciation provision is only required at 31 May 19–8 on remaining *old* plant.

5 *On 31 December 19–7 the following balances stood in the books of the Barrell Manufacturing Co. Ltd*

	£
Motor vehicles purchased 1 January 19–4 at cost	14,000
Plant and machinery purchased 1 January 19–0 at cost	26,000
Provision for depreciation on motor vehicles	7,000
Provision for depreciation on plant and machinery	26,000

On 1 January 19–8 half the vehicles, cost price £7,000, were sold on credit to Van Agents Ltd for £2,000 and the whole of the plant and machinery was sold for scrap for £500. Van Agents Ltd sent a cheque for £2,000 on 5 January 19–8.

Prepare ledger accounts to record the sale of these assets, indicating clearly *the amounts to be transferred to profit and loss account. The balances remaining on the asset and provision accounts should also be clearly shown.* (LOND)

Note

It is suggested that two separate depreciation provision a/cs be used. Deal with motor vehicles transactions in full first *then* plant and machinery. Similarly, it is easier to use two disposal a/cs. (In Chapter 6 there are final accounts questions introducing the various end of year adjustments.)

MC1 Given the following details –

Trade debtors, per trial balance	£10,000
Provision for bad debts	£ 1,000
Provision for discount allowed to debtors	5%

– the amount shown as a current asset in the balance sheet is

A *£8,500*
B *£8,550*
C *£8,590*
D *£9,000.* (AEB–S)

MC2 Which one of the following would result from a decrease in the provision for bad and doubtful debts?

A *An increase in gross profit*
B *A reduction in gross profit*
C *An increase in net profit*
D *A reduction in net profit.* (AEB–S)

MC3 Using the straight line method, the annual depreciation at 20% for a motor-car which cost £2,000 now valued at £1,200 would be

A *£160*
B *£240*
C *£400*
D *£800.* (AEB–S)

Answers to multiple choice questions:

MC1 **B**; *MC2* **C**; *MC3* **C**.

5 Accounting adjustments at year end – 2

A basic concept in accounting is that income referring to any one accounting period is to be matched with expenses incurred in the same period; in other words, the relevant factor is *when* the income or expenditure arises, *not* when cash is received or paid. As with credit purchases or sales, which are counted in the period the transaction occurs, it is now necessary to use the same system for revenue expenditure and income items. The basic rule is: How much would have been paid in any one accounting period if nothing was in arrear nor in advance?

Underpayment of expenses

If at the end of the accounting period money is owing to a creditor for a service provided, then the expense account involved must be adjusted. Examples which might arise:

(a) Rent, gas or electricity;
(b) Building or motor vehicle repairs.

Care is needed with category (a) because the period for which the service is charged may not coincide with the accounting period.

Example

Vehicle servicing bills were paid in 19–1. 21 Feb. £65.30, 25 April £39.64, 5 Oct. £126.51. At 31 Dec. 19–1 £88.50 was owing to the garage (subsequently paid 12 Jan. 19–2). Write up the vehicle servicing a/c for 19–1 and show balance sheet extract at 31 December 19–1.

Increase the charge to vehicle servicing a/c and show the £88.50 owing as a creditor thus:

Vehicle servicing a/c

	£		£
19–1	£	19–1	£
21 Feb. Bank	65.30	31 Dec. P&L	319.95
25 Apr. Bank	39.64		
5 Oct. Bank	126.51		
31 Dec. Balance owing c/d	88.50		
	£319.95		£319.95
19–2		19–2	
12 Jan. Bank (etc.)	88.50	1 Jan. Balance owing b/d	88.50

Balance sheet at 31 December 19–1 (extract)

			£
		Current assets	x
		less	
		Current liabilities	
		Creditors	y
		Expenses owing	£88.50

Notes

1 Expenses owing also called 'accrued expenses' or 'expenses outstanding' (o/s).

2 The effect of the above is to count the £88.50 in 19–1 instead of in 19–2. The debit and credit in 19–2 offset each other.

3 Sometimes the exact amount owing is not known – it has to be estimated. Thus if £80 had been used in the above example, the expenses would have been £8.50 understated in 19–1, but this would be corrected in 19–2, thus:

Vehicle servicing a/c

19–2		19–2	
12 Jan. Bank	£88.50	1 Jan. Balance owing b/d	£80.00

Example

A firm commenced business on 1 January 19–2 and chose 31 October as its financial year end. Rates payments were made as follows:

12 Feb. for 3 months to 31 March 19–2 based on *annual* charge of £2,460.

16 May for 6 months to 30 Sept. 19–2 based on a new *annual* charge of £3,000.

At 31 October rates were owing for the 6 months 1 October 19–2/31 March 19–3 (subsequently paid 16 November 19–2). Prepare the rates account for financial year ended 31 October 19–2 and also show the 16 November payment.

Rates 19–2

19–2	£		£
12 Feb. Bank (**a**)	615	31 Oct. P&L (**d**)	2,365
16 May Bank (**b**)	1,500		
30 Oct. Balance o/s c/d (**c**)	250		
	£2,365		£2,365
19–2		19–2	
16 Nov. Bank (**e**)	1,500	1 Jan. Balance o/s b/d	250

Notes

(**a**) 3 months (¼ of year) at £2,460 p.a.
(**b**) 6 months (½ of year) at £3,000 p.a.
(**c**) 1 month (October) at £3,000 p.a.
(**d**) Proof 10 months (Jan. to Oct.) – 3 months at old rate, 7 months at new rate.
(**e**) Payment for 6 months was made in the year 19–2/–3 but only 5 months of this will be chargeable to that year (£1,500 – £250).

Overpayment of expenses

Sometimes a payment may cover part of the following accounting period (e.g. accounting year January to December 19–1; a new yearly insurance policy taken out 1 Oct. 19–1 – thus it includes 9 months' payment covering 19–2). Or an advance payment may be for several years (e.g. two years' advertising paid in advance to secure a discount). The same principle applies as with underpayments. Adjust the expense account so that any overpayment is carried forward to the following accounting period.

Example (part 1)

Premises are rented as from 1 May 19–1, at an annual rental of £6,000 payable 6 months in advance. £3,000 was paid on 3 May and a further £3,000 was paid on 4 Nov. Write up the rent a/c for the year to 31 December 19–1 and the balance sheet extract at 31 December 19–1.

Rent a/c

19–1	£	19–1	£
3 May Bank	3,000	31 Dec. P&L a/c	4,000
4 Nov. Bank	3,000	31 Dec. Balance prepaid c/d (**a**)	2,000
	£6,000		£6,000
19–2			
1 Jan. Balance prepaid b/d	2,000		

Notes

(**a**) This is calculated before P&L transfer is made. The £2,000 represents 4 months in advance at £500 per month (Jan., Feb., March, April 19–2).

Balance sheet at 31 December 19–1 (extract)

	Current assets	
	Debtors	y
	Prepaid expenses	£2,000

Example (part 2)

Assume that the rent was increased from May 19–2 to £7,200. 6 months' rental was paid on 2 May 19–2 and a further 6 months on 1 November 19–2. Carry on writing up the rent account.

Rent a/c

19–2	£	19–2	£
1 Jan. Balance b/d	2,000	31 Dec. P&L a/c (**a**)	6,800
2 May Bank	3,600	31 Dec. Balance prepaid c/d	2,400
1 Nov. Bank	3,600		
	£9,200		£9,200
19–4			
1 Jan. Balance b/d	2,400		

Notes

(**a**) *Proof*: 4 months at £500 = £2,000. 8 months at £600 = £4,800, (thus 12 months has been charged against profits). 4 months (£2,400) carried down covers 1 January to 30 April 19–3.

Outstanding revenue (other than sales)

If a customer owes us money for credit sales, this is automatically shown in the accounts because at the time of dispatch the invoice is prepared and the appropriate entries made in the books – (**a**) sales day book, (**b**) a debit in customer's personal account. It is other sorts of revenue income accounts (e.g. rent receivable, interest receivable which need adjustment. Little difficulty should arise – the same principle applies as with expense items. If revenue has been earned in an accounting period, but the cash has not been received, the amount involved must still be included as income. The correct credit to profit and loss account is the sum that would have been received if the debtor had paid up in the correct period in respect of that period.

Example

A firm sublets part of its offices on 1 January 19–1 at a monthly rental of £240 payable four months in arrears. Rent is to be increased by 25% from 1 September 19–1. From the following details write up the rent account for 19–1 and also show the receipt of rent on 13 January 19–2).

19–1
4 May Received £960 for 4 months to 30 April 19–1
8 Sep. Received £960 for 4 months to 31 August 19–1
19–2
13 Jan. Received rent for 4 months to 31 December 19–1

Rent receivable a/c

19–1	£	19–1	£
31 Dec. P&L (**b**)	3,120	4 May Bank	960
		8 Sep. Bank	960
		31 Dec. Balance due c/d (**a**)	1,200
	£3,120		£3,120
19–2		19–2	
1 Jan. Balance due b/d	1,200	13 Jan. Bank	1,200

Notes

(**a**) Revenue owing to the firm – 4 months at £300.

(**b**) *Proof*: 8 months Jan./Aug. at £240 = £1,920; 4 months Sep./Dec. at £300 = £1,200. Total £3,120.

At 31 December the £1,200 would be included in current assets.

A worked example

(The likely breakdown of marks is shown in brackets.)

1 (*a*) *From the following information write up the advertising expenses account for 19–1, balancing it as appropriate.*

1 Jan. Balance b/d (representing a payment covering January, February and March 19–1 made during 19–0), £450.

17 May Payment made in respect of 1 April to 30 September 19–1, £1,260.

31 Dec. Owing to advertising agency for period 1 October to 31 December 19–1, £630.

(*b*) *At 31 Dec 19–1 where will the balance on the advertising account be shown in the balance sheet?*

(*c*) *How much would be charged to profit and loss account for 19–1 in respect of advertising?*

(*d*) *If, during 19–2, £1,950 is paid to the advertising agency, all of which is in respect of 19–2 expenditure, how much will be charged to profit and loss account for 19–2 in respect of advertising, assuming nothing is owing at 31 December 19–2?*

(*e*) *Will there be a balance sheet entry at 31 December 19–2 in*

respect of advertising? If so what will it be? (Give a reason for your answer.) (RSA I) ***(16 marks)***

(a) *Advertising expenses a/c*

19–1	£	19–1	£
1 Jan. Balance b/d **3**	450	31 Dec. P&L	2,340
17 May Bank **6**	1,260		
31 Dec. Balance o/s c/d **3**	630		
	£2,340		£2,340
		19–2	
		1 Jan. Balance o/s c/d	630 (7)

Notes

The bold figures **3, 6, 3** indicate the number of months covered by the sums shown (so 12 months have been charged). The £450 was *paid* in 19–0 but is *counted* in 19–1 as it is for a service provided in 19–1.

(b) Under current liabilities – because it is owing to the supplier of the service. *(2)*

(c) As shown £2,340. *(1)*

(d) This can either be solved by continuing the above account for 19–2 or by a purely arithmetical calculation. *Either*:

Advertising expenses a/c

19–2		£	19–2		£
–	Bank	1,950	1 Jan	Balance o/s b/d	630
			31 Dec	P&L	1,320
		£1,950			£1,950

or:

	£
Payments in 19–2 covering 19–1 & 19–2 items	1,950
less 19–1 items	630
∴ referring to 19–2	£1,320 *(4)*

(e) No balance sheet entry at 31 December 19–2 (nothing owing). *(2)*

Practice work

2 *On 1 January 19–2 the following appear in E.X. Ton's balance sheet:*

Rates in advance, £150.

During the year the following rates payments were made: 11 May 19–2, £400; 23 November 19–2, £400.

The second £400 covers the period from 1 October 19–2 to 31 March 19–3.

Write up the account for the year ended 31 December 19–2, showing clearly the amount to be charged to the profit and loss account for the year ended on that date.

Write down the amount which should appear in E.X. Ton's balance sheet on 31 December 19–2, and indicate whether the amount is an asset or a liability. (RSA I)

Notes

£150 of 19–2 rates was paid in 19–1 – this was an asset at 31 December 19–1 so it will be a debit balance at 1 January 19–2 (similar to the £450 in the previous example). The 11 May payment but only part of the 23 November payment refer to 19–2. Make sure that 12 months' rates payment is charged to profit & loss a/c – carry forward the advance payment for the 3 months 1 Jan to 31 March 19–3.

(This question was allocated 8 marks – it should not take more than 10 minutes.)

3 *On 31 May 19–1, R. Gee's balance sheet showed the following:*

Items outstanding	£	*Items in advance*	£
Stationery	30	Insurance	20
Salaries	700		
Rates	300		

During the year ended 31 May 19–2, the following payments were made by cheque:

	£
Insurance	240
Stationery	70
Salaries	10,000
Rates	2,700

On 31 May 19–2 the balance sheet showed the following:

Items outstanding	£	*Items in advance*	£
Stationery	10	Insurance	30
Salaries	800	Rates	360

Prepare the ledger accounts for each of the above items for the year ended 31 May 19–2, showing clearly the amount charged to profit and loss account in each case. (LOND)

Notes

Examination questions will often include several expense accounts (in arrears and in advance). Tackle it this way:

1 Open the three accounts with credit balances and the fourth with a debit balance.

2 Then write up the first account (stationery) fully, showing the P&L transfer, and remember to enter the credit balance brought down at 1 June 19–2 (because R. Gee owes £10). To help you, the P&L charge will be £70 – £30 + £10, because the £70 includes the arrear of £30 which refers to the previous year and the £10 is a current item. The others are then dealt with one by one.

6 The trial balance and preparation of final accounts

The trial balance

Every transaction has a debit entry and a credit entry. It follows therefore that if the individual accounts are listed in two columns, one for the total debits and one for the total credits, then, when added, the same overall totals should result. The following example (dates omitted) shows this:

Cash a/c

	£		£
Sales (**a**)	790	Rates (**c**)	155
Sales (**b**)	500	Rent (**d**)	600
		G. Smith (**f**)	100

Sales a/c

			£
		Cash (**a**)	790
		Cash (**b**)	500

Rent and rates a/c

	£		
Cash (rates) (**c**)	155		
Cash (rent) (**d**)	600		

Purchases a/c

G. Smith (**e**)	£180		

G. Smith a/c

Cash (**f**)	£100	Purchases (**e**)	£180

List of debits/credits

	Dr	Cr
Cash	1,290	855
Sales		1,290
Rent and rates	755	
Purchases	180	
G. Smith	100	180
	£2,325	£2,325

However, overall totals that agree will also be obtained if the balances only are entered, i.e. the amounts by which one side exceeds the other. This is called a trial balance, and assuming the date it was taken out was 31 October 19–1, the following would result.

Trial balance at 31 October 19–1

	Dr	Cr
Cash	435	
Sales		1,290
Rent and rates	755	
Purchases	180	
G. Smith		80
	£1,370	£1,370

Notes

1 Remember that a debit balance is the amount by which the total debits exceed total credits and vice versa.
2 Students often forget to date a trial balance.
3 If both sides total the same, the account can be omitted entirely – thus if G. Smith had been paid £180 instead of £100, his account would not be entered in the trial balance.

Use and limitations of the trial balance

A trial balance is *not* proof that the accounting is correct. All it shows is that for every debit entry there has been an equal and opposite credit entry. Various errors can arise which will not show up in the trial balance. Examples are:

1 Both entries needed for a transaction missed out entirely.
2 Both entries are made using the same incorrect amount, e.g. item (**a**) above entered as £970 in both cash and sales a/c.
3 The correct amount is entered on the correct side of the wrong account, e.g. item (**d**) above entered correctly in the cash a/c but £600 debited to repairs a/c instead of rent and rates.

You will find more about trial balance errors and how they are corrected in Chapter 8.

Preparation of final accounts

Before trading and profit and loss accounts and balance sheet are prepared at financial year end, a trial balance will be taken out. At this stage the individual accounts will be totalled in pencil and balances calculated. If there is a difference on the trial balance, the error(s) need to be traced and corrected. Then the year-end adjustments (e.g. depreciation, bad debts provision, outstanding and prepaid expenses) are put through the books. Businesses with a considerable number of adjustments to make may well take out another trial balance after these have been dealt with. The final accounts can then be prepared from this trial balance. The reader will realize that basically the final accounts are just a rewrite in a different form of the trial balance. Some items will be included in the trading a/c, some in the profit and loss a/c, and the remainder in the balance sheet.

Final accounts examination questions

These appear in many papers. With care a good mark can be earned, but there are definite pitfalls to be wary of. A typical question might set out a trial balance, provide certain items of additional information underneath it (adjustments), and ask for preparation of final accounts. Total mark allocation may well be up to about 25/26, but the maximum will not be earned unless a methodical approach is made.

A worked example

Guidance on methods of operation are given below, in addition to a complete model answer. A possible marking scheme is also shown. The trial balance is set out on p. 86–7 below.

Method

1 Mark each trial balance item with a *T*, *P* or *B* to indicate whether an entry will be made in the trading profit and loss accounts or balance sheet.
2 Decide how the adjustments will affect the trial balance figures. You will see that:
  (a) increases wages and is entered under current liabilities ('expenses owing') in balance sheet;
  (b) reduces insurance and will be a current asset (prepaid expenses) in balance sheet;
  (c) depreciation charge (£560 + £750) debited in profit and loss a/c, and deducted from fixed assets in balance sheet;
  (d) a *reduction* on the debit side of the trading a/c; included as a current asset in balance sheet.

  The author recommends (certainly in the early stages of final accounts work) that the action to be taken on the adjustments should be written on the question paper. Use a 'shorthand', (e.g. Wages + : c/l in BS).

Note that each of these adjustments alters the profit and will also affect the balance sheet.

3 Mark with an *X* the balances affected in the trial balance.
4 Remember that a *debit* balance will be either an expense item in trading or profit and loss a/c or an asset in the balance sheet. (Drawings has slightly different treatment – instead of being counted as an expense it is a deduction from the capital a/c in balance sheet – which in principle is the same thing. See Chapter 3).
5 If a combined wages and salaries balance is shown, treat as a profit and loss a/c item. Sometimes you are instructed to charge part to trading and part to profit and loss.
6 Remember that trading and profit and loss is for an accounting period, and the balance sheet is as at the last day of the period.
7 Provided you show closing stock as indicated, you get cost of sales automatically.
8 Be as neat as you can and don't cramp your work – notice particularly how insetting of figures helps.
9 Subtotals are needed for fixed and current assets and current liabilities.
10 The layout illustrated is recommended for the balance sheet, though normally you will not be penalized if you include current liabilities on the other side (as specimen in Chapter 3). However, you may be asked to lay out in such a way as to show working capital within the balance sheet; in this case that specimen will not do.
11 Tick each item as you use it. Each trial balance item will have one tick; each adjustment item will have two ticks.

Andrew Roberts has an established business as a wholesaler and the following is his trial balance at 31 December 19–1.

	Dr £	Cr £
Capital 1 January 19–1		25,840*B*
Drawings	5,632*B*	
Debtors and creditors	5,852*B*	5,658*B*
Bank overdraft		646*B*
Land and buildings	15,400*B*	
Equipment	2,800*XB*	
Vehicles	3,000*XB*	
Unsold stock 1 January 19–1	8,800*T*	
Purchases and sales	42,870*T*	62,438*T*
Rent received from tenant		1,000*P*

Wages and salaries	8,608XP	
Rates and insurances	548XP	
Light and heat	370P	
Sundry office expenses	638P	
Selling expenses	1,064P	
	£95,582	£95,582

The following additional information is to be taken into account:

(*a*) Balance owing for wages for the last few days of the accounting year is £272.

(*b*) Insurance premiums prepaid £52.

(*c*) Depreciate the equipment by 20% and the vehicles by 25%.

(*d*) Unsold stock at 31 December 19–1 is valued at £10,300.

You are asked to prepare trading and profit and loss accounts for the financial year to 31 December 19–1 showing clearly in the accounts the cost of goods sold. Also a balance sheet at 31 December 19–1.

Answer

Andrew Roberts: Trading and profit and loss accounts for year to 31 December 19–1

	£		£
Opening stock 1 Jan. 19–1	8,800	Sales	62,438
add Purchases	42,870+		
	51,670		
less Closing stock 31 December 19–1	10,300–		
Cost of goods sold	41,370		
Gross profit c/d	21,068		
	£62,438		£62,438
Wages and salaries	8,880	Gross profit b/d	21,068
Rates and insurances	496	Rent received	1,000
Light and heat	370		
Sundry office expenses	638		
Selling expenses	1,064		
Depreciation:			
Equipment 560			
Vehicles 750	1,310		
	12,758		
Net profit to capital a/c	9,310		
	£22,068		£22,068

Balance sheet as at 31 December 19–1

		Fixed assets			
	£			£	
Capital 1 Jan. 19–1	25,840	Land and buildings		15,400	
add Net profit for year	9,310	Equipment	2,800		
		less Depreciation	–560	2,240	
	35,150	Vehicles	3,000		
less Drawings –	5,632	*less* Depreciation	–750	2,250	19,890
		Current assets			
		Unsold stock		10,300	
		Debtors	5,852		
		Prepayments	52	5,904	
				16,204	
		less			
		Current liabilities			
		Creditors	5,658		
		Expenses owing	272		
			5,930		
		Bank overdraft	646	6,576	9,628
	£29,518				£29,518

Possible marking scheme

Trading a/c	6
P&L a/c	10
Balance sheet	10
	26

Deductions

Each error of principle 2

Each arithmetic error 1 (but not 'double penalized')

Layout up to 3

Subtotals not shown 1 or 2

Other errors, e.g. incorrect headings 1

Checking for errors

With this sort of question it does *not* follow that you must be correct if both sides of the balance sheet agree – but if they do not agree you are certainly wrong somewhere. The important thing is not to panic, and never move a figure from one position to another merely to reduce the difference!

Another fatal mistake is to stop writing up the balance sheet in the middle just because you realize that the two totals are obviously not going to agree.

Steps

1 First just look at your accounts in case there is an obvious error – for example are all the debit entries in the profit and loss a/c expenses? Have you used each balance given in the trial balance?

2 Recheck your arithmetic being careful to see that where a subtraction is necessary you have not added in error.

3 Check your book-keeping on the adjustments. Have you made use of each figure twice? Do your expenses-owing items increase expenditure? Do your prepayments reduce expenditure?

4 Last step will be to check each entry from the examination paper against your answer book. Change the order of working by taking each trial balance figure in turn, and tick it off in your accounts.

5 Do not spend too long on this checking exercise, but go on to another question and return to the final accounts one if time allows. (Reread advice given about examination technique, p. 13.)

Service businesses

Increasingly, examination bodies, instead of setting a final accounts question on a buying and selling business, choose one which is providing a 'service', and students often do not do as well as they might, largely because some of the accounts will not have such familiar names. In previous years the following have appeared: a professional consultant; a hotel; a café; a hairdresser; a private school.

Sometimes a business which both sells and provides a service is given, e.g. a garage selling cars and fuel as well as repairing vehicles, or a shoe shop which also repairs boots and shoes.

Again, from time to time, trading and profit and loss accounts in columnar form may be required.

Example

1 Jane Jones is in business as a hairdresser. From the figures below prepare her profit & loss account for the year ended 31 December 19–1 and a balance sheet on that date.

	£	£
Capital 1 January 19–1		9,740
Drawings	4,500	
Motor-car (cost £1,800)	1,320	
Petty cash	40	
Cost of new hair dryer	120	
Equipment (cost £1,000)	600	
Freehold premises	6,000	
Advertising	230	
Cash at bank	5,400	
Motor-car expenses	480	
Rates	140	
Telephone	110	
Revenue from hairdressing		10,400
Sundry expenses	1,200	
	£20,140	£20,140

The following should be taken into consideration:

(*a*) Rates prepaid 31 December 19–1 £30.
(*b*) One-third of motor-car expenses including depreciation for the year is to be regarded as private use.
(*c*) Provide for cleaning costs £50.
(*d*) Depreciate all equipment on hand at 31 December 19–1 by 10% of cost.
(*e*) Motor-car is to be depreciated by 20% on reduced balance. (RSA I) *(26 marks)*

Notes

1 Often it is not possible to divide into trading and profit and loss a/cs in this type of business. Revenue from hairdressing is her income item (being the equivalent of sales in a buying/selling firm).

2 *Adjustments*

(*a*) Rates £110. Balance sheet £30 prepaid (current assets).
(*b*) Car expenses { £320 charged to P&L
£160 charged to drawings (also see *e*).
(*c*) Sundry expenses £1,250. Balance sheet £50 expenses owing (current liability).
(*d*) 'All' equipment at cost will be £1,000 + £120, i.e. £1,120; depreciation at 10% = £112. It is easy to make the error of using the written-down value of £600 instead of the original cost of £1,000.
(*e*) 'Reduced balance' means 'book value', i.e. £1,320. 20% of £1,320 = £264 allocated thus

{ $^2/_3$ charged to P&L, i.e. £176
$^1/_3$ charged to Drawings, i.e. £88.

3 *Drawings*
Total charge £4,500 + £160 (refer to (b) above) + £88 (refer to (e) above).

Practice work

2 P. Brown is in practice as a professional adviser. The figures below relate to his affairs for the year ended 31 May 19–2. Prepare a profit and loss account for the year ended 31 May 19–2 and a balance sheet on that date.

	£	£
Capital 1 June 19–1		6,200
Drawings	4,000	
Office furniture and equipment (at cost)	1,400	
Subscriptions to professional bodies	120	
Money held in trust for clients		2,000
Postage and stationery	450	
Rent and rates	700	
Interest on bank deposit account		150
Money on deposit account	3,000	
Professional charges for services		12,000
Unpaid accounts for services	400	
Petty cash	30	
Cash in bank	5,500	
Salaries office staff	4,000	
Travelling expenses	750	
	£20,350	£20,350

The following should be taken into consideration:

(*a*) Salaries unpaid, £80.
(*b*) Rent and rates unpaid for April and May may be calculated from the figure of £700 which covers ten months.
(*c*) Travelling expenses for private journeys by P. Brown (included in the £750 travelling expenses), £50.
(*d*) Of the interest received the following amount is interest on client's money, £100.
(*e*) Depreciate furniture and equipment by 10% on cost.
(RSA I)

Notes

This was a rather difficult question for a Stage I examination; again notice that a trading a/c cannot be prepared.

1 *Adjustments*
(*b*) Sometimes you are required to calculate, from information

provided, the amount owing or prepaid. It is £70 per month for two months.

(*c*) Brown should not charge his firm with private expenses; reduce travelling expenses to £700 and add £50 to drawings.

(*d*) This refers to 'Money held in trust for clients, £2,000'. The £2,000 is not Brown's money – he is merely looking after it – in the same way as a solicitor may be holding a deposit on a house on behalf of a client. So only £50 of the interest is debited to profit and loss – the remaining £100 is owing to the client. The balance sheet entry is:

Current liabilities	
On trust for clients	£2,000
+ interest due to them	£100

(*e*) As with the previous example depreciation is calculated on cost.

2 *Revenue income*

Look at the two items 'professional charges for services' £12,000, and 'unpaid accounts for services' £400. Normally you would expect to find the unpaid accounts as an adjustment to be actioned. As it is in the trial balance it has already been entered in the books. So the total credit must have been £11,600 before the £400 was entered, thus:

Professional charges a/c

19–2		£			£
31 May	P&L	12,000	–	Total for year	11,600
			31 May	Balance owing (to P. Brown) c/d	400
		£12,000			£12,000
19–2					
1 June	Balance b/d	400			

So enter the £12,000 as the income item and merely show the £400 as a current asset (fees owed by clients).

In questions *3* and *4* below, further extracts from past examination questions are given with notes on how they should be dealt with.

Sometimes the list of balances given is not divided into debits and credits. Normally you can tell by the name of the account whether it is asset, liability, expenditure or income; in the few cases where this cannot be done, the paper will provide the necessary information.

3 *The following were among the balances extracted from the books of S. Drive on 31 December 19–1. From this information prepare trading and profit and loss accounts. (NB Only some of the balances given in the question are shown below.)*

	£
Purchases	15,750
Sales	20,500
Returns inwards	456
Returns outwards	278
Carriage on purchases	84
Interest on loan (debit)	30
Discount allowed	210
Discount etc. received	140

(RSA I)

Adjustments
(*a*) Provide £100 for doubtful debts.
(*b*) A half-year's interest £30, is due on the loan.

Notes

1 Notice that no balance sheet is required.
2 Returns inwards (sales returned by customers of S. Drive) reduces sales figure given, i.e. £20,500 less £456. Conversely, returns outwards are goods he rejects (so purchases is £15,750 less £278).
3 Discount allowed – expense. Discount received – income.
4 There is no existing provision for bad and doubtful debts, so create one. Charge £100 as an expense. In a full question the provision would be deducted in the balance sheet from total debtors.
5 Interest on loan is an expense item (information given). When the interest was paid by Drive the entry was Cr cash; Dr interest. Charge £60 as an expense and show £30 as a current liability.

4 *A trial balance included the following balances (amongst others), together with the adjustments shown below. (The question required final accounts to be prepared.)*

Trial balance 31 December 19–1

	Dr £	Cr £
Capital		36,000
Furniture and fittings	1,200	
Purchases	88,120	
Sales		106,640
Drawings	4,500	
(etc.)		

Adjustments
On 31 December 19–1 Rail (the trader) bought a motor van for the business for £2,000 and furniture for the business costing £200. He paid for both with cheques drawn on his private bank account. He also took from the business goods costing £250 for his own private use. No entries have been made in the books of the firm recording these transactions. (RSA II)

Notes

1 As he paid £2,200 from his private funds for business assets this is the equivalent of paying in additional capital. So capital must be increased by this amount and the two assets added.

2 Goods taken from the business is the same as cash taken. Therefore, drawings should be increased by £250. The trading a/c entry can be dealt with in two ways:

Either:

	£	
Purchases	88,120	
less Stock taken by owner	250	£87,870

or:	£	
Sales	106,640	
Stock taken by owner at cost	250	£106,890

The first choice is the better one, and is recommended.

Considerable practice is essential on final accounts questions. Remember to be methodical and adopt the methods suggested in this chapter. The following are sole trader examples. In Chapters 10, 14, 15 there are questions involving departmental accounts, partnerships and limited companies.

5 *The following trial balance was extracted from the books of F. Wood, proprietor of the Woodstock Hotel, on 31 March 19–2:*

	£	£
Proprietor's capital		40,000
Purchases and sales of food	18,000	47,100
Stock on 1 April 19–1	1,300	
Trade creditors		1,500
Debtors for banquets	1,700	
Rent and rates	900	
Wages and salaries	9,950	
Light and heat	1,550	
Repairs and renewals	780	
Furniture	3,800	
Kitchen equipment	4,400	

China and cutlery	1,660	
Drawings	110	
Cash at bank	550	
Leasehold premises	44,000	
Provision for bad debts		100
	£88,700	£88,700

You are required to prepare the hotel's trading and profit and loss account for the year ended 31 March 19–2, and a balance sheet as at that date after taking into account the following:

(*a*) the final stock of provisions was valued at £1,400;
(*b*) the provision for bad debts is to be adjusted to 5% of the debtors;
(*c*) provisions are to be made for depreciation as follows:

Furniture	10%
Kitchen equipment	£400
Leasehold premises	£2,000
China and cutlery to be revalued at	£1,420;

(*d*) the cost of staff meals, provided free of charge, is estimated at £1,600;
(*e*) entries have not yet been made in the accounts in respect of purchases on credit amounting to £100;
(*f*) a sum of £200 for a wedding banquet is still owing and has not been recorded in the books;
(*g*) the item repairs and renewals includes an amount of £140 in respect of repairs to the proprietor's house. (JMB)

Notes

Adjustments

(*b*) 5% of debtors £1,900 (see adjustment (*f*) – £1,700 + £200) is £95; bad debts provision is already £100 so it has to be *reduced*. A credit entry in the profit and loss a/c is needed as follows: PBD written back £5. Balance sheet entry will be debtors £1,900 *less* PBD £95.

(*c*) The revaluation method of depreciation is often used in cases where the length of life cannot be estimated with any degree of accuracy (also used by builders and engineers for loose tools). The difference between old book value of the china and cutlery £1,660 and the new book value £1,420 is the depreciation charge.

(*d*) 'Perks' for the staff – if ignored the gross profit suffers, though obviously the net profit cannot be affected. It is assumed that £1,600 is the equivalent menu price. Therefore, add an extra item of £1,600 as a credit in the trading a/c and show it as an expense in profit and loss a/c.

(*e*) Making the double-entry will increase purchases and trade creditors.

(*f*) Similarly this increases sales and debtors.

(*g*) The business must not pay for Mr Wood's private repairs, so reduce repairs and renewals and increase drawings.

6 *From the following trial balance and the notes appended below, prepare the profit and loss account for the year ended 31 December, 19–1 and a balance sheet as at that date.*

Trial balance of A. M. Dealer 31 December 19–1

	£	£
Capital		66,365
Cash at bank – deposit a/c	50,000	
Cash at bank – current a/c	14,622	
Cash-in-hand	374	
Debtors	30,003	
Creditors		34,681
Drawings	10,000	
Investments	5,000	
Office furniture and fittings	10,100	
Office machines	4,000	
Motor-car	1,600	
Commission received		53,740
Consultation fees		1,250
Interest		2,476
Rent and rates	5,240	
Salaries and national insurance	21,478	
Travel and entertaining	2,472	
Advertising	728	
Insurance	224	
Trade subscriptions	1,280	
Telephone and cables	1,284	
Sundry expenses	107	
	£158,512	£158,512

Adjustments

(*a*) No trading a/c is required.

(*b*) Depreciate office furniture and fittings and office machines by 10%.
Depreciate motor-car by 20%.

(*c*) Insurance paid in advance £34.

(*d*) Rates paid in advance £80.

(*e*) Advertising expenses accrued £72. (RSA I)

Notes

1 A. M. Dealer is obviously some sort of professional consultant.
2 The adjustments are straightforward.
3 Note that there are three credit (income) items in the profit and loss a/c, £53,740, £1,250 and £2,476.
4 No information is given about the type of investment – is it a semi-permanent one Mr Dealer has made with surplus business cash? Best solution is to show it separately between the fixed assets and the current assets.

6 *C. Fix, a wholesaler, produced the profit and loss account given below to the local inspector of Taxes. Fix stated at the time of presentation that the account represented his net revenue for the year ended 31 August, 19–2.*

C. Fix Profit & loss a/c

	£	£	£
Stock 31 August 19–2		17,000	
Purchases for year		35,000	
Salaries		3,500	
Carriage outwards		500	
Stock 31 August 19–1		12,000	
			68,000
less Sales			100,000
Gross profit			32,000
less			
Wages (warehouse)		3,000	
Cash discount on purchases		600	
Depreciation			
Furniture (at cost)	5,000		
10% depreciation thereon	500		
		4,500	
			8,100
			23,900
add			
Bad debts			800
Bank charges			200
Stationery			200
Motor expenses (including £800 depreciation)			1,200
Carriage inwards			300
Returns (from a customer)			1,000
Total net revenue			£27,600

The local Inspector of Taxes is not satisfied with the account. You are required to:

Produce an amended trading and profit and loss account, for presentation to the Inspector of Taxes, for the year ended 31 August, 19–2, showing clearly therein cost of materials sold, cost of sales, gross profit and net profit. (RSA I)

Notes

No doubt the reader will feel that the trader should be called C. Fixit rather than C. Fix! Note that all the figures but one will be needed in your amended accounts (the omission will be £5,000 for furniture – it is only the annual depreciation that is charged against profits). Points to watch:

1 *Cost of materials sold* – remember that carriage inwards is part of the cost of the goods. So cost of materials sold will be – opening stock + (purchases + carriage inwards) – closing stock.

2 *Cost of sales* – i.e. the cost of getting the goods on the shelves ready for sale. Wages (warehouse) should therefore be added to 1 above.

3 *Other items* – Cash discount on purchases = discount received. Carriage outwards is a selling expense. Returns from a customer = returns inwards. Show motor expenses and depreciation as two separate items.

7 The journal

In Chapter 1, books of original entry (or subsidiary books) were introduced in connection with credit transactions (purchases, sales, returns), showing that a credit purchase will first be recorded in the purchase day book; a cheque payment will be entered first in the bank column of the cash book. In fact the vast majority of transactions in a business will first see the light of day in one of the above books (the cash book is regarded both as a subsidiary book and a ledger account).

However, this still leaves a number of other transactions (generally not too many in number) which require special treatment and for these the **general journal** (or **journal proper**) is used. Remember, the basic principle is that all transactions should first be recorded in a book of original (or prime) entry. One of the advantages is that more detail can be recorded than with direct entries into the ledger. Again, especially where there is a considerable volume of accounting work, the ledgers may well be subdivided in various ways (see Chapter 11 on control accounts).

What should be entered in the journal?

1 Correction of errors.
2 Adjustments (e.g. outstanding expenses).
3 Year-end transfers (e.g. to trading a/c).
4 Any special entries (e.g. introduction of new capital; opening entries of a business).
5 Credit purchase or sale of assets (as distinct from goods for resale). Some firms, however, enter these in a special column in the normal day books.

Journal entry layout

Regard a journal entry as the authority to make the necessary ledger entries – it shows the accounts that are to be entered. The following is an example:

Date	*Details*	*Folio ref.*	*Dr*	*Cr*
19–1				
15 June	Bad debts a/c	GL29	£120.54	
	L. Smith a/c	SL75		£120.54
	Amount written off, authorized by credit control memo 10/6/–1 reference cc/GkN			

It is essential that the explanation for the action to be taken (the narration) gives all relevant information. From the above the ledger clerk will:
Debit bad debts account on folio 29 of the general ledger and credit L. Smith's account on folio 75 of the sales ledger.

Examples of journal entries

Date	*Details*	*Folio ref.*	*Dr*	*Cr*
19–1			£	£
29 Oct.	G. Stephenson & Co.	SL82	65.40	
	George Stevenson Ltd	SL85		65.40
	Invoice 894, 16 October, wrongly debited to latter account now corrected			
31 Oct.	Rent 19–1	GL20	85.50	
	Rent 19–2	GL20		85.50
	Rent for October owing to ABC Property Co. carried down unpaid			
31 Oct.	Drawings	PL4*	100.00	
	Purchases	GL11		100.00
	Goods taken from stock during the month by owner			
31 Oct.	Office equipment	GL17	640.00	
	Ofco Ltd	PL19		640.00
	Purchase on credit of typewriters (invoice 754) for office use			

* PL = private ledger; really a subdivision of the general ledger, it will contain the confidential items directly affecting the owner(s).

Composite journal entries

Where three or more accounts are involved, a composite entry can be made. Thus the following entry shows the transfer of three expense accounts totals to the profit and loss a/c.

31 Oct.	Profit and loss	PL3	720.77	
	Telephone	GL24		210.35
	Heating and lighting	GL26		184.60
	Rates	GL21		£325.82
	Balances transferred			

NB In the profit and loss a/c the three totals will still be shown separately.

Practice work

Many examination questions requiring journal entries (especially those dealing with correction of errors) also ask for the arithmetical effect of the entries on the final accounts. The latter are dealt with in Chapter 8.

1 A number of business transactions of a non-routine nature require special treatment in the books of account. A sample of such transactions is given hereunder relating to the retail shop owned by Mr J. Jackson, for the four weeks ending 31 August 19–1.

(*a*) Commission on turnover due to Mr R. Brown, manager: 3½% on a turnover of £14,000.

(*b*) J. Jackson took from the stock each week, for his personal use, £20 of goods.

(*c*) E. B. Tate, a supplier, agreed to take J. Jackson's motor van, valued at £1,800, in part payment of the amount owing to him.

(*d*) Discount received, £30 from T. D. Smith, was disputed by Smith and has now been disallowed.

You are required to:

(*i*) *Prepare the journal entries necessary to record the above transactions.*

(*ii*) *Show clearly in the journal folio column, to which ledger, each entry would be posted.* (RSA I) *(16 marks)*

Notes

1 Question does not say 'Pay Mr Brown'. So debit a commission (or salaries and commission) account and credit a personal account. The latter account will be in the general ledger (because Brown is not a trade customer).

2 See specimen entries earlier in this chapter.

3 Remember you are Jackson. You have to eliminate the van in your books (general ledger) by crediting motor vans account and debiting E. B. Tate (purchase ledger) as if you had paid him in cash.

4 This can cause difficulty. Imagine the ledger position (with fictitious entries) before the item is disallowed:

T. D. Smith a/c

	£		
6 Feb. Bank	1,470	11 Jan. Purchases	£1,500
Discount	30		
	£1,500		

In Chapter 1 you saw that the individual discount items are entered in the cash book for convenience and the total transferred to the ledger account. However, below, the £30 is shown as an individual entry in the appropriate expense account.

Discount received a/c

	6 Feb.	T. D. Smith	£30

Smith has refused to agree to the discount (either because the contract did not contain this concession or because Jackson paid too late) so the double-entry needs to be cancelled. This will be achieved if you credit Smith (as you owe him the £30) and debit the discount account. Suitable narrations are essential in all cases – in practice, almost the exact words given in the question can be used. Thus a narration for (*c*) would be: 'Motor van taken by the supplier in part payment of his account.' (Some reference to the correspondence would in practice, also be included).

2 *Set out journal entries including short narrations to adjust the following matters:*
   - *(a) Transfer of £80 balance of rent receivable account to the final accounts.*
   - *(b) Goods taken by the proprietor for private use, retail price £150 (mark-up is 20% on cost) had not been recorded in the books.*
   - *(c) Discount allowed £6 had been posted from the cash book to the credit of discount received account.*
   - *(d) An allowance of £60 to a debtor for goods returned had been omitted from the books.*
   - *(e) The sum of £500 had been debited to freehold premises account for repairs and alterations. It was decided that one-fifth of this amount be dealt with as revenue expenditure.* (RSA I)

Notes

(*a*) Rent receivable is an income a/c so the £80 will be a credit in the profit and loss a/c.

(*b*) See example 1, p. 000. The owner 'charges' himself at cost price but you will not arrive at this by deducting 20% from the £150. The problem is: goods cost *x*, add 20% to it to arrive at selling price £150, find *x*. Calculation is based on the following:

Assume CP is 100, then SP will be 120.
Therefore CP is $^{100}/_{120}$ of SP, i.e. $^{5}/_{6}$ of £150 = £125
(*check*: CP £125 + Profit £25 = £150).

(*c*) Discount allowed is an expense item (we have accepted £6 less than the sum charged on the invoice). In error there is the following ledger entry in the books:

Discount received a/c

	Mr Customer £6

This has to be cancelled by debiting the account and debiting discount allowed account. There are two debit entries because the £6 was posted to the wrong side of the wrong account.

The journal entry will be:

		Dr
Date—	Discount allowed	£6
	Discount received	£6

Correction of incorrect posting on—(cash book folio—refers).

(*d*) A journal entry is made here to explain the reason for omission from returns inwards a/c and therefore also from the customer's personal account (possibly the error may not have been discovered till the subsequent accounting period). Debit returns inwards a/c; credit the customer.

(*e*) Repairs and decorations are revenue expenditure, ie a charge against profit (refer back to Chapter 3); structural alterations and additions are capital items. The £500 has been debited to premises a/c, so reduce this to £400 by a credit entry of £100 and charge this to an expense account.

3 *Show by means of journal entries how the following errors would be corrected in the books of A. Vickers:*

(a) Machinery valued at £2,000 purchased on credit from Valient Engineering Company had been debited to the purchases account.

(b) A sale to Wyatt & Company amounting to £364 had been entered in the sales day book as £346, and this latter figure had been posted to the respective ledger accounts.

(c) When paying R. Mead, a creditor, A. Vickers had deducted £8 cash discount. Mead has disallowed this discount.

(d) An allowance for returns of £3 had been agreed by a creditor and posted to his account, but the corresponding entry in the returns account had not been made. (RSA I)

Notes

(*a*) A straightforward correction.

(*b*) The sales day book total will be £18 short, and therefore so will the sales a/c entry. The personal account has been posted from the sales day book, hence the error in that too.

The £18 should not be added to the day book; an £18 double-entry will be made (from the journal authority) in the sales a/c and the customer's account.

Note that (*a*) and (*b*) are examples of errors not showing up in the trial balance (Chapter 8).

(*c*) Similar principle to 1(*d*) above (p. 101); remember, it is the books of Vickers (the purchaser) that are being kept.

(*d*) A single-sided journal entry is needed because one entry is correct. This will be:

		Cr
Date—	Returns outward	£3

(with a suitable narration).

One or more responses to the following question may be correct.

MC1 Which of the following are books of original entry?

1. *The cash book*
2. *The journal*
3. *The sales returns book.* (AEB–S)

Answer to multiple-choice question:

MC1 All.

8 Accounting errors, their correction and effect on financial results

Errors not reflected in trial balance

These errors were referred to in Chapter 6, and journal entries correcting them were shown in Chapter 7. There are six types of error:

1 Error of omission
Both entries missed entirely from the accounts.

2 Error of commission
An entry is made in the correct *class* of account but the wrong individual account is chosen.

Examples
(a) A rates payment debited to rent a/c (both are expense accounts).
(b) A sale on credit debited to A. Brown instead of A. Browning (both are personal accounts).

This type of error should not affect the final net profit figure, nor the balance sheet totals – (ii) produces the same total debtors figure.

3 Error of principle
This is a more serious type of error than (2) because it will result in an incorrect net profit and a basic error in the balance sheet. This arises as a result of an entry being made in the wrong *class* of account.

Example
Equipment bought for office use debited to purchases account instead of office equipment account. The effect will be: purchases overstated – gross profit understated – net profit understated – office equipment book value understated in balance sheet.

4 Compensating error
By sheer coincidence, an equal and opposite error is made in two separate instances.

Examples

(a) An entry of £100 made on debit side of repairs a/c instead of £10, and a similar error made on the credit side of sales a/c.

(b) Rent a/c overcast by £1 and salaries a/c undercast by £1.

This type of error can have a variety of effects on the accounting results, depending on the accounts involved. Thus in (a) gross profit is overstated by £90, but it is corrected in profit and loss a/c. In (b) there is no change in trading or profit and loss a/cs.

5 Error of original entry

Arithmetically this is the same as (4) but it does not arise by sheer coincidence. Either the original posting document is incorrect or alternatively it is correct but it is posted wrongly in the first instance.

Examples

(a) Sales invoice shows £110 instead of £100. The effect will be that the sales day book and subsequently the sales a/c will show £110, and so will the personal account.

(b) Sales invoice correctly shows £100. In error it is entered in sales day book as £110, and if the posting to the personal account is made from the day book then that will also show £110. Note, however, that some businesses post personal accounts from the invoice; in that case the error will show up in the trial balance.

Errors of original entry can have a variety of effects on the final results.

6 Reversal of Entries

Example

£150 received from Z. Jones & Co. is entered as a payment (instead of as an income item) in the cash book, and is then debited (instead of credited) to their personal account.

The correction of this type of error sometimes causes difficulty, so the incorrect entries are shown here and the corrections made, after the journal entry, are placed in brackets.

Cash book

(Z. Jones & Co.	*£300)*	*Z Jones & Co.*	*£150*

Z. Jones and Co. a/c

Cash	£150	(Cash	£300)

It is necessary to reverse the entry in each in cancellation, then to make the actual entry – thus twice the sum has to be journalized:

	Dr	Cr
	£	£
Cash	300	
Z. Jones & Co.		300

being a reversal of incorrect entries – a payment of £150 by the latter originally entered as a payment *to* the latter.

Errors reflected in trial balance

Any one-sided error, however it arises, will show up in a trial balance. They can be:

1 Incorrect additions of totals, either in a subsidiary book or a ledger a/c.
2 One entry omitted in a transaction, e.g. cash sales entered in cash a/c but omitted from sales a/c.
3 Different amounts used, e.g. rates paid £175 correct in cash book but shown as £157 in the expense account.

Sometimes these errors may not have been traced by the time the final accounts have to be prepared, and then a **suspense** account is opened purely as a temporary measure; the difference in the trial balance is entered in this account as follows:

Trial balance at 31 March 19–1

	£	£
Totals of all accounts	79,300	79,420
Suspense account	120	
	£79,420	£79,420

Suspense a/c

31 March	TB difference £120	

Many examination questions are set on the assumption that the errors have not been traced by the time accounts have to be prepared. It does not follow that there is only one error of £120; the likelihood is that there will be several, the net effect of which will account for the difference.

Example

After checking all transactions (Chapter 6 suggested the order in which this should be tackled), errors were found as follows:

1 18 April 19–1. Cash purchases £160 has been entered in cash book on 12 February 19–1 but had been omitted from purchases a/c.

2 26 April 19–1. £20 paid to G. Brown on 12 March had been wrongly debited to G. Browning.
3 27 April 19–1. Salaries account had been overcast on 31 March by £40.

Item 2 will not affect the suspense a/c as it is an error of commission, (see p. 105).

Journal entries

		Dr	Cr
		£	£
18 April	Purchases	160	
	Suspense		160

Omission of debit entry in former account on 12 February now corrected.

		Dr	Cr
26 April	G. Brown	£20	
	G. Browning		£20

Payment to G. Brown on 12 March wrongly debited to latter account now corrected.

27 April	Suspense	£40	
	Salaries		£40

Overcasting of latter account at 31 March now corrected.

Suspense a/c

		£			£
31 March	TB difference	120	18 April	Purchases	160
	Salaries	40			
		£160			£160

Purchases a/c

18 April	Suspense	£160			

G. Brown a/c

26 April	G. Browning	£20			

G. Browning a/c

			26 April	G. Brown	£20

Salaries a/c

			27 April	Suspense	£40

Effect of errors

Here are some worked examples of examination questions.

Balance sheet of A. Dearman as at 31 December 19–1

	£		£
Capital	4,000	Fixtures and equipment	5,000
Net profit for year	3,460	Stock	2,000
		Debtors	840
	7,460	Cash	20
Drawings	1,800		
	5,660		
Creditors	1,740		
Suspense a/c	460		
	7,860		7,860

1 When the above balance sheet was prepared, there was a difference in the trial balance and it was necessary to open a suspense account with the balance of £460 as shown.
Since the date of preparation the following errors have been discovered:

(*a*) a new typewriter costing £250 had been debited to purchases account instead of to the fixtures and equipment account;
(*b*) the balance of £120 on F. Brown's account in the sales ledger had been brought forward as £12;
(*c*) discounts allowed of £40 had been posted to the credit of the discounts received account;
(*d*) the sales day book had been undercast by £180;
(*e*) depreciation of equipment had been entered in the profit and loss account as £864 instead of £468.

You are required:
(i) to provide journal entries necessary to correct the errors, and
(ii) to produce a corrected balance sheet, showing the amended balance on the suspense account. (LOND)

Answer

Abbreviated journal enries	*Dr* £	*Cr* £
(*a*) Fixtures and fittings a/c	250	
Purchases a/c		250
(*b*) F. Brown a/c	108	
Suspense a/c		108
(*c*) Discount received a/c	40	
Discount allowed a/c	40	
Suspense a/c		80
(*d*) Suspense	180	
Sales		180
(*e*) Suspense	396	
Profit and loss		396

Suspense a/c

	£			£
– Sales	180	31 Dec.	Difference in TB	460
– Profit and loss	396	–	F. Brown	108
– Balance c/d	72	–	Discount received	40
		–	Discount allowed	40
	£648			£648
		–	Balance b/d	72

Notes

(*a*) is error of principle not affecting trial balance.
(*b*) refers to the *opening* balance of Brown's account for 19–2, therefore the closing balance on 31 Dec. is understated on 1 Jan.
(*c*) requires double the £40 to be credited to suspense as original posting was on *wrong* side (and also on wrong account).
(*d*) requires sales to be increased.
(*e*) as the debit in profit and loss a/c was £396 overstated (£864 – £468) a credit for this sum is needed in profit and loss a/c.

The errors do *not* eliminate suspense a/c – see the last sentence in the question.

Effect of correction of errors on results

	Net profit	*Balance sheet*
(*a*)	+ £250	F and E + £250
(*b*)	—	Debtors + £108
(*c*)	– £80	–
(*d*)	+ £180	–
(*e*)	+ £396	–

Notes

1 Some questions ask the 'effect of the errors' but here it is the 'effect of the corrections' that is needed. Thus the effect of error (*a*) was to show profit £250 understated – therefore the correction increases profit by £250.
2 It is assumed that the transposition error (*e*) affected profit and loss a/c only and that the correct figure had been entered as the depreciation provision.
3 Combine the net profit amendments gives a net plus of £746 (£250 + £180 + £396 – £80).

Corrected balance sheet

	£		£
Capital	4,000	Fixtures and equipment	5,250
Net profit	4,206	Stock	2,000
	8,206	Debtors	948
– Drawings	1,800	Cash	20
	6,406		
Creditors	1,740		
Suspense a/c	72		
	£8,218		£8,218

2 Oswald Bennett, a sole proprietor, had been advised that his capital account for the year ended 31 December 19–1, was as follows:

	£
Opening balance	11,500
Net profit for the year	5,750
	17,250
Less drawings	4,900
	12,350

Further investigation showed that the books contained the following errors:

1 A motor vehicle costing £1,100 had been incorrectly debited to material purchases account. Depreciation on the vehicle should have been provided at 20% on cost.

2 Wage payments of £100 to employees had been incorrectly debited to drawings account.

3 Bennett had taken £75 of goods from the business for his own use. No entries had been made in the books.

4 A. Smith, a debtor, had paid £150 on his account but unfortunately the amount had been treated as a payment received in the account of A. Smythe, another debtor.

5 Cash sales of £950 had been omitted from sales account.

6 Rates account had been debited with an amount of £50 instead of the correct amount of £500.

Required:

1 Journal entries recording the necessary corrections, assuming that a suspense account had been opened with a credit entry of £500. (Narrations are not required.)

2 A corrected capital account showing clearly any adjustments to the net profit and/or drawings. (AEB)

Abbreviated journal entries

			Dr £	Cr £
1	31 Dec.	Vehicles	1,100	
		Material purchases		1,100
1		Depreciation	220	
		Depreciation provision		220
2		Wages	100	
		Drawings		100
3		Drawings	75	
		Purchases		75
4		A. Smythe	150	
		A. Smith		150
5		Suspense	950	
		Sales		950
6		Rates	450	
		Suspense		450

5 and 6 will clear the suspense credit balance.

Effect of corrections

Increase in net profit	(1) £1,100 (3) £75 (5) £950	+ £1,355
Decrease in net profit	(1) £220 (2) £100 (6) £450	
Increase in drawings	(3) £75	– £25
Decrease in drawings	(2) £100	

Corrected profit £5,750 + £1,355 = £7,105.

Amended capital account £11,500 + £7,105 – £4,875 = £13,730.

Practice work

MC1 *A suspense account can be used as a temporary measure to balance the*

A *trading and profit and loss account*
B *manufacturing account*
C *trial balance*
D *appropriation account.* (AEB–S)

MC2 *If a posting is made to the correct class of account on the correct side, but in the wrong account, it is an error of*

A *omission*
B *principle*
C *commission*
D *compensation.* (AEB–S)

MC3 *A trial balance fails to agree by £40. Which one of the following errors, subsequently discovered, could have caused the disagreement?*

A *A sale of goods, £40, to A. Brown had been debited to B. Brown's account.*
B *A cheque for £20 received from C. Green had been debited to C. Grey's account.*
C *A machine sold for £40 had been credited to the sales account.*
D *A payment for rent £40 had been debited to the wages account.* (AEB–S)

3 The following balance sheet has been prepared by a sole trader, B. James, with inadequate book-keeping knowledge. He asks your advice.

Balance sheet from 1 August 19–1 to 31 July 19–2

	£		£	£
Drawings	2,160	Creditors	11,054	
Delivery van	3,730	*less* Debtors	3,720	7,334
Equipment and furniture	3,000			
Buildings	11,500	Capital	20,000	
Stock	5,092	*less* Loss	600	19,400
Cash	1,252			
	£26,734			£26,734

You make the following comments with which the trader agrees:

(*a*) Provisions should be made for the depreciation of the delivery van of 20%, equipment and furniture of 5% and a provision for doubtful debts of 5% of the debtors.

(*b*) An adjustment is required for the fact that during the financial year the trader drew from stock, goods amounting to £400 for his own use.

(*c*) an allowance should be made for expenses due, of £102 at 31 July 19–2.

Required:

1 James's balance sheet as at 31 July 19–2 in suitable form, after the necessary adjustments have been made; (10 marks)

2 an explanation of the significance of making a provision for depreciation on the delivery van, equipment and furniture. (AEB–S) *(7 marks)*

Notes

1 You may find it easier to write out in rough the ledger accounts which the adjustments will affect. Note that the balance sheet heading is inaccurate.

2 Refer back to Chapter 4 if in difficulty. There is a fairly high

mark allocation given here so a reasonably detailed answer is needed – you can, of course, illustrate the answer with reference to the depreciation items above.

4 *R. James drew up the following balance sheet on 31 December 19–1:*

Balance sheet

	£	£		£	£
Capital 1 Jan. 19–1	7,690		*Fixed assets*		
add Net profit	3,040		Furniture and fittings	1,540	
	10,730		Motor vehicles	2,980	
less Drawings	2,860				4,520
		7,870	*Current assets*		
Sundry creditors		1,850	Stock	2,724	
			Sundry debtors	1,241	
			Cash at bank	1,235	
					5,200
		£9,720			£9,720

When checking the books, the following errors and omissions were found:

(*i*) A purchase of fittings, £140, had been included in the purchases account.
(ii) Motor vehicle should have been depreciated by £280.
(*iii*) A debt of £41 included in sundry debtors was considered to be bad.
(*iv*) Closing stock had been overvalued by £124.
(*a*) *Show your calculations of the correct net profit.*
(*b*) *Draw up a corrected balance sheet as at 31 December 19–1.* (AEB)

Answers to multiple-choice questions:

MC1 C; MC2 C; MC3 B.

9 More on banking; petty cash

Banking

Deposit accounts

All current account transactions are shown either in the bank column of the cash book or in the bank cash book (as illustrated in Chapter 1). However, account holders who are likely to have at various times a balance on current a/c in excess of their normal requirements may well open a deposit a/c at their own branch. The advantage is that interest is paid by the bank, calculated on a daily basis. However, there are no payment facilities available on a deposit a/c – it is really a savings a/c. Seven days' notice of withdrawal is strictly required, but in practice the banks do not insist on this; they action the withdrawal immediately but backdate it by seven days. Normal practice with many account holders is to transfer from current a/c to deposit a/c and vice versa, so that a reasonable but not excessive balance is maintained on current a/c (on which no interest is paid). Instructions are generally given by letter.

An ordinary general ledger a/c should be kept for the deposit a/c. The following example illustrates a transfer from current to deposit a/c:

Cash book

1 March Balance b/d	£4,231	2 March Deposit	£2,000

Deposit a/c

2 March Cash	£2,000		

Generally, interest gained will be credited by the bank twice yearly when the entries will be: Dr deposit; Cr interest receivable.

Loans and overdrafts

A customer of a bank may find from time to time that his actual cash resources are likely to be insufficient for a limited period. An example would be a retailer stocking up in the autumn for the

Christmas season. Provided the customer is creditworthy, the bank is likely to allow him to overdraw, i.e. write cheques in excess of his balance in hand. The usual arrangement is that the bank agrees that the account may be overdrawn up to a certain sum (say, £1,000) for a stated period (say, 2 months).

A separate account is not required. The amount actually owing to the bank is likely to vary from day to day; interest is only charged on a daily basis on the actual sum owing.

Cash book

		£			£
1 November	Balance b/d	530	11 November	XYZ & Co.	600
15 November	Sales	150	13 November	Electricity	174
18 November	Sales	210			

Notes

11 Nov. Overdraft of £70 for two days.
13 Nov. Overdraft increase to £244 for two days.
15 Nov. Overdraft reduced to £94 for three days.
18 Nov. Account now in credit £116.

An overdraft will show in the balance sheet under current liabilities (although the bank will grant it for a definite period in the first instance they reserve the right to request repayment at any time without notice).

A bank loan is a sum of money borrowed at a fixed rate of interest for a fixed period. Various repayment methods may be arranged. In the case of a loan to a business it is quite common to find that a lump-sum capital repayment is required at the end of the agreed period, interest being charged at six-monthly intervals.

A loan a/c should be opened in the ledgers, the double-entry on receipt of the money being: Dr bank; Cr loan a/c.

Assuming there is no partial repayment of capital, there will be a constant balance in the loan account which will show as a liability in the balance sheet. Generally, the bank will debit the customer's current account with the interest, and the double-entry will be: Cr bank; Dr interest on loan – this will be charged as an expense in the profit and loss a/c.

Payments other than by cheque

Standing orders Bank A's customer arranges for a fixed sum to be paid at regular intervals (e.g. monthly, quarterly, yearly) by his own bank to bank *B* for the credit of one of its customers. The standing order will either be 'till further notice', or will state the number of payments to be made. Provided there are funds available, the drawer's bank will make each payment without any reminder from the drawer.

Credit transfer (multiple payments) Increasingly, businesses are paying staff salaries as well as their trade and expense creditors by this method. Basically, the business draws one cheque in favour of its own bank for the total sum involved and prepares a credit-transfer slip for each creditor, stating the individual sum to be transferred and giving the creditor's bank account details, i.e. bank, branch name, branch-code (e.g. 60–12–37), current account number. The paying bank arranges the necessary transfers through normal interbank channels. In the case of salaries, the employee will receive a payslip from the employer showing how the amount paid is arrived at; business creditors will be sent a remittance advice stating that payment by credit transfer has been made and giving details of the breakdown of the payment

Direct debits In both the above cases it is the drawer's bank which commences the operation by debiting their customer's current account and then passing the items through the banking system. In the case of direct debiting, it is the *payee* who requests his own bank to collect an amount from the drawer's account. The creditor must, of course, obtain written authority from the debtor before direct debiting can take place.

Direct debiting can be used for fixed amounts at fixed dates or for varying amounts at irregular intervals. Many creditors, e.g. the Automobile Association, will not now accept annual subscriptions by standing order, because the individual member will have to amend his standing order each time the subscription increases.

Direct debiting simplifies the clerical work; therefore the banks prefer it to the standing order method. From the debtor's point of view, there is virtually no difference, and certain safeguards have been introduced to ensure that he is protected from the demand for unauthorized sums.

The banker's clearing system

Every working day there are several million banking transactions (the majority by cheque, the remainder by one of the payment methods referred to above). In a large proportion of cases the drawer and the payee use different banks, and so an interbank settlement is needed. It is the banker's clearing house which deals with the transfers, and the work is largely computerized.

The following diagram illustrates how a cheque for £15 drawn by A. N. Other (his bank is Midland, Radford, Coventry) in favour of N. O. Boddie (his bank is Barclays, Walsall) is cleared.

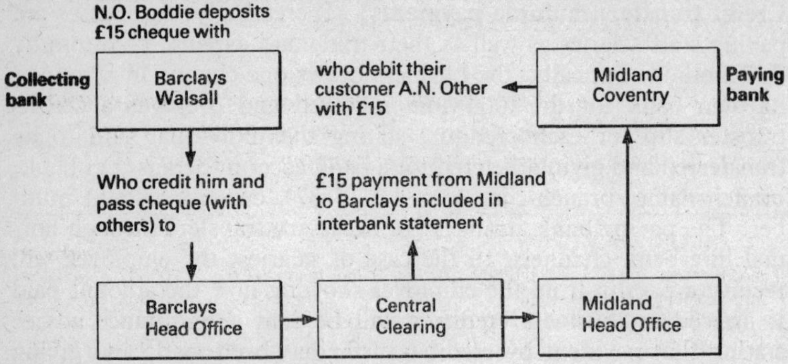

How a cheque is cleared

Bank reconciliation statements

At regular intervals each customer receives a bank statement which sets out the balance in hand at the beginning of the period involved, and details of each and every transaction that has taken place; the last item on the statement is the balance in hand (or overdraft balance) at the end of the period.

Obviously it is in the customer's interest to compare his cash book entries with those on the bank statement. In practice the two accounts will rarely show the same balance. The reasons for this are:

1 An error on the part of the customer or the bank (e.g. one party has made an incorrect entry).
2 The time-lag before details of a transaction are recorded by the bank (e.g. the cashier will enter a payment when he draws a cheque; allowing for postal delivery and the clearing process, it may be a week before his firm is debited by their bank).
3 The bank has made entries details of which are not known by the customer until he receives his statement (e.g. bank charges, interest on overdrafts, receipt of sums by credit transfer from debtors).

Preparation of bank reconciliation statements

This is an arithmetical exercise by the business to 'explain' the difference between the balance on the cash book and the one on the bank statement. Remember that there may be a number of items which need to be taken into account; and the combined effect of these accounts for the difference. A recent examination question is used here to explain the technique needed.

Example

1 J. B. King & Co. receive weekly bank statements and consequently balance their cash book weekly. The following are the (1) cash book, (2) bank statement for the week ending 12 January 19–1.

Cash book

Date	Details		Total	Date	Details	Cheque no.	Amount
8 Jan.	Balance		b/d 569.00√	9 Jan.	Irving & Co.	200802	69.80√
10 Jan.	C. Atkin	100.00			Angel Ltd	200803	145.20√
	A. Brown	220.50	320.50√	10 Jan.	B. Benn	200804	11.10√
12 Jan.	Cash sales		70.90x	11 Jan.	Wessex Gas Board	200805	9.44x
				12 Jan.	Balance		c/d 724.86
			£960.40				£960.40
15 Jan.	Balance		b/d 724.86				

Bank statement

Date	Details	*Dr*	*Cr*	*Balance*
8 Jan.	Balance			569.00√
10 Jan.	Credit		320.50√	889.50
10 Jan.	Credit transfer (Dee & Co.)		68.95x	958.45
11 Jan.	200802	69.80√		888.65
12 Jan.	200803	145.20√		
12 Jan.	200804	11.10√		732.35
12 Jan.	Charges (foreign exchange)	2.00x		730.35

(a) You are asked to bring the cash book up to date, and then reconcile the new cash book balance with the statement balance.

(b) Why is it necessary to reconcile the bank statement, when received, with the cash book?

(c) How is it that the date given for a transaction is not necessarily the same in each document?

(d) Why is it that the bank statement does not show individually the two cheques from C. Atkin and A. Brown that make up the deposit of £320.50? (RSA I)

Method

(a) Check the cash book against the bank statement, ticking each item which appears on both documents – this has already been done above. There remain two items in the cash book missing from the bank statement, and two on the bank statement not yet in the cash book (these four figures are each marked with a X). You will notice that a debit in the cash book is a credit as far as the bank is concerned – the latter keeps its books from its own point of view, just as the seller and purchaser of goods will have equal and opposite entries of transactions.

The reasons for the difference can be explained:

(i) £70.90 is group 2 above (p. 118) – an amount deposited by J. B. King & Co, that has not yet been added to their account.

(ii) £9.44 is another group 2 item – a cheque paid by J. B. King & Co. that has not yet been deducted by their bank.

(iii) Both the above are 'time-lag' items.

(iv) £68.95 is group 3 – the bank receive details of the credit transfer directly from the paying bank.

(v) £2.00 is also group 3 – the bank has made a charge for a foreign exchange transaction.

(b) The group 3 items now need to be entered into the cash book; unless this is done, the cash book will never show the up-to-date position.

	£		£
15 Jan. Balance b/d	724.86	12 Jan. Bank charges	2.00
10 Jan. Dee & Co.	68.95	15 Jan. Balance c/d	791.81
	£793.81		£793.81
16 Jan. Balance b/d	791.81		

In practice, the bank statement will not be received until several days after 15 January, so space should be left if it is known a statement is due.

(c) The reconciliation statement can now be prepared – to explain the difference between £730.35 and the amended balance of £791.81. It is the group 2 items that need to be taken into account. It is probably easier to start from the bank statement balance.

Bank reconciliation statement 15 January

	£
Balance on bank statement	730.35
add	
Deposit (12 Jan.) not yet credited	70.90
	801.25
deduct	
Cheque 2C0805 not yet presented	9.44
Balance in cash book (agreed)	£791.81

Of the remainder of the question, (*b*) and (*c*) are already answered in this chapter; a satisfactory answer to (*d*) is to state that the bank credits the customer with the total on the paying-in slip – the statement does not show individual cheques making up the total.

Example

Often in examination questions, instead of giving the bank statement and the cash book, only the errors and omissions are listed. To eliminate guesswork by the student, questions may omit one of the balances, as in the following which introduces the added complication of an overdraft.

2 *On 30 June 19–1 B. Back's cash book showed a balance of £40.00 overdrawn on his bank account. After checking his cash book with his bank statement, Back located the following errors and omissions:*

(*a*) Cheques drawn and entered in the cash book on 29 June £35.00 in favour of C. White and £25 in favour of J. Green had not been passed through the bank for payment.

(*b*) Interest charges of £15, shown in the bank statement, had not been entered in the cash book.

(*c*) £80 cash banked by B. Back on 30 June was not credited by the bank until 1 July, although it had been entered in the cash book.

You are required to:

(a) Make the necessary entries to amend the cash book balance.

(b) Prepare a bank reconciliation between the bank statement balance and the revised cash book balance.

(c) Briefly describe the reason for preparing a bank reconciliation statement. (RSA I)

Notes

(*a*) Only the £15 interest charge has to be introduced into the cash book, so the amended balance becomes £55 overdrawn.

(*b*) As the statement balance has not been given, it is easier to commence with the cash book balance.

Bank reconciliation statement 30 June 19–1			£
Balance on cash book		o/d –	55.00
add Cheques not presented			
C. White	£35.00		
J. Green	£25.00	+	60.00
			5.00
less Deposited 30 June not yet credited		–	80.00
Balance on bank statement was o/d			£75.00

This is a rather difficult one. It can be proved as follows:

Bank statement

o/d 75.00

When the two cheques are presented o/d *increases* by £60 to o/d £135.

When the deposit is credited by bank o/d *reduces* by £80 – o/d £55.00 agreed.

Starting from cash balance in the reconciliation requires care. What is being said is: *this 'cash book shows £55.00 – bank has not dealt with the £60.00 payment, so (just taking this £60 into account) their balance is higher*. Similarly progressing from the subtotal £5.00 – as they have not dealt with the £80.00 then balance is lower.

The author personally always prefers to start with the bank figure in all reconciliations, as it seems more logical.

Alternative reconciliation

	£
Bank statement balance	?
add Deposit	80 +
	?
less Unpresented cheques	60 –
Cash book balance	o/d £55

Unknown figure *plus* £80 *less* £60 = –£55 (o/d). Unknown figure *plus* £20 = –£55. Therefore –£75 (o/d) *plus* £20 = –£55. Alternatively, work backwards reversing the signs: – 55 + 60 – 80 = +5 – 80 = – 75.

Practice work

3 *On 31 December 19–1 the balance in the bank account as shown in the cash book of N. Small & Co. was £874. On checking the cash book with the bank statement, the cashier discovered the following differences:*

(*a*) The bank statement did not include cheques totalling £312 received and paid into the bank on 31 December and entered in the cash book for that day.

(*b*) Cheques drawn during the month but not yet presented for payment totalled £524.

(*c*) The bank had debited the firm's account with charges of £25 and had credited the account with £120, being a dividend received by the bank on behalf of the firm. Neither of these items had been entered in the cash book.

You are required:

(i) *To show how the necessary entries would be recorded in the cash book, and*

(ii) *To reconcile the adjusted cash book balance with the bank statement, showing the balance which appears on the bank statement on 31 December 19–1.* (RSA I)

Notes

The two items in (*c*) need to be entered in the cash book – the £25 reduces balance and the £120 increases it (a credit transfer – see earlier in this chapter.

4 (*a*) *Smith receives his bank statement showing a balance in bank of £1,340 on 31 May 19–1. Cheques totalling £130 paid to creditors have not yet been presented for payment, and a sum of £75 credit transfer received by the bank has not been entered in his cash book. Calculate the balance which Smith's cash book should show before any corrections are made.*

(*b*) *Smith receives a statement of account from one of his suppliers. It shows a balance due of £180. The account in Smith's ledger indicates that the amount due is only £50. Explain how this difference could arise without any mistakes being made.* (RSA I)

Notes

(*a*) merely requires cash book to be updated.

(*b*) It could be a number of things:

(i) a payment of £130 has been made by Smith not yet recorded by the supplier, or:

(ii) invoice(s) from supplier not yet checked and passed for payment by Smith, or:

(iii) Smith has returned goods as unsatisfactory and has debited supplier's account in advance of receiving a credit note; or:

(iv) a combination of the above.

5 *Ben Bailey had recently received his bank statement showing that he had £1,051 to the credit of his current account.*

Unfortunately, he had not been keeping his own private record of his bank account, but at least he had details in his cheque book and paying-in book regarding his recent transactions. Items not *included in the bank statement were:*

(*a*) *cheque payable to A. Smith for £125.*

(*b*) *cash and cheques paid into the bank of £459.*

(*c*) *a recently submitted standing order of £28.50 per annum for fire insurance due immediately.*

(d) cash withdrawn to be used in paying wages £157. (RSA I)

The following item appeared in the bank statement:
A monthly direct debit payable to a HP company was incorrectly debited twice in the same month

Required:
An updated bank statement.

Notes

Start with £1,051, debit the payments (there are three) and credit the direct debit amount which will cancel the duplicate payment made by bank. It is best to present a standard-type bank statement:

B. Bailey Current a/c

Date	*Detail*	*Dr (payments)*	*Cr (receipts)*	*Balance*
?	Balance b/d			1,051.00
	A. Smith	125.00		926.00
	(etc.)	(etc.)		

Most bank statements, in fact, give cheque numbers and not name of payee.

MC1 The bank column of your cash book shows a credit balance. This would appear in the balance sheet as a
A *current asset*
B *long-term liability*
C *current liability*
D *fixed asset.* (AEB–S)

MC2 The bank statement shows an overdraft of £300. A creditor has not presented a cheque for £75. When this is presented for payment, the bank balance will be
A *£375*
B *£225*
C *£225 overdrawn*
D *£375 overdrawn.* (AEB–S)

The following is a multiple-completion question.

MC3 Which of the following is/are the reason(s) for preparing a bank reconciliation statement?
1 *To see if the bank has made any mistakes on the account.*
2 *To see if there are any mistakes on the bank account in the books of the business.*
3 *To see what cheques have not yet been paid by the bank.* (AEB–S)

Petty cash

Though businesses will make the vast majority of payments by cheque or credit transfer, there remain various minor items of expenditure which it is more convenient to settle in cash. In many businesses it is necessary to retain some cash in individual departments, branches or sites.

The usual procedure is to appoint a petty cashier who accepts responsibility for maintaining a petty cash account. It is convenient to use the 'imprest' or 'float' system, whereby an advance of cash considered adequate is made to the petty cashier, and at a fixed interval (probably weekly or monthly) he draws from the main cashier the sum he has spent.

Staff requiring cash complete petty cash vouchers, and at any point in time the cash-in-hand plus the total value of the vouchers should equal the 'imprest'.

Instead of each item of expenditure being posted to the appropriate expense account (an unnecessary chore), the totals of the analysis columns are posted. If the bank cash book system is in use, the petty cashier is likely to be given a cheque, which he will cash at the local bank.

At GCE O or equivalent level examinations, a practical petty cash question is very unlikely. It is possible for Stage I Book-keeping, and therefore a worked example is now shown. A VAT column is not included – this tax is dealt with in Chapter 10.

Example

(*a*) *You are in charge of your department's petty cash account which is kept on a weekly imprest system, the 'float' being £50. Complete the account for the week commencing 14 April 19–1.*

14 April Balance of cash available £6.40
14 April Received from chief cashier the sum necessary to restore imprest.
16 April Voucher 197 Taxi to station £2.75; lunch with area representative £8.50
16 April Voucher 198 Wages for student labour £35.00
17 April Additional cash received from chief cashier (in view of high expenditure to date this week) £25.00
18 April Voucher 199 Registered parcels to Glasgow branch £5.70
18 April Voucher 200 First-aid materials for office £4.14
18 April Voucher 201 Bus and rail fares to Middlesbrough £11.32; refreshments £1.75
18 April Balance petty cash book carrying down the balance available and restore imprest

(*b*) *Why will the chief cashier need to see vouchers 197 to 201 when you present the petty cash box to him? How will he check the accuracy of the payments analysis columns?*

Petty cash book

Received		Date	Particulars	Voucher number	Total paid out		Casual labour		Office expenses		Travelling		Meals	
6	40	14/4	Balance	b/d										
43	60		Cashier											
		16/4	Taxi and lunch	197	11	25					2	75	8	50
			Wages – students	198	35	–	35	–						
25	–	17/4	Cashier											
		18/4	Parcel postage	199	5	70			5	70				
			First aid	200	4	14			4	14				
			Fares and meals	201	13	07					11	32	1	75
					69	16	35	–	9	84	14	07	10	25
		18/4	Balance	c/d	5	84	GL	29	GL	18	GL	21	GL	27
75	–				75	–								
5	84		Balance	b/d										
44	16		Cashier											

Notes

A common error is to use one line per item for expenditure, instead of one line per voucher as above. In some firms, vouchers may have to be countersigned by a supervisor. The folio reference under each analysis indicates the posting of the column total to the expense account. It is important to cross-cast the totals to ensure arithmetical accuracy. A trial balance taken out on 18 April would need to have the petty cash balance included.

Answers to multiple-choice questions:

MC1 **C**; *MC2* **D**; *MC3* **All**.

10 Departmental accounts; VAT

A business with several departments will find it useful to know the trading results of each department. This can only be done if each income and expenditure item can be allocated to a particular department or 'work station'. A good example of an organization which will operate an analysed accounting system is a retail department store where it is quite possible to keep accurate records of trading account items but is difficult to split overhead expenses between departments.

Departmental trading accounts

It is necessary to use suitably designed accounting books to be able to provide separate departmental figures. Thus day books and the cash book will require additional columns, as will the purchases, sales and returns ledger a/cs. As an example, a sales day book with analysis columns is shown below.

Analysis sales day book

Date	Customer	SL folio	Total sales	Dept A	Dept B	Dept C
1 June	ABC & Co.	16	£820.50	£600.00	£220.50	
4 June	G. Kent. Ltd	29	£150.42			£150.42

(i.e. Sales invoice on 1 June to ABC & Co. included goods from both department A and department B.)

Similarly, in a retail store, daily takings will need to be analysed. Mechanized methods simplify the task – the electric cash register in a supermarket has a coding device, operated by the cashier, indicating the type of sale (e.g. groceries, household goods). Stock records too will have to be maintained on a departmental basis.

Departmental profit and loss accounts

This presents greater problems. Often an expense item will have to be split between departments on an estimated basis. There are various logical ways of doing this. Examples are:

Lighting and heating Rent/rates	} – according to floor area.
Wages and salaries	– in proportion (approximately) to the amount of time on any department's work.
Delivery vehicle expenses	– according to turnover.

However, the analysis system used will vary from business to business.

Balance sheet

It is rarely possible to show assets and liabilities split between individual departments, simply because it is not practical to do so. For example, how would you divide up the bank balance (or the overdraft)? Or the owner's capital?

Example

1 T. Upman runs a business which is divided into two departments, furniture and electrical goods. The following trial balance was extracted from his books on 31 March 19–1.

	£ 000s	£ 000s
Capital 1 April 19–1		100
Premises	72	
Furniture and fittings	14	
Delivery vans	12	
Sales: furniture		22
electrical goods		10
Purchases: furniture	6	
electrical goods	4	
Drawings	4	
Stocks on 1 April 19–1: furniture	3	
electrical goods	1	
Van expenses including drivers' wages	6	
Rates	2	
Wages of shop assistants	3	
Heating and lighting	2	
Creditors		2
Debtors	4	
Cash in hand and bank	1	
	134	134

Prepare a trading and profit and loss account in columnar *form to show the profit or loss on each department for the year ended 31 March 19–1, and a balance sheet on that date.*

The following are to be taken into consideration:

(*i*) Furniture to the value of £2,000 purchased by the furniture department had been taken from that department and used to equip a new office and reception room. A shop assistant booked this furniture out on a sales invoice, and the amount had been debited to an account in the sales ledger.

(*ii*) Included in the purchases of electrical goods is a quantity of fittings used in the shop. Cost price: £1,000.

(*iii*) Divide rates, heating and lighting equally between the two departments.

(*iv*) Depreciate delivery van by 25% of book value.

(*v*) Divide shop assistants' wages, van expenses and depreciation in proportion to sales.

(*vi*) Stocks on 31 March 19–2: furniture £2,000; electrical goods £1,000. (LOND)

Notes

1 This example is not worked in full – refer back to Chapter 6 if difficulty arises. It is advisable to provide *three* columns – one for furniture dept, one for electrical dept and the last one as a total column. Otherwise the accounts are not as informative as they would otherwise be. The following layout is suggested:

Trading a/c for year to

Furniture	*Electrical*	*Total*	(similarly three credit-columns)
£	£	£	

In the examination, use a double page to avoid cramping. Note that the figures are given in thousands. However, the same style cannot be adopted in the answer because adjustment (*v*) does not quite give round thousands when split departmentally.

2 *Adjustments*

(*i*) Furniture £2,000 must be added to the asset account. Therefore, reduce purchases by £2,000 and increase furniture and fittings to £16,000 (if Upman had decided at time of purchase that the furniture was for use in the business, he would not have debited it to purchases). Also, cancel the sales invoice and reduce debtors by £2,000 (unsolved problem – which debtor did he charge? However, it is not necessary to know this to answer the examination question). This is the type of transaction which a business would journalize and as revision journal entries are now given (suitable narrations are also necessary):

		Dr	Cr
		£	£
31 March	Furniture and fittings	2,000	
	Purchases (furniture dept)		2,000
	Sales	2,000	
	Personal account of debtor		2,000

(*ii*) Similarly reduce purchases (electrical) and increase furniture and fittings by £1,000.

(*iii*) Straightforward arithmetic.

(*iv*) As revision – supposing question had said '25% of *original* cost' and the trial balance entry was 'vans (cost £20,000) . . . Dr £12,000' then the depreciation would have been £5,000 and not £3,000.

(*v*) 'In proportion to sales'. But it is not 22:12 because adjustment (*i*) has reduced sales (furniture) from £22,000 to £20,000. So it will be 20:12, or 5:3, i.e. ⅝ and ⅜.

NB Normal balance sheet required.

Practice work

2 D. Jewel a hardware merchant divides his business into three departments namely: glass, china and miscellaneous. During October 19–1 Jewel made the following sales:

1976		
4 Oct.	to John Dove	
	10 dozen buckets	@ £6.00 per dozen
	4 dozen pans	@ £7.20 per dozen
	10 jugs (china)	@ £1.00 each
	4 dozen teapots (china)	@ £4.00 per dozen
17 Oct.	to D. Brown	
	12 dozen glasses	@ £4.00 per gross.
20 Oct.	to F. James	
	6 dozen teasets (china)	@ £22.00 per dozen
	6 buckets	@ £ 6.00 per dozen
	18 glass flower bowls	@ £ 5.00 per dozen

You are required to:

(a) Prepare D. Jewel's tabular sales journal and to enter the above listed items therein; and

(b) Post from the sales journal to the nominal and the personal ledgers. (NB: Ignore VAT) (RSA I)

Notes

This type of comparatively routine question comes up occasionally at Stage I level, probably not at GCE. Though some textbooks still give details of goods in the subsidiary books, this is quite unnecessary – they appear on the invoice.

Buckets and pans are miscellaneous. It is suggested that the calculations should be clearly shown. Note that the price *unit* varies. In practice there would be a VAT column, but the VAT cannot be departmentalized (see later in this chapter). One entry has been done below:

Sales day book

Date	*Customer*	*Total*	*Glass*	*China*	*Misc.*
1976					
4 Oct.	John Dove	£114.80	—	£26.00	£88.80
(etc.)					

Note

1 Sales journal = sales day book.
2 Ruling would include columns for invoice number and folio reference and the day book sheet would be numbered, e.g. SDB17.
3 Remember to cross-cast totals before posting to ledger.
4 Analysis columns will be needed in the sales account but *not* in the customer's account (because balance sheet cannot normally be 'departmentalized').

3 *J. Last sells and repairs boots and shoes. On 31 December 19–1 he extracted the following trial balance from his books:*

	Dr	*Cr*
	£	£
Capital		1,500
Drawings	2,000	
Sales		5,125
Receipts from repairs		4,280
Purchases: materials for repairs	523	
boots and shoes	3,810	
Stocks (1 Jan. 19–1): materials for repairs	176	
boots and shoes	840	
Wages: shoe repairer	988	
shop assistant	614	
Tools and equipment (1 Jan. 19–1)	315	
Power, light and heat	196	
Rent and rates	996	
Insurance	32	
Packing materials	21	
Trade creditors		213
Shop furniture and fittings	280	
Cash in hand and balance at bank	327	
	£11,118	£11,118

Prepare Last's trading account (in columnar form) and his profit and loss account for the year ended 31 December 19–1 and a balance sheet as at that date. (LOND)

Notes

1 Three columns for trading: total, sales, repairs. Wages costs are direct expenses, so charge both to trading a/c; shop assistant is sales department; for the majority of his time would be spent on this side of the business.

2 Packing materials cannot mean the boxes in which shoes are sold, because the item sold is the shoes in the box. Either way the examiner must have intended it to be charged as an overhead expense because no split is given.

Value added tax (VAT)

For about ten years a government tax has been charged on a very wide range of goods and services. Examples of items *not* subject to VAT are foodstuffs, newspapers, bus and rail fares, insurance premiums. At one time certain goods attracted a higher rate of VAT, but since 1979 a standard rate of 15 per cent has been charged (which, of course, is likely to be varied from time to time).

With the exception of businesses with very low turnover, for whom registration is optional, all traders must register with HM Customs and Excise for VAT purposes. They are compelled to keep certain VAT records which will show the VAT they themselves have paid to their suppliers (input) and the VAT they have charged to their customers (output). Periodically the trader pays over to the government the excess of output over input, or receives a refund if input exceeds output. Note that when selling to the final consumer at retail level, an inclusive price is often charged to include the VAT – though a VAT invoice will be provided if required.

The following diagram illustrates clearly that it is the final consumer who in practice bears the VAT, even though its collection takes place at each point in the manufacturing and distribution chain. (The tax collector for VAT is the Customs and Excise Department and not the Inland Revenue).

VAT and books of account

For firms registered for VAT, it is necessary to vary the traditional layout of the normal buying/selling accounting records.

Invoices prepared will need to show the VAT as a separate item.

The charge is calculated on the *net* amount of the invoice, i.e. after deduction of any trade discount. Also, if a cash discount is offered, the VAT is worked out on the amount that the customer would pay if he took advantage of the cash discount.

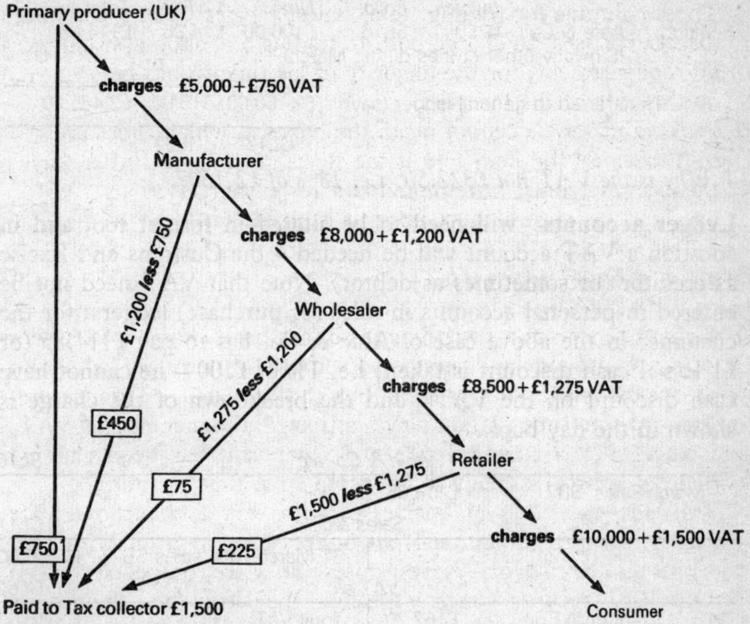

How VAT (15 per cent) is collected

Example

Goods are invoiced on 1 March to Able & Co. at a gross selling price of £125 subject to a 20% trade discount and a cash discount of 1% if settled within 14 days.

	£
Goods	125
less Trade discount 20%	25
	100
add VAT 15% of £99	14.85
Charged to customer	114.85

1% must be deducted from the £100 before the VAT is added – this applies whether the customer takes the cash discount or not.

Day books will need an additional VAT column, because of the £114.85 only £100 represents sales; the remainder will have to be accounted for to the Customs and Excise.

Sales day book

		Invoice	Folio	Net	VAT	Total
1 March	Able & Co.	6250	SL16	£100.00	£14.85	£114.85
	(Similarly other entries during March)					
	Transferred to general ledger (say)			£2,150.00	£315.00	£2,465.00
				GL12	GL62	

4 Why is the VAT not £322.50, i.e. 15% of £2,150?

Ledger accounts will need to be altered in format too, and in addition a VAT account will be needed – the Customs and Excise as creditor (or sometimes as debtor). Note that VAT need not be entered in personal accounts in sales (or purchase) ledgers; for the customer in the above case of Able & Co. has to pay £114.85 (or £1 less if cash discount is taken, i.e. 1% of £100 – he cannot have cash discount on the VAT), and the breakdown of the charge is shown in the day book.

Able & Co. a/c — *SL16*

1 March	Sales SB7	£114.85		

Sales a/c — *GL12*

			31 March Total sales SB7	£2150.00

VAT a/c — *GL62*

(31 March	Total VAT on purchases	£152.20	Total VAT on sales SB7	£ 315.00

A fictitious entry in brackets shows total VAT *paid* to suppliers in March. Assuming a balance sheet was prepared as at 31 March the VAT owing to Customs and Excise would show in current liabilities. When payment is made it will be debited to VAT a/c – this is usually monthly or quarterly.

Credit notes will also have to have the VAT element taken into account. Supposing one-fifth of the goods by value were returned by Able & Co. as unsatisfactory, then they will be entitled to a credit note of one-fifth of the total invoice charge. For they have been charged VAT on all the goods but are only paying for four-fifths of them. This makes for complicated arithmetic as it also does if an additional charge is needed. Therefore, many firms now prefer to issue a credit note cancelling the invoice fully and then issue a new invoice for the correct sum.

Trading account will never include any VAT element.

Analysed (departmental) day book (with VAT)
When departmental analysis is shown, the appropriate proportion of VAT must *not* be added to the analysis; because, as already seen, the VAT element is not part of the firm's sales income. A suitable ruling (with one specimen entry) would be:

Sales day book

Date	*Customer*	*Invoice no.*	*Folio ref.*	*Dept A*	*Dept B*	*Net invoice*	*VAT*	*Total invoice*
1 July	Jones & Co.	17	SL 61	£69.55	£50.45	£120.00	£18.00	£138.00

The total of the net invoice column is the sum credited to sales, the total VAT column credited to VAT and the individual items in the end column debited to the customer in the usual way.

11 Control accounts

In an organization where the volume of accounting work is fairly light, it will not be necessary to break down the books further than the divisions already mentioned, i.e. a sales day book, a purchase day book, one or two returns and allowance books, a purchase ledger, a sales ledger. In the event of trial balance error, the checking process should not be too lengthy.

However, in a larger organization, some method is needed to simplify the checking procedure. This can be done by introducing a control account system, which limits the area of search.

In a normal buying/selling business (say, a wholesaler) the vast majority of entries are going to be those connected with sales and purchases documents. Under the book-keeping methods already proposed in this textbook, error tracing can be difficult – one entry could be in the cash book, the other in a personal account in the purchases or sales ledgers or in an expense account in the general ledger. However, a control account system for both purchase and sales ledgers will pinpoint in which one there are errors. Furthermore, if the accounting work warrants it, a control can be placed on a section of a ledger, e.g. sales A–K, Sales L–Z.

Preparing a control account

Imagine it has been decided to subdivide the sales ledger into A–K and L–Z. The various accounting books and ledgers will need to be rearranged so that all A–K entries can be grouped and total figures for A–K given (similarly with L–Z). Individual entries in day books/cash book are made in the correct column and postings made normally to personal accounts. However, *independently*, the totals are posted to the A–K control account. At the end of the accounting period (probably monthly), individual A–K balances are extracted, and in total this should agree with the control account total.

Example

The procedure is illustrated with just a few entries and only three personal accounts.

Transactions:

Credit sales	–	1 Jan. ABC £200; 15 Jan. CDE £130; 16 Jan. ABC £75; 23 Jan. CDE £30; 28 Jan. FGH £80.
Returns	–	13 Jan. from ABC £10; 24 Jan. from CDE £20.
Receipts	–	29 Jan. from ABC £185, £5 cash discount; 30 Jan. from CDE £100 on account.

A deliberate mistake is made in the individual posting of 15 Jan. item (encircled below).

Sales day book

	A–K	L–Z
	£	
1 Jan. ABC	200	
15 Jan. CDE	130	
16 Jan. ABC	75	
23 Jan. CDE	30	
28 Jan. FGH	80	
	£515	

Sales returns book

	£
13 Jan. ABC	10
24 Jan. CDE	20
	£30

Cash book

	Discounts allowed		*Receipts*	
	A–K	L–Z	A–K	L–Z
	£		£	
29 Jan. ABC	5		185	
30 Jan. CDE			100	
	£5		£285	

Sales ledger *ABC a/c*

	£		£
1 Jan. Sales	200	13 Jan. Returns	10
16 Jan. Sales	75	29 Jan. Cash/discount	190

CDE a/c

	£		£
15 Jan. Sales	(180)	24 Jan. Returns	20
23 Jan. Sales	30	30 Jan. Cash	100

FGH a/c

28 Jan. Sales	£80		

Sales ledger control a/c

	£		£
31 Jan. Total sales	515	31 Jan. Total returns	30
		31 Jan. Total cash	285
		31 Jan. Total discount	5
		31 Jan. Balance c/d	195
	£515		£515
1 Feb. Balance b/d	£195		

		Dr
Balances per sales ledger	ABC	75
	CDE	90
	FGH	80
		£245

Notes

1 Assuming the L–Z control agreed then it would only be necessary to check only the A–K section to find the error(s).
2 The control accounts are normally kept in the general ledger by a different person from the one operating the sales ledger – the latter will submit the list of individual balances to the former.
3 The system is capable of considerable expansion, e.g. a control system for each letter of the alphabet. Invariably it will be employed with a mechanized and computerized system.
4 The basic rule to remember is this: If an entry is made in the personal account then it must be in the control account – generally in the totals figure, though sometimes as an individual amount, e.g. a journalized correction of error. Thus, if an item referring to Blow & Co. is entered into Stowe & Co.'s account, then, when found, it has to be transferred from the A–K section to the L–Z section (both in the individual accounts *and* in the two controls).

Example

The following figures for the month of May 19–1 relate to the sales ledger of South & Son:

Totals of ledger balances

19–1	£
30 April debit	3,740
30 April credit	12
31 May debit	3,996
31 May credit	8
Sales for month	2,408
Sales returns	102
Cash received	1,974
Discount allowed	46
Bad debts written off	16

Required:

1 Prepare the sales ledger control account for May 19–1.

2 What conclusion do you draw from the control account you have prepared? (AEB)

Notes

1 A word of explanation is needed regarding the balances. Normally on sales ledgers there would be debit balances. However, a few individual accounts may be in credit, i.e. the supplier owes money to the customer: two reasons why this could arise are:

(a) Posting errors – supposing the invoice to the customer is debited to the wrong account, then when he pays he may be in credit until the correction is made.

(b) A payment on account before invoice charge is made – for example, a new customer may be asked to make a part or full payment on a cash with order basis.

Similarly on purchase ledger there will normally be credit balances but there are likely to be a few debit balances.

Answer

1 *Sales ledger control a/c May 19–1*

		£			£
30 April	Balance b/d	3,740	30 April	Balance b/d	12
31 May	Total sale	2,408	31 May	Total returns	102
			31 May	Total cash	1,974
			31 May	Total discount	46
			31 May	Bad debts w/o	16
			31 May	Balance (net) c/d	3,998
		£6,148			£6,148

2 There are obviously errors somewhere in the sales ledger as the net balance according to the totals of the individual accounts

should be £3,988 (£3,996 – £8). As the error is exactly £10 it is possibly just one item, though this is not certain.

The error could be either:

(a) an incorrect posting from a subsidiary book to a personal account; or
(b) an error in totalling in a subsidiary book; or
(c) an error in calculating/extracting balances in the personal accounts.

It must *not* be assumed that the error is in any one particular area.

Example

1 The following figures relating to the year 19–1 have been extracted from the books of Pylon, a trader. All sales and purchases have been entered in the accounts of customers and suppliers.

	£	
Sales ledger balances (debit) as at 1 January 19–1	15,728	DS
Bought ledger balances (debit) as at 1 January 19–1	240	DB
Bought ledger balances (credit) as at 1 January 19–1	13,480	CB
Returns outwards	790	DB
Returns inwards	648	CS
Cheques received from customers	164,349	CS
Cheques paid to suppliers	101,440	DB
Discounts allowed	3,942	CS
Discounts received	2,984	DB
Sales	158,423	DS
Purchases	102,481	CB
Cash paid in respect of a credit balance on a sales ledger account	26	DS
Bad debts written off in 19–1	2,490	CS
Credit balances on sales ledger accounts as at 31 December 19–1.	58	DS

You are required to prepare a sales ledger control account and a bought ledger control account for 19–1. (RSA II)

Notes

This is a more difficult question, as two control accounts are required. It is better to complete one first before tackling the other. To assist, the entries have been marked:

DS = DR Sales control; CS = CR Sales control;
DB = DR Bought control; CB = CR Bought control.

The first eleven items are straightforward if the rule is followed – what happens to individual items in the personal account happens to totals in the control accounts. Thus purchases are credited and returns outwards debited in bought ledger control a/c. *Re* the £26 – Pylon has paid a customer the credit balance owing to him.

Individual bad debts would have been written off by crediting customer, so sales control a/c is credited.

The credit balance on sales ledger at the end of the year is given, therefore the debit balance can be calculated. There is no debit balance on bought ledger at the end of the year.

Practice work

L. Renton keeps several sales ledgers and a purchases ledger. From the following details write up Renton's sales ledger no. 1 control account and the purchases ledger control account for the month of November 19–1.

19–1		£
1 Nov.	Balance of sales ledger no. 1 control account	2,670
	Balance of purchases ledger control account	4,140
30 Nov.	Sales for month	2,890
	Purchases for month	3,960
	Receipts from debtors	2,405
	Payments to creditors	3,920
	Discounts allowed	125
	Discounts received	195
	Sales returns	65
	Purchase returns	45
	Transfer of a debit balance from the purchases ledger to sales ledger no. 1	120

Notes

1 Tackle each control a/c separately.

2 The last item £120. This is a case where L. Renton deals with another business both as a buyer and a seller. Normally there would be a credit balance on purchase ledger and a debit balance on sales ledger, thus:

XYZ & Co. a/c (SL)

Balance	£200			

XYZ & Co. a/c (PL)

			Balance	£350

In that case the £200 owing by XYZ & Co. could be transferred to purchase ledger reducing amount due to XYZ & Co. to £150, and accordingly: sales control would be credited, and purchase control would be debited.

However, in this question there is a debit balance on purchase ledger (see above for possible reason), so it is necessary to credit purchase ledger and debit sales ledger – entries shown in brackets:

XYZ & Co. a/c (PL)

30 Nov.	Balance b/d	£120	(30 Nov.	transferred to S/L)	£120

	XYZ & Co. a/c	(SL)
(30 Nov. transferred from P/L £120)	30 Nov. Balance b/d (say)	£275

Therefore you must:
Dr sales control; Cr purchases control.
These are called **contra** entries.

(a) What is meant by a control or total account?
(b) What is it that a sales ledger control account seeks to control?
(c) From such of the following information as is required, prepare the sales ledger control for the month of April 19–1.

	£
Cheques received from debtors	11,270
Cash discounts allowed	940
Cash discounts received	290
Amounts owing by debtors 1 April 19–1	31,500
Goods sold on credit	15,100
Debtors cheques returned by their banks unpaid	1,100
Interest charged on debtors' overdue debts	150
Returns inwards	750
Returns outwards	810
Bad debts written off	190

Notes

(*c*) Cheques returned unpaid; that is, debtors' banks refused to pay the cheques as insufficient funds were available. When the individual debtors sent in cheques they would have been credited and the sum included in 'cheques received from debtors', which would be credited to sales control a/c.

Therefore, when the cheques are returned the individual debtors must be debited and sales control will likewise be debited.

Interest charged (an unusual thing) is debited to debtors, so the same happens in the control.

2 *Brown Ltd keeps a sales ledger in which there are* five *accounts. The balances on 1 May 19–1 were as follows:*

		£
	C. Edmunds Ltd	250
	J. Barton Co. Ltd	130
	Thissell Co. Ltd	200
	Lightfittings Ltd	190
	The Downs Co. Ltd	85
Sales during the month were as follows:		
5 May	J. Barton Co. Ltd	240
	Lightfittings Ltd	70
6 May	Thissell Co. Ltd	140
7 May	C. Edmunds Ltd	85

19 May	Thissell Co. Ltd	150
26 May	J. Barton Co. Ltd	250
28 May	Lightfittings Ltd	100

Returns during the month were as follows:

10 May	C. Edmunds Ltd	10
	Thissell Co. Ltd	20

All debtors settled their balances brought forward from April 19–1 (except The Downs Co. Ltd) on the 5 May 19–1, C. Edmunds Ltd and Thissell Co. Ltd taking 2% cash discount. On the 31 May it was decided to write off the amount owing by The Downs Co. Ltd.

Write up the accounts in the sales ledger and compile a control account to make the ledger self-balancing.

Extract a trial balance from the ledger. (LOND)

Notes

1 Write up the five personal accounts (remembering the opening debit balances) from the information given, i.e. sales, returns, receipts, discount.

2 Write off the sum owing by The Downs Co. Ltd, thus closing their account.

3 *Sales control a/c*

1 May Total balance b/d	31 May Total returns
31 May Total sales	31 May Total cash
	31 May Total discount
	31 May Bad debt w/o
	31 May Total balance c/d

It will be helpful to write up in rough a cash a/c with a discount column.

The total of the individual balances should equal the overall total balance in the control a/c.

12 Incomplete records and single-entry

Many small businesses do not maintain a full double-entry system. The records they keep will be adequate for the owners for day-to-day business operations, particularly if there are few credit transactions and limited fixed assets. An accountant is likely to be able to produce adequate accounts from the incomplete set of records the trader keeps. Thus details of receipts and payments plus two batches of invoices (one paid, one unpaid) will provide a foundation on which the accountant can work. The general term 'single-entry' is used to cover any book-keeping system which does not record fully the 'double' aspect of each transaction.

Questions on this subject are very common in examinations and cannot be dealt with unless the student understands certain basic accounting principles.

Net profit calculation from incomplete records

It was shown in Chapter 1 that net profit (after allowing for drawings) must be reflected in increased net assets. Thus, if net profit is £6,000, of which £2,900 is withdrawn by the owner, then the total net worth of the business (total assets *less* total liabilities) at the end of the period will be £3,100 greater than at the beginning of the period. Therefore, if only the net profit figure is needed, the calculation can be quite straightforward. Examination questions are unlikely to give a complete list of the values needed and some information may have to be deduced from data given.

Example

1 Maurice's balance sheet as at 31 December 19–1 was as follows:

Balance sheet as at 31 December 19–1

	£			£
Capital	12,400	Fixed assets		9,890
Creditors	3,210	Current assets:		
		Stock	3,200	
		Debtors	1,908	
		Bank	612	
				5,720
	£15,610			£15,610

The following information was extracted from Maurice's books at 31 December 19–2:

	£
Stock	3,900
Debtors	2,420
Bank	1,290
Creditors	3,800

During 19–2, Maurice drew £3,000 from the business for his own personal use.

Depreciation during 19–2 is to be provided for by charging 10% on the opening value of the fixed assets.

Required:

A calculation of Maurice's profit for 19–2. (RSA II)

Most textbooks in dealing with single-entry refer to the need to complete a 'statement of affairs'. The author thinks it better to use the term already known – balance sheet. The way to tackle this question is to commence writing up a balance sheet for 31 December 19–2. All the information (except one item) is given directly or indirectly.

Balance sheet 31 December 19–2

	£		£	£
Capital 1 Jan. 19–2	12,400	Fixed assets	9,890	
add Net profit for 19–2	? +	*less* Depreciation	989	8,901
	?			
		Current assets		
less Drawings	3,000–	Stock	3,900	
		Debtors	2,420	
		Bank	1,290	
			7,610	
		less Creditors	3,800	£ 3,810
	£12,711			£12,711

Notes

1 This style of balance sheet is preferable (refer to Chapter 3).

2 The net worth side is complete so the total £12,711 can be inserted on the left-hand side. Net profit can now be calculated: £12,400 – £3,000 = £9400. Therefore net profit is £12,711 – £9,400, i.e. £3,311. Alternatively, work backwards, changing the signs:

£12,711 + £3,000 – ? = £12,400
£15,711 – ? = £12,400
∴ ? = £3,311

Calculating credit purchases/sales

In another type of question it is necessary to produce a trading a/c but neither credit purchases nor sales are given.

However, sufficient other information is provided to enable these to be calculated. Remember that it is goods bought or sold in the period that are included in purchases/sales whether payment has been made or not. It is a common mistake in examinations to use the cash paid or received figures only.

The following information might for example be included in a question:

		1 Jan. 19–1	31 Dec. 19–1
Debtors		£2,960	£3,155
Creditors		£1,792	£1,570
Cash sales in a year	£5,240		
Received from debtors	£9,351		
Paid to creditors	£6,572		
Discount received	£98		
Bad debts written off	£100		

Method

Prepare total debtors and total creditors a/c – the equivalent of control a/cs. It is like imagining that you are only dealing with one debtor and one creditor.

Total debtors summary a/c

19–1		£	19–1		£
1 Jan.	Balance b/d	2,960	31 Dec.	Total receipts	9,351
31 Dec.	Total credit sales	(9,646)	31 Dec.	Bad debts w/o	100
			31 Dec.	Balances c/d	3,155
		12,606			12,606

Total creditors summary a/c

19–1		£	19–1		£
31 Dec.	Total payments	6,572	1 Jan.	Balances b/d	1,792
31 Dec.	Total discount	98	31 Dec.	Total purchases	(6,448)
31 Dec.	Balances c/d	1,570			
		£8,240			£8,240

Notes

1 Missing figures calculated (shown in brackets above).

2 In the trading a/c, cash sales would need to be shown as well as credit sales; cash sales would not be debited to a personal account because there is no debtor involved – they will not be in the above summary a/c.

Preparation of final accounts from incomplete data

This is a more formidable task. Even if you cannot immediately spot how to tackle the question fully, it is important to work out any figures that are likely to be needed. In the following example, even if the question did not stipulate parts (1) and (2) in the instructions, it would be necessary to calculate these figures because they will be needed for the balance sheet. Again, set out calculations clearly as shown below – this is a fairly difficult question and it is essential not to lose marks because the examiner cannot follow the script.

Example

2 *D. Quox, a retailer, did not keep proper books of account, but he was able to supply his accountant with the following information on 1 April 19–1:*

	£
Trade debtors	2,400
Bank	7,709
Cash	401
Fixtures and fittings	2,500
Freehold premises	15,500
Trade creditors	2,362
Stock	5,000

Further information was provided on transactions during the year ended 31 March 19–2:

	Cash	Bank		Cash	Bank
	£	£		£	£
Receipts from goods sold	28,450		Payments to suppliers of goods		17,500
Interest from private investment		108	Cash paid into bank	24,400	
Cash receipts paid into bank		24,400	Wage and salaries payments	2,900	
			Rates		590
			Advertising		140
			Insurance		150
			Drawings	150	4,500
			Repairs and decorations	10	375
			Carriage outwards	170	

Adjustments

(*a*) Fixtures and fittings were to be depreciated by 10% of the book value at the beginning of the year.
(*b*) Insurance had been paid for the period from 1 April 19–1 till 30 September 19–2.
(*c*) £150 was still owing for wages.
(*d*) Discounts allowed for the year were £1,564.
(*e*) At 31 March 19–1 the following balances were provided:

Stock	£4,700
Trade debtors	£2,386
Trade creditors	£4,562

Required:

1 A calculation of the capital of the business at 1 April 19–1.
2 A calculation of the cash and bank balances at 31 March 19–2.
3 A trading and profit and loss account for the year ended 31 March 19–2 and a balance sheet as at that date. (AEB)

Notes

1 Opening capital £33,510 – £2,362 = £31,148.
2 Cash balance £28,450 – £27,630 = £820. Bank balance £24,508 – £23,255 = £1,253.
3 **Gross profit calculation** Calculation of credit purchases and sales is required (see above example).

Total creditors summary a/c

	£		£
Payments	17,500	Opening balances	2,362
Closing balances	4,562	Purchases	(19,700)
	£22,062		£22,062

Total debtors summary a/c

	£		£
Opening balances	2,400	Receipts	28,450
Sales	(30,000)	Discounts allowed	1,564
		Closing balances	2,386
	£32,400		£32,400

Trading a/c can now be prepared.

Net profit calculation Note that £50 insurance is prepaid as £150 covers 18 months. (*a*) and (*c*) should present no difficulty. Note that repairs is £385 as there are both cash and cheque payments. Carriage outwards is a selling expense. The £108 interest is *not* an income item arising from business activities, so it must not be credited to profit and loss a/c.

Balance sheet The opening capital is known from (1), cash and bank from (2). Fixed assets – the only change is the depreciation, premises remain as in opening balances. The £108 interest is *additional* capital.

Practice work

3 On 1 August 19–1 S. Pea started his business with £10,000 in his bank account. After the end of his first year of trading he realized that because of his lack of book-keeping knowledge he was unable to prepare a balance sheet. S. Pea was, however, able to produce the following data for the year ended 31 July, 19–2:

	£
Furniture (cost £900)	800
Motor vehicles (cost £2,100)	1,600
Stock-in-trade	2,700
Creditors	3,300
Cash-in-hand	50
Balance at bank (overdrawn)	1,000
Debtors	1,600
Loan to B. Smith	200
Drawings	3,000

You are required to:

1 Ascertain S. Pea's profit or loss for the year ended 31 July, 19–2.

2 Prepare S. Pea's balance sheet as at 31 July 19–2, showing clearly all the totals and subtotals normally found in a balance sheet. (RSA I)

Notes

This is a Stage I example rather below O level standard. Proceed to draw up closing balance sheet (as already shown) and you will finish up with one missing figure, i.e. the profit and loss.

(a) Opening capital is £10,000.

(b) The only action regarding the two depreciation items is to show written down book values in balance sheet as usual, e.g. furniture £900 *less* depreciation £100 = £800.

(c) Overdraft is a current liability. Include the £200 loan to Smith as a current asset (it is hardly likely to be a long-term investment).

4 *L. Rank, a trader, does not keep complete books of account. His balance sheet at 1 April 19–1 was as follows:*

	£		£
Capital	9,800	Freehold property	6,000
Trade creditors	2,620	Furniture and fittings	600
Creditor for motor van	1,000	Motor van	1,200
		Stock	2,900
		Trade debtors	2,500
		Cash at bank	220
	13,420		13,420

On 31 March 19–2 the following balances were known: trade debtors £3,200, trade creditors £2,900, stock £3,600, cash at bank £425.

The following additional information was available:

(*i*) Rank won £1,400 in a competition which he paid as additional capital into the business and from which he paid the amount owing on the motor van.

(*ii*) Depreciation of £120 is to be allowed on the motor van and £30 on the fixtures and fittings.

(*iii*) Rank's drawings for private use during the year were £1,850.

Required:

Calculate the net profit for the year to 31 March 19–2 by compiling a balance sheet as at that date. (RSA I)

Notes

This is similar to earlier examples. Again, draft the closing balance sheet to find the missing piece of information. Note the £1,400 additional capital. Layout as follows:

	£
Capital 1 April	9,800
add Extra capital	1,400
	11,200
add Net profit	?
	?
less Drawings	1,850
	?

5 J. Bowman is a dentist. On 1 April 19–1 his assets were as follows:

	£
Premises	15,000
Furniture	1,000
Equipment	3,000
Debtor: National Health Service	2,000
Balance at bank	500

During the year ended 31 March 19–2 his cash records showed the following:

	£		£
Balance 1 April 19–1	500	Rates	500
Payments by private patients	1,500	Salaries	3,000
Receipts from National Health Service	9,500	Materials etc.	1,700
		Private expenses (drawings)	4,000
		New equipment	1,000
		Redecoration of house	800
		Balance	500
	11,500		11,500

Prepare an account to show the dentist's net income from his practice for the year ended 31 March 19–2 and a balance sheet on that date. Take into account the following:

(i) Work done for the National Health Service during the year valued at £10,300.
(ii) One-quarter of the redecoration to be charged to the practice; the rest applies to private rooms.
(iii) One-fifth of the rates to be charged to the practice.
(iv) Equipment costing £500 was scrapped during the year. (LOND)

Notes

This is the type of business which cannot produce a trading a/c (refer back to Chapter 6).

(*i*) Total income is NHS £10,300 + private practice £1,500 = £11,800 (remember it is value of service provided in year and not receipts that is counted as income). £1,500 receipts from private patients is however used because there are no debtors/creditors affecting these patients.

To calculate closing NHS debtors, prepare the usual total debtors summary.

Total debtors (NHS)

	£		£
Opening balances	2,000	Receipts	9,500
Total work done	10,300	Closing balances	(2,800)
	£12,300		£12,300

(*ii*) Confusion can arise about use of words 'private rooms' – this must be the non-surgery part of the property, so the division of the £800 should be £200 business expense, £600 drawings.

(*iii*) Similarly rates: £100 expense, £400 drawings.

(*iv*) Fixed assets. Equipment £3,000 + new equipment £1,000 *less* disposals £500 = £3,500. Presumably he replaced obsolete equipment which had no scrap value.

Remember to include the £500 cash-in-hand in the balance sheet opening capital – there were no creditors, so total the assets listed.

MC1 A trader prepares balance sheets at the beginning and end of the financial year which show:

1 January 19–1	Capital account	£20,000
31 December 19–1	Capital account	£30,000

During the year he received a legacy of £11,000, which he paid into the business bank account. His drawings for the year amounted to £8,000.

His profit for the year is

A *£7,000*
B *£8,000*
C *£10,000*
D *£13,000.* (AEB–S)

Answer to multiple-choice question:

MC1 **A.**

13 Receipts and payments accounts; income and expenditure accounts

So far in this book, the accounts of businesses have been dealt with; that is, enterprises that exist primarily for profit-making purposes. However, other organizations exist whose main functions are not trading or profit making. Examples are clubs, societies and associations, which are run on behalf of a group of persons with an interest in a particular type of activity (often social or athletic). The normal practice is for these organizations to appoint a committee to control activities with one or two of its members carrying out certain administrative and accounting functions (often on an unpaid basis). One of these officers would be the treasurer.

Receipts and payments accounts

A club or society finds it useful to maintain a receipts and payments record which is merely an extension of the normal cash book. Analysis columns are provided so that each income or expenditure item can be shown under a particular heading. This is really nothing more than a limited style of double-entry, for each analysis column replaces an income or expense ledger a/c. An example might be:

Blackheath Social Club

Receipts

Date	*Details*	*Subs*	*Bar*	*Misc*	*Total*

Payments

Date	*Details*	*Fees*	*Bar*	*General expenses*	*Misc.*	*Total*

If this record is maintained accurately, then a receipts and payments a/c can be prepared for the members which lists the totals of each classification of receipts and payments.

However, if just this statement is prepared, then there will be in many sets of circumstances important information lacking. This includes:

1 Assets owned by the club. It may have a considerable amount

of furniture, fittings, equipment, even if it does not own premises.

2 Money may be owing to the club (subscriptions in arrear, etc.) or by the club (e.g. suppliers of refreshments, affiliation fees).

3 Members do not know whether there is a surplus (profit) or loss from the year's activities – all they do know is the difference between cash in hand at the beginning and end of the year and how this came about. All they have been presented with is a flow-of-funds statement – where did all the money go (or come from)?

Income and expenditure accounts

An income and expenditure a/c is the non-profit-making organization's equivalent of the trader's trading and profit and loss a/cs. So it records income and expenditure arising in the year, whether payment has been made or not. In the same way, the business counts as income/expenditure its sales/purchase/expenses that relate to the current accounting period (refer back to Chapter 5, on adjustments).

Balance sheet

Again, there is one difference in the use of terms. The capital a/c is generally (but not always) referred to as the accumulated fund, because there is no owner's capital in the sense of a business investment on which it is hoped to have a financial yield.

Thus the same accounting principles apply as with a business, though there will be somewhat different procedures adopted. Also a different accounting policy may be adopted in certain cases; for example, though you may pursue a debtor who owes money, it is very doubtful if you will take any action about a member who leaves the club owing subscriptions.

Example 1

1 *From the following particulars prepare the income and expenditure account of the Barnhill Drama and Music Club for the year ended 31 December, 19–1 and its balance sheet as at that date:*

	£
Accumulated fund at 1 January, 19–1	368
Cash-in-hand	5
Cash at bank	92
Musical equipment	150

Drama equipment	190
Postages and stationery	12
Receipts from sale of tickets for performances	323
Hire of costumes for plays	33
Subscriptions received from members:	
For 19–1	99
For 19–2	4
Donations from supporters	15
Royalties paid on plays performed	21
Rent of hall for weekly meetings	76
Hire of theatre for special performances	230

Provision is to be made for the following matters which have not yet been passed through the books of the club:

1 Rent paid in advance amounts to £4.
2 Subscriptions still due for 19–1 amount to £6.
3 Depreciation at 10 per cent is to be written off the musical and drama equipment. (RSA I)

Answer

Prepare an income and expenditure account, remembering to include only items referring to 19–1, not 19–2.

Adjustments

1 Rent £76 – £4.
2 Subs income £99 + £6. The £6 will be a debtor in balance sheet; the £4 subscriptions paid *by members* in advance for 19–2 is a liability – club has received their cash for 19–2 but has not yet provided the services for that year. In other words, there is £4 included in the cash-in-hand at 31 December 19–1 which does not relate to 19–1 (but you cannot alter the cash balance).
3 Depreciation is $^1/_{10}$ of £340.

Income and expenditure a/c for year to 31 December 19–1

	£		£
Rent of hall	72	Subscription	105
Theatre hire	230	Donations	15
Costume hire	33	Tickets receipts	323
Royalties	21		
Postages and stationery	12		
Depreciation	34		
	402		
Surplus of income over expenditure	41		
	£443		£443

Balance sheet at 31 December 19–1

	£		£	
		Fixed assets		
Accumulated fund 1 Jan. 19–1	368	Musical equipment	150	
add Surplus for 19–1	41	*less* Depreciation	15	135
		Drama equipment	190	
		less Depreciation	19	171
				306
		Current assets		
		Rent in advance	4	
		Subscriptions owing	6	
		Cash in hand	5	
		Cash in bank	92	
			£107	
		less		
		Current liabilities		
		Subs in advance	4	103
	£409			£409

Example 2

2 The balance sheet of the Players Club at 31 December 19–1 is as follows:

	£	£		£
Accumulated fund		51,790	Investments at cost	25,300
Creditors			Furniture and equipment at cost	
Bar purchases	2,390		less depreciation	16,100
Expenses	140		Bar stocks	7,700
			Bank balance	5,220
		2,530		
		£54,320		£54,320

A summary of the club's bank account for 19–2 is as follows:

	£		£
Balance 1 Jan. 19–2	5,220	Bar purchases	46,110
Subscriptions received	6,930	Wages and salaries	8,930
Bar sales	61,120	Rent and rates	2,600
Interest on investments	2,170	General expenses	2,840
		Cost of new investment	13,500
		Balance 31 Dec. 19–2	1,460
	£75,440		£75,440

On 31 December 19–2 bar stocks were valued at £9,650, and

£2,610 was owing for bar supplies; £118 was owing for expenses; rates paid in advance amounted to £200.

There are no subscriptions in arrears or in advance; depreciation should be charged on the furniture and equipment at the rate of 10% per annum on the value at 31 December 19–1.

You are required to prepare:

(i) Bar trading account and income and expenditure account for 19–2 and

(ii) A balance sheet dated 31 December 19–2. (RSA II)

Answer

Although the club does not trade in the accepted business sense, there is a buying and selling operation in its bar and it wants to have its bar a/c shown separately. This bar a/c can either be shown separately or within the income and expenditure a/c itself. The former is probably easier for most students.

Bar a/c for 19–2

	£	£		£
Stock 1 January 19–2		7,700	Sales	61,120
Payments for goods	46,110			
less In respect of 19–1	2,390			
	43,720			
add Owing for 19–2	2,610	46,330		
		54,030		
less				
Stock 31 Dec 19–2		9,650		
		44,380		
Profit on bar c/d		16,740		
		£61,120		£61,120

Income and expenditure a/c for 19–2

	£	£		£
Wages/salaries		8,930	Bar profit	16,740
Rent and rates	2,600		Subscriptions	6,930
less Prepaid	200	2,400	Investment interest	2,170
General expenses	2,840			
less In respect of 19–1	140			
	2,700			
add Owing for 19–2	118	2,818		
Depreciation		1,610		
		£15,758		
Surplus		10,082		
		£25,840		£25,840

Balance sheet at 31 December 19–2

	£				£
Accumulated fund 1 Jan. 19–2		Furniture and equipment			14,490
	51,790	at cost *less* Depreciation			
add 19–2 Surplus	10,082				
		Investments at cost			38,800
		Current assets			
		Bar stocks		9,650	
		Rates prepared		200	
		Cash at bank		1,460	
		Less creditors		11,310	
		Bar supplies	2,610		
		Expenses	118	2,728	
					8,582
	£61,872				£61,872

Notes

1 If you have difficulty seeing how £46,330 for purchases is calculated, try the alternative of constructing a total creditors bar a/c (as if there were only one supplier). Thus:

Creditors bar a/c 19–2

	£		£
Payments	46,110	Balance owing from 19–1 b/d	2,390
		Purchases 19–2 ∴	(46,330)
	£48,720		£48,720

The missing figure has been calculated by deduction.

2 Similarly with expenses:

Total expense creditors a/c 19–2

	£		£
Payments in 19–2	2,840	Balance owing from 19–1 b/d	140
Balance owing for 19–2	118		
		Expense 19–2 ∴	(2,818)
	£2,958		£2,958

There is no need to show the detail in the accounts you prepare, but if you do not then your method of calculation must be clearly shown.

Practice work

On 1 Jan 19–1 a club owed its bar suppliers £650. During 19–1 it paid its suppliers £4,659, and at 31 December 19–1 it owed them £250. How much should be charged as purchases for 19–1?

On 1 January 19–2 the subscription position was as follows:

Owing by members for 19–1	£65
Paid in advance for 19–2	£155
Subscriptions received in 19–2	£2,650

At 31 December 19–2 members owed £130 but there were no payments in advance to be taken into account.

How much should be credited as subscription income for 19–2?

Refer back to the worked examples earlier in this chapter for assistance with the above questions.

3 *The Brownlee Tennis Club has 500 adult members paying £5 a year subscription, and 700 junior members paying £2 a year.*

1 January 19–2: 50 adults and 10 juniors had not paid their subscriptions for 19–1. 20 adults and 5 juniors had paid their 19–2 subscriptions in advance during December 19–1.

31 December 19–2: All members had paid their 19–1 arrears during 19–2. 40 adults and 14 juniors

had not paid their 19–2 subscriptions. 20 adults and 10 juniors had paid their subscriptions for 19–3 in advance during December 19–2.

Write up the club's subscription account in columnar form, using one column for adults and one for juniors. Show clearly the cash received during the year on account of each year 19–1, 19–2 and 19–3, and the amounts transferred to the income and expenditure account for the year ended 31 December 19–2. (LOND)

Notes

The clue is given in the first sentence. The transfers to income and expenditure for 19–2 must be £2,500 for adults and £1,400 for juniors. The opening entries are shown below.

Subscriptions a/c

19–2		*Adults*	*Juniors*	19–2		*Ad.*	*Jr.*
			£				
1 Jan.	Owing for 19–1	250	20	1 Jan.	In advance for 19–3	£100	£10
31 Dec.	19–2 subscriptions transferred to I&E a/c	2,500	1,400				

MC1 The balance on the accumulated fund of a club can be established at any date by:

A *preparing a balance sheet*
B *looking only at the bank statement*
C *preparing an income and expenditure account*
D *calculating the current balance on the subscription account.* (AEB–S)

4 On 31 December 19–2 you are given the following information regarding the Little Barr Social Club:

		£
1 January 19–2	Cash in bank	50
	Subscriptions 19–1 unpaid	30
	Subscriptions 19–2 in advance	20
	Rent unpaid for 19–1	20
During year ended 31 December 19–2	Subscriptions received (including 19–2 arrears and 19–3 in advance)	450
	Rent paid	140
	Lighting and heating paid	100
Annual dance	Sale of tickets	150
	Printing of tickets	2
	Hire of dance hall	20
	Band fee	20
	Prizes for events	10

31 December 19–2	Furniture repair account due and unpaid	30
	Electricity account due and unpaid	20
	Subscriptions 19–2 unpaid	10
	Subscriptions 19–3 received	15

Prepare:

(a) Receipts and payments account for the year ended 31 December 19–2.

(b) A subscription account and a dance account, showing clearly in each case the amount to be transferred to income and expenditure account.

(c) Income and expenditure account for the year ended 31 December 19–2.

(d) A short statement explaining the club's financial position.

NB A balance sheet is not required. (LOND)

Notes

(*a*) A summarized cash a/c is needed commencing with the £50 balance and including only actual receipts and payments, thus enabling you to calculate the closing balance (refer back to the example about the Players Club).

(*b*) Subscription account will commence as follows (√the figures are given; ? missing figure):

	£		£
1 Jan. Owing by members b/d	30	1 Jan. In advance b/d	20
31 Dec. In advance c/d	√	31 Dec. Total sub received	450
31 Dec. Transferred to I&E	?	31 Dec. Owing by members c/d	√

The dance a/c should give no trouble – all relevant items are listed under annual dance, surplus is transferred to I&E a/c.

(*c*) The income items for the income & expenditure a/c have just been calculated. Expenses are:

(i) Rent – of the £140 paid £20 is not for current year.

(ii) Lighting and heating. Increase the £100 by the £20 unpaid at 31 December 19–2 so that you get the amount referring to 19–2.

(iii) Furniture repair. The only item is the £30 relating to current year but unpaid.

(*d*) No balance sheet can be prepared as no information is given about assets (if any) other than cash. Previous year's results are not known so the only useful information is:

(i) Cash position 31 December compared with 1 January.

(ii) Reference to the financial results as shown in the income and expenditure a/c.

Answer to multiple-choice question:

MC1 **A.**

14 Partnerships

A business partnership is a firm with a minimum of two and a normal maximum of twenty partners. It is a very common form of business unit and it can be created with very little formality. The partners have unlimited liability for the debts of the business; that is, each partner is liable to the full extent of his personal property and possessions for all the debts of the partnership should the firm be unable to meet them.

The Partnership Act 1890 deals with partnership law, and it lays down rules to be followed in cases where the partners have made no clear arrangement to the contrary. The ones that are of interest to accounting students at this level are those in Section 24:

(a) Partners share profits and losses equally.
(b) No partner is entitled to a salary or interest on his capital.
(c) A partner *lending* money to the firm is entitled to interest at 5 per cent.
(d) No new partner may be introduced without agreement of the other partners.

In practice, partnerships are very likely to draw up a written agreement (or deed of partnership) setting out the arrangements under which the partnership will operate, and these may well supersede the provision of the Act.

Accounting records of partnerships

The basic books and accounts used by a sole trader will be kept in the same way by a partnership; the gross and net profits are calculated using the same principles. However, whereas with a sole trader the net profit is transferred to capital account, in a partnership the net profit will have to be divided amongst the partners in the agreed ratio. Furthermore, drawings may not be the same for each partner. Thus from this point there is some variation in the accounts kept.

Fixed capital accounts and current accounts

The normal procedure is to have two accounts for each partner. If there are just two or three partners only, columnar accounts can be used.

(a) A fixed capital a/c, which remains at the fixed original amount invested (plus additions for any new capital introduced).

(b) A current a/c, which will be credited with the appropriate share of profit, or debited if a loss and also debited with any drawings.

The current a/c should be regarded as an extension of the capital a/c; the two balances together represent the partners' claim on the business. A partnership need not keep separate current a/cs, in which case all additions or reductions are entered into capital a/c in the normal way.

Interest on capital and partnership salary

Sometimes the partnership deed provides for each partner to be credited with interest on his fixed capital. It is purely 'book-keeping interest', because there is no organization actually paying interest to each partner. The example below shows that the effect of crediting interest is merely to vary the division of profit.

In some businesses, one or more partners may be working full-time in the firm and others may not. It is reasonable in these cases to reward the former with a salary. Again, it is not treated in the books in the same way as payment to an employee is; for a partner is a self-employed person, and it is not possible to be both an employer and an employee in the same organization.

Profit and loss appropriation account

This is just an extension to the normal profit and loss a/c and all it contains are the entries dividing up the profits amongst the partners.

Example

High and Low enter into partnership on 1 January 19–1, agreeing to share profits in the ratio of High 3: Low 2. High invested £24,000 and Low £18,000. It was arranged that because Low would be doing more work in the business than High he should be credited with a salary of £1,500 before division of profits. It was also agreed that interest at 5% p.a. on capital should be allowed to each partner before division of profits. The net profit for the year 19–1 was £11,900. During the year, High had withdrawn £3,150 and Low £2,880. Show the appropriation a/c, the partners' capital and current a/cs, and an extract of the balance sheet at 31 December 19–1.

Profit and loss appropriation a/c for the year to 31 December 19–1

	£		£
Salary – Low	£1,500	Net profit b/d	11,900
Interest on capital			
High	1,200		
Low	900		
Profit share			
High 3/5	4,980		
Low 2/5	3,320		
	£11,900		£11,900

Capital a/c

		High	Low
19–1			
1 Jan.	Bank	£24,000	£18,000

Current a/cs

19–1		High	Low	19–1		High	Low
		£	£			£	£
31 Dec.	Drawings	3,150	2,880	31 Dec.	Salary		1,500
31 Dec.	Balances c/d	3,030	2,840		Interest on capital	1,200	900
					Profit share	4,980	3,320
		£6,180	£5,720			£6,180	£5,720
				19–2			
				1 Jan.	Balances b/d	3,030	2,840

Balance sheet 31 December 19–1

		£	£
Capital a/c	High	24,000	
	Low	18,000	42,000
Current a/c	*High*:		
	Interest	1,200	
	Profit share	4,980	
		6,180	
	Drawings	3,150	3,030
Current a/c	*Low*:		
	Salary	1,500	
	Interest	900	
	Profit share	3,320	
		5,720	
	Drawings	2,880	£2,840

Notes

1 Drawings must *not* be debited to appropriation a/c.

2 If in any year drawings exceeded the total credit balance available to a partner, then he would have a debit (overdrawn) balance carried down. The partnership agreement sometimes limits drawings, otherwise a partner who withdraws all his credit balance is securing an advantage over one who does not. Sometimes there is an interest on drawings arrangement, so that the individual partner suffers a penalty if he takes out for his own purposes more than his colleagues. The entry is: Dr current a/c, Cr profit and loss appropriation a/c.

Goodwill

An established on-going business is generally worth more than the amount of the net assets, because there is a 'value' attached to the fact that the business may have acquired a good reputation; even if ownership changes hands, customers are likely to continue dealing with the firm. The difference between the selling price and the book value of the business is called goodwill. The method of valuing goodwill varies from trade to trade – it may be directly related to the takings of the business, or it may just be an arbitrary figure agreed by the parties. The goodwill will be shown in the first place as an asset – it is neither a fixed nor a current one. The term 'intangible' is used to describe it. Goodwill is just a book-keeping entry in the accounts, it cannot be turned into cash until the business is sold again; even then it does not follow that the goodwill will be assessed at the same figure. Because of the intangible nature of goodwill it is often written off over a period of years out of profits, or even eliminated from the accounts entirely.

Example

The book value of a going concern is £30,500 (assets £35,000 less liabilities £4,500). The business is sold for £40,000 to J. Jones.

Notes

Alternative treatments

1 *Balance sheet of J. Jones at —*

	£		£
Capital	40,000	Goodwill	9,500
Creditors	4,500	Fixed current assets	35,000
	£44,500		£44,500

2 Capital shown as £30,500 and goodwill omitted entirely. In a sole-trader business there is really little point in showing the goodwill.

Introduction of a new partner

1 This can be a very straightforward operation if there is to be no goodwill adjustment, i.e. the new partner's cash payment will be credited to his capital a/c; the new profit-sharing ratio may be arranged so that he is penalized – he will then be making a goodwill payment indirectly.

Example
A and *B* (capital of each £40,000) share profits equally. *C* is admitted without any goodwill adjustment and contributes £40,000 capital. However, the new profit-sharing ratio is agreed as *A*3, *B*3, *C*2, for a period of three years, after which they will share equally.

2 *A* and *B*, equal partners, £40,000 capital each. *C* is admitted as equal partner, £40,000 capital invested plus £10,000 cash premium paid.

Journal entries (see Chapter 7) are required for this category of transaction (it can hardly go through a day book):

	Dr £	*Cr* £
Cash a/c	50,000	
C's capital a/c		40,000
A's current a/c		5,000
B's current a/c		5,000

being payment of capital and premium to the business by new partner.

A and *C* would then be free to withdraw the premium received. Alternatively, the £10,000 premium payment could be dealt with by direct payments to *A* and *C*, thus eliminating the need for any entries of the premium transaction.

3 A third possibility would be that *A* and *B*'s capital a/cs are increased by the creation of a goodwill a/c. A suitable profit-sharing arrangement would be made. The three could share equally, in which case there would be no immediate material gain to *A* and *B* unless interest on capital was to be paid.

Example
On admission of *C* as partner, a goodwill element of £10,000 is introduced into the business for the benefit of existing partners. This is credited to them in their profit-sharing ratio (in this case it is the same as the ratio of their capitals). The journal entries would be:

	Dr	Cr
	£	£
(a) Goodwill a/c	10,000	
Capital a/c *A*		5,000
Capital a/c *B*		5,000

(b) Another journal entry also needed debiting cash and crediting *C*'s capital a/c with £40,000.

Dissolution of partnership

Though this is unlikely to be included in examinations at this level, students should note that as with any other type of business unit, outside creditors must be paid first. Certain ones will get preference – for example, rates and taxes collectors, wages, mortgages (see Chapter 15, dealing with debentures). The remaining cash is shared between partners in the ratio of their capitals.

Final accounts of partnerships

Preparation of final accounts of sole traders was dealt with in Chapter 6. The same procedures are followed for a partnership.

Example

1 Gold and Silver are in partnership sharing profits in the ratio of 2:1 and the following trial balance was extracted from their books on 31 December 19–1:

	£	£
Capital: Gold		15,000
Silver		13,000
Purchases and sales	101,429	125,983
Debtors and creditors	9,955	8,240
Stock-in-trade 31 December 19–0	14,100	
Cash-in-hand	360	
Balance at bank	8,410	
General expenses	2,405	
Fixtures and fittings	2,500	
Discounts allowed and received	2,300	1,200
Drawings: Gold	3,400	
Silver	2,100	
Insurance	940	
Wages and salaries	12,980	
Lease of premises	1,800	
Lighting and heating	744	
	£163,423	£163,423

You are given the following additional information:

(*a*) Stock-in-trade 31 December 19–1, £16,400.

(*b*) Silver is to be credited with a salary of £2,900 per annum.

(*c*) The lease of the premises will expire on 31 December 19–2.

(*d*) Wages accrued 31 December 19–1 £420.

(*e*) Insurance paid in advance 31 December 19–1 £180.

(*f*) A provision for bad debts of £310 is required.

(*g*) Fixtures and fittings are to be depreciated at the rate of 10% per annum on the balance at the beginning of the year.

(*h*) Gold ordered goods for his own use at a cost of £415, and this amount was paid by the firm and debited to purchases.

Required:

A trading and profit and loss account for 19–1 and a balance sheet at 31 December 19–1. (RSA II)

This example is not worked in full, as solutions to several final accounts were given in Chapter 6. The following notes should help:

1 *Adjustments*

(*c*) This is an indirect instruction to depreciate. As lease expires 31 December 19–2, one-half is now to be written-off book value.

(*f*) Create a bad debts provision by debiting profit & loss a/c and showing the £310 as a deduction from debtors.

(*h*) This counts as drawings; so, as in earlier examples, reduce purchases and increase Gold's drawings.

2 *Appropriation account*

Silver's salary must be debited to appropriation a/c before profit is shared in the rates given.

3

Notice that there are no current a/cs, so items to be credited/debited to partners will appear in capital a/c.

Dealing with a loss

Supposing there had been a net loss in the above example. Silver would still be credited with his salary, then the loss would be borne in the 2:1 ratio, thus:

Profit and loss appropriation a/c

	£		£
Net loss (say)	2,131	Share of loss	
Salary – Silver	2,900	Gold	3,354
		Silver	1,677
	£5,031		£5,031

Thus the net loss of £2,131 is allocated:	Gold	– £3,354
	Silver	+ £1,223
		– £2,131

Practice work

1 *In the absence of any agreement to the contrary, how are profits and losses dealt with in a partnership?*

X and Y each have £70,000 capital invested in their business, and share profits and losses equally. Is there any point in allowing each of them 5% interest on capital?
NB If you cannot spot the answer immediately, try a practical example.)

2 *Towin and Hack are partners in a retail business sharing profits and losses equally. The following balances were extracted from their books at 30 April 19–2:*

	Dr	*Cr*
Fixed capital: Towin		10,000
Hack		5,000
Current accounts: Towin		2,000
Hack		3,000
Drawings: Towin	6,000	
Hack	4,000	
Partners' salaries: Towin	5,000	
Hack	7,000	
Shop fittings (cost £10,000)	6,500	
Stock at 1 May 19–1	3,300	
Wages of assistants	2,200	
Sales		52,000
Purchases	24,500	
Heating and lighting	800	
Rent and rates	6,200	
Debtors	1,100	
Creditors		880
Motor vans (cost £7,500)	5,000	
Bank	1,280	
	72,880	72,880

The following matters are to be taken into account:

(*a*) The partners are entitled to 5% interest on capital.
(*b*) Motor vans are to be depreciated at the rate of 20% and shop fittings at 10% both on written-down value.
(*c*) Stock at 30 April 19–2 was valued at £2,700.
(*d*) Rent and rates amounting to £500 have been paid in advance.

You are required to prepare a trading and profit and loss account and an appropriation account for the year ended 30 April 19–2 and a balance sheet as at that date. (JMB)

Notes

1 Calculation of gross and net profits should cause no particular difficulty – rent and rates have to be reduced (*d*).

2 Appropriation needs care. The partners have drawn their salaries in cash already – if they had not, the amounts could not have appeared in the trial balance. So their salaries are *not* credited to their current a/cs, merely debited to appropriation a/c. Then, after allowing them their interest on capital, the balance will be divided equally.

3 Set out the liability side of the balance sheet, as shown earlier in this chapter, remembering that each partner has a credit balance on current a/c to start with. Thus:

Towin Current a/c

Balance	£2,000
add Interest on capital	?
add Profit share	?
	?
less Drawings	?

(etc.)

Remember that if a partner is overdrawn, it will show up in the trial balance in the debit column. If this arises, show the balance sheet entry thus:

Jones Current a/c

Balance	£1,500	Dr
add Profit share	£6,000	
	£4,500	

15 Limited liability companies

The last hundred years have seen enormous increases in the size of business enterprise; this has demanded large amounts of capital investment. The limited liability company has proved the best medium for raising capital. The three main advantages are:

1 The liability of the individual shareholder (member) is **limited** to the amount he has agreed to invest. Sole traders and partnerships do not have limited liability, and therefore their owner(s) will have to use their non-business assets to meet the firm's debts in the event of financial difficulties.

2 Limited liability provides a convenient way for persons to invest either small or large sums.

3 With the exception of **private** limited companies (see below), it is a simple matter to transfer one's **shares** to another party.

A company has 'corporate personality' – it is a separate legal being which can contract, sue and be sued in its corporate name. Almost all companies are incorporated under the Companies Act with limited liability.

The basic principle is that the capital is subscribed by **shareholders** whilst management is in the hands of an elected **board of directors** who control the work of paid staff. Directors are often large shareholders (and in small companies may well be the only shareholders). A shareholder is, in effect, a part-owner and shares in the profits of the company according to the size and type of his holding. There is a clear division between ownership and control – the shareholder as such is not concerned with the management and the operational activities of the company.

Formation of a company

The Companies Act 1948 lays down the procedure for registration of a company, for raising capital and for commencing business. The Act exists to provide protection for both the prospective shareholders and the creditors; and the Department of Trade has extensive powers to investigate a company's affairs. A company's objects are defined by its **memorandum of association**; but, to avoid the possibility of legal action on the grounds the company is acting *ultra vires* (beyond its powers), the clause is drawn up widely (for example, a large grocery supermarket might use the words 'retailing generally' rather than 'retailing foodstuffs').

The **articles of association** are the internal regulations – laying down rights of shareholders, how directors are elected, how meetings are to be conducted, etc.

The nominal **capital** of a limited company is the amount the company has power to raise. Capital is divided into shares which may be in units of 25p, 50p, £1, etc. – the choice is purely a matter of convenience. Thus a company may have a nominal capital of £1 million divided into one million £1 units (or four million units at 25p each). The **issued capital** is the amount of share capital the company has actually issued. So, if the company referred to above has issued 900,000 £1 units, then the remainder (100,000) is **unissued** and may be issued for expansion later.

Furthermore, a company may not ask the shareholders to pay the full amount on issue. Thus, if the company had issued 900,000 £1 shares, 75p **called** and **paid up**, then the remaining 25p per share (i.e. £225,000) may be called by the company at any time; in the event of financial difficulty it would certainly be demanded. Once a share has been fully called and paid, there is no further liability on the individual shareholder.

Public and private companies

1 **Private** Membership limited to fifty excluding employees and ex-employees;* the articles must provide for some restriction on transfers of shares;* an invitation to the public to subscribe for share or loan capital is prohibited.

The advantage of the private company is that whilst providing limited liability it prevents outsiders obtaining a majority of the shares; thus it is a convenient type of unit for the family business. There are over 500,000 private companies in the United Kingdom.

2 **Public** Minimum number of members is seven; the company may advertise its shares publicly in order to raise capital (provided that the provisions of the Act are observed), and its shares may be transferred freely.

* These two provisions are no longer mandatory for new companies, nor for existing ones provided they change their Articles.

Capital of a joint stock company

Much of the country's large-scale business enterprise is in the hands of public limited companies. Obviously a limited company can only succeed if it is able to raise money successfully. This can be done in two ways.

1 Shares

Preference These shares pay a fixed rate of interest; and as preference shareholders take priority over ordinary shareholders, they attract the investor who is concerned with obtaining a steady interest rate with a limited risk (thus insurance companies, banks, etc. may invest surplus funds in good preference shares). As preference shareholders attach much importance to financial safety, it follows that only prosperous and well-established companies can successfully issue preference shares. If preference shares are cumulative (e.g. 10% £1 cumulative preference stock), this means that until preference shareholders are up to date with dividend payments no other category of shareholder is entitled to be paid a dividend. An example:

	Dividends paid		
	in 19–0	*in 19–1*	*in 19–2*
Cumulative pref.	*nil*	19–0	19–1 and 19–2
Ordinary	*nil*	*nil*	*entitled*

It is not until 19–2 that ordinary shareholders can be considered for a dividend – even there is no absolute right to it. It is the board of directors which recommends a dividend payment to the company's annual general meeting. The AGM can accept or reject the proposal, they cannot alter it, but would have to pass a vote of 'no confidence' to force the board's resignation.

Ordinary These shareholders take the major risks in a business, and their dividend payment depends on profits. In a good year they are likely to receive a better reward than the preference shareholders. Generally, ordinary shareholders posses all or the majority of the voting power in a company.

By far the majority of share capital in companies is in ordinary shares. The ratio between ordinary and preference is called the 'gearing'.

2 Loan capital

Debentures Sometimes a company raises money by borrowing; the lenders are not shareholders but **creditors**. The advantage of this is that in event of liquidation they are entitled to repayment before shareholders.

Debentures (written acknowledgements of loans) are issued and they are generally secured on the assets of the company, thus guaranteeing that holders are secured creditors (mortgage debentures). Fixed interest is paid, which is a charge against the company whether a profit is made or not. Generally, debentures are dated, e.g. 6% debenture stock 19–4–6 – this means that the company *may* redeem them (pay back) in 19–4 but *must* do so by 19–6. A company may decide to issue a dated debenture stock when it considers it will only require the capital for a limited number of years; for example, for a major redevelopment project. Mortgage debentures often attract large institutional investors (insurance companies, pension funds, trade unions) because of the additional security offered.

Accounts of limited companies

The full accounting provisions of the Companies Acts are outside the scope of this book. Gross and net profits can be calculated in the usual way; as with a partnership, an appropriation account will be prepared. However, there is one basic difference: whereas with a partnership the whole of the net profit will be divided amongst the partners in an agreed manner, this cannot be achieved with a company. The individual shareholder's portion of the profits is paid to him by way of an annual dividend (or sometimes in two instalments – interim and final).

A typical appropriation account, with explanatory notes, is given below (assume this is the first year of operations).

Appropiation a/c

19–1		£	19–1		£
31 Dec.	Corporation tax	35,600	31 Dec.	Net profit b/d	69,250
	Preliminary expenses	1,000			
	General reserve	5,000			
	Preference dividend	2,000			
	Ordinary dividend	15,000			
	Balance c/d	10,650			
		£69,250			£69,250
			19–2		
			1 Jan.	Balance b/d	10,650

Notes

1 Corporation tax is the company's equivalent of income tax. The

amount, subject to agreement with the Inland Revenue, will be paid at a later date.

2 When a company is formed, the legal and administrative costs involved (including those of the share issue) must not be written off as an expense. They are a fictitious asset, and normal practice is to write them off out of profits.

In this case, it is assumed that the preliminary expenses were £5,000 (see ledger a/c).

3 A reserve is an appropriation of profit as distinct from a provision (e.g. for depreciation) which is a charge against profits. Here it is nothing more than a book-keeping entry, because if a general reserve was not created the appropriation balance would be £15,650. Companies often feel that the creation of these reserve accounts gives shareholders confidence.

4 The dividend remains a current liability until the AGM approves the recommendation and then it will be paid.

5 Journal entries would be required for these appropriations.

Each one of these items will be credited to a separate general ledger a/c; only two of them are shown:

Preliminary expenses

19–1		19–1	
1 Jan. Eastern Bank	£5,000	31 Dec. Appropriation	£1,000

General reserve a/c

		31 Dec. Appropriation	£5,000

Balance sheet layout

Using the above appropriation account figures, a balance sheet extract might look like this:

Balance sheet of XYZ Ltd at 31 December 19–1

		Authorized	*Issued*
£1 Ordinary shares fully paid		300,000	200,000
10% £1 Preference shares fully paid		20,000	20,000
		320,000	220,000
Revenue reserves			
General reserve		5,000	
Balance on profit and loss Appropriation a/c		10,650	15,650
			235,650
8% Debenture stock 19–1			50,000
			£285,650

Notes

1 Full details of the capital structure must be given. The remaining £100,000 of ordinary shares can be issued if necessary, though existing share-holders cannot be *required* to subscribe. Sometimes a 'rights' issue is arranged, i.e. shareholders are offered preferential terms to take up further shares, any balance not taken up being issued through normal procedures.

2 Interests on debenture stock would have been debited in profit and loss account as this is a charge against profits.

Fixed and current assets and current liabilities would be presented as normally, with the preliminary expenses (and goodwill where appropriate) shown separately. In outline the following might be the layout:

		£	£
Preliminary expenses		5,000	
less Written off		1,000	4,000
Fixed assets		(say)	210,000
Current assets	(say)	135,750	
less Current liabilities (say)			
Corporation tax	35,600		
Preference dividend	2,000		
Ordinary dividend	15,000		
Creditors	11,500	64,100	71,650
			£285,650

Practice work

1 *The following trial balance was extracted from the books of Loach Ltd as on 31 December 19–1.*

	£	£
Share capital authorized and issued 50,000 ordinary shares of £1 each		50,000
Share premium		5,000
10% Debentures repayable 1990		10,000
Freehold land and buildings	40,000	
Fixtures and fittings at cost	15,000	
Provision for depreciation of fixtures and fittings as at 1 January 19–1		2,250
Bad debts	720	
Wages and salaries	15,200	
Rent and rates	2,200	
Purchases	65,200	
Sales		100,500
Stock-in-trade as at 1 January 19–1	14,100	
Directors' remuneration	13,000	
Debenture interest	500	
Debtors	20,010	
Creditors		14,900
Provision for doubtful debts as at 1 January 19–1		610
Balance at bank	1,400	
Profit and loss account balance at 1 January 19–1		4,070
	£187,330	£187,330

You are given the following additional information:

(*a*) Stock in trade 31 December 19–1 £17,900.

(*b*) Rates paid in advance 31 December 19–1, £130.

(*c*) Wages outstanding at 31 December 19–1 amounted to £560.

(*d*) Depreciation of fixtures and fittings is to be provided for at 5% per annum on cost.

(*e*) Provision for doubtful debts is to be reduced to £540.

(*f*) Provision for a dividend of 5p per share is to be made.

(*g*) Debenture interest for the half year to 31 December 19–1 was paid on 1 January 19–2.

(*h*) The directors propose to transfer £2,000 to general reserve.

You are asked to prepare a trading and profit and loss account for the year 19–1 and a balance sheet at 31 December 19–1. NB Ignore taxation. (RSA II)

Notes

1 *Adjustments*

(*d*) Note the separate depreciation provision a/c. Dr profit and loss £750; Cr depreciation provision £750, thus increasing it to £3,000.

Balance sheet: at cost	£15,000	
less Depreciation to date	£3,000	£12,000

(*e*) Note this is a reduction. So Cr profit and loss £70; balance sheet £20,010 *less* £540.

(*g*) £500 debenture interest is owing at 31 December, so charge £1,000 against profits.

2 Directors' remuneration means fees (not dividends), so charge against profits.

3 Remember that the appropriation a/c will start with a credit balance £4,070 from previous year, to which profit will be added. Only two items will be debited – (*f*) and (*h*).

4 Share premium £5,000. Shares have been issued at a premium, in this case it could have been the whole 50,000 issued at £1.10 each. The premium must not be used for ordinary revenue purposes and will show separately in the balance sheet.

5 Extract from balance sheet:

Authorized and issued share capital	
50,000 £1 ordinary shares fully paid	£50,000
Revenue reserves	
General reserve	£2,000
Profit and loss balance	?
Share premium	5,000
10% Debentures 1990	£10,000

2 The following information has been obtained from the books of Drayfuss Ltd:

Authorized capital	100,000	8% £1 preference shares
	400,000	50p ordinary shares
Profit and loss account balance 1 April 19–1 cr	£355,000	
General reserve	£105,000	
Issued capital	80,000	8% £1 preference shares (fully paid)
	250,000	50p ordinary shares (fully paid)
Net trading profit for the year to 31 March 19–2	£95,000	

The preference share interim dividend of 4% had been paid and the final dividend of 4% had been proposed by the directors.

No ordinary share interim dividend had been declared, but the directors proposed a final dividend of 15p per share.

The directors agreed to transfer to general reserve £150,000.

Required:

The profit and loss appropriation account for the year ended 31 March 19–2. (Ignore taxation.) (AEB)

Notes

1 Note that there is unissued capital – layout as in the balance sheet of XYZ Ltd earlier in this chapter.

2 Appropriation a/c

General reserve√	Balance b/f√
Preference shares	Net profit√
Interim dividend√	
Final dividend√	
Ordinary shares:	
Final dividend√	
Balance c/f√	

3 In the balance sheet the interim preference dividend would not be a creditor, as it was paid earlier in the year. Dividends are calculated on the issued capital figures not the authorized ones.

MC1 A company is registered with an authorized capital of £100,000. This means that £100,000 is
- **A** *the maximum which the company may use for the purchase of fixed capital items*
- **B** *the minimum amount of working capital permitted before the company starts trading*
- **C** *the value of shares which a company must issue before starting business*
- **D** *the maximum amount of capital which a company may raise now by the issue of shares.* (AEB–S)

MC2 The amount of share capital registered with the Registrar of Companies is known as
- **A** *fixed capital*
- **B** *uncalled capital*
- **C** *authorized capital*
- **D** *issued capital.* (AEB–S)

One or more responses may be correct in the following questions.

MC3 Which of the following items would be included in the current liabilities of a limited company?
- **1** *Proposed dividend*
- **2** *Bank overdraft*
- **3** *Retained profit.* (AEB–S)

MC4 Which of the following items should be debited to the appropriation account of a limited company?
- **1** *A transfer to general reserve*
- **2** *Debenture interest*
- **3** *Director's remuneration.* (AEB–S)

Answers to multiple-choice questions:

MC1 **D**; *MC2* **C**; *MC3* **1/2**; *MC4* **1.**

16 More about stock and its valuation

Chapter 2 dealt with stock valuation in the elementary way. Further work on the topic is now necessary.

In many businesses it is difficult if not impossible to identify the cost price of goods that have been sold or materials and components that have been used in manufacturing (see next chapter). For example, different batches will have been bought at different prices at different times from a number of suppliers. The administrative costs of trying to link a particular sale with a particular purchase will be so high in many businesses that it will not be worth while attempting it.

(Note that although financial statements have traditionally always been produced on 'historical' accounting, i.e. using the *cost prices* of assets, within the next decade there will be a general change to 'current cost' accounting, i.e. using *replacement costs* for assets. This will have the effect of reducing stated profits because of the drastic effects of inflation. However, this is outside the scope of this textbook.)

Stock valuation can therefore be a very complicated matter, particularly in manufacturing businesses. There are a number of methods used, and the individual firms will make its own decision, bearing in mind the advice of its accountants and auditors as well as decisions on the subject by the Inland Revenue.

Methods of valuation

1 Weighted average

	Quantity	*Price*	*Value*	*Total value to date*	*Total quantity to date*	*Average price*
March	6,000	40p	£2,400	£2,400	6,000	40p
April	10,000	50p	£5,000	£7,400	16,000	46.25p

Thus at the end of April all stock in hand would be valued at 46.25p (total £7,400 ÷ total quantity 16,000).

2 'First in, first out' (FIFO)

Here it is assumed that the oldest stock goes out first. Assume there was no purchase in May and the balance left at the end of May was 11,000. Therefore 5,000 (i.e. 16,000 – 11,000) have been used (or sold) and they are treated as coming from the March batch (leaving 1,000), which gives a stock valuation of:

1,000 @ 40p =	400
10,000 @ 50p =	5,000
11,000	£5,400

i.e. approximately 49.1p each.

3 'Last in, first out' (LIFO)

This is the reverse of 2. So the 11,000 left is valued thus:

5,000 @ 50p = 2,500 (5,000 used counted as April leaving another 5,000 of April in hand)

6,000 @ 40p =	2,400
11,000	£4,900

i.e. 44.5p approx. each.

Remember that the above methods are used only if it is not possible to match easily the 'issued' with a definite 'received'.

4 Replacement price

On occasions, because of a slump in the market, the firm can replace the articles from suppliers at a lower price than it paid originally. Thus, if goods bought at 25p by a business can, at stocktaking time, be bought at 21p, then this price will be used.

Practice work

1 *The financial year of a business ended on 30 June 19–1, but due to a shortage of available staff, stocktaking was not completed until the close of business 5 July 19–1, when the value of stock at cost price was £8,342.*

You are given the following information for the period 1 to 5 July 19–1:

Purchases, all of which were received before 5 July amounted to £725.

Sales, all of which were dispatched before 5 July amounted to £1,060.

Goods sold on 30 June for £185 were not dispatched until 8 July, but the sale had been entered in the books on 30 June.

The percentage of gross profit on all sales is 20%.
Required:

(*a*) *A statement showing the value of the stock at cost price on 30 June 19–1.*

(*b*) *An explanation of the two methods of valuing stock, last in, first out (LIFO), and first in, first out (FIFO), showing which will produce a higher figure of stock valuation in times of rising stock prices.* (AEB)

Notes

(*a*) First calculate the cost price of the 1–5 July sales also the £185 sale on 30 June (by deducting 20% in each case).

Then from the 5 July stock figure deduct the 1–5 July purchases of £725 because they were not in stock on 30 June.

Also deduct the 30 June sale (at cost price), because as the invoice went through on 30 June the value must not be included in stocktaking. Finally, add the sales (at cost price) 1–5 July, because if stocktaking had been done on its correct date these goods would have been included.

(*b*) If you cannot spot the answer immediately, use some fictitious figures:

June	Purchases	600 items at £1 each
July	Purchases	850 items at £1.30 each
June/July	Sales	1,200 items.

2 *A firm buys the following goods:*

1 March	250 of item *A* at 26p each
3 March	1,000 of item *B* at 71p each
10 March	550 of item *B* at 72p each
12 March	600 of item *A* at 25p each
15 March	750 of item *B* at 72p each

At 31 March unsold stock was 375 of item A, 1,330 of item B. Value the unsold stock using (a) FIFO; (b) LIFO; (c) 'weighted' average.

Notes

(*a*) FIFO. Unsold stock will be from latest purchases.

(*b*) LIFO. Unsold stock is the oldest stock. Is quantity greater than that purchased on first batch?

(*c*) Take item *A* first:

250 @ 26p = ?
600 @ 25p = ?
∴ 850 cost ?

17 Manufacturing accounts

In the case of businesses whose main activity is manufacturing, it will be necessary to be able to identify the costs incurred in actually making the finished goods. A manufacturing firm can be divided for our purposes into three parts:

1 Factory
2 Warehouse
3 Office.

At its simplest, expenditure incurred in each of these will be taken into account in the:

1 Manufacturing account
2 Trading account
3 Profit & loss account.

All expenditure can be allocated as follows:

Expenditure			
(a) Direct materials (b) Direct labour (c) Direct expenses	**Prime costs**	**Factory cost of production**	**Overall costs**
to which is added (d) Factory overhead or indirect expenses			
to which is added (e) Selling, distribution and administration costs			

Note that prime costs can be described as direct costs or variable costs – they increase more or less in line with output. Indirect costs can be described as fixed costs or oncosts – examples are factory rates, lighting and heating, machinery repairs, factory managerial salaries.

Basically, prime costs can be directly charged against a unit of production (e.g. a machine-operative's wages), whereas indirect costs are charged against a production unit as a whole.

Manufacturing account

Consider the accounting period 1 January to 31 December. On each date there will be partly finished goods (or work in progress). These have to be taken into account in arriving at total manufacturing costs, because it is the total cost of goods completed in any accounting period that has to be used. Valuation of work in progress is a complicated technical matter; for not only have 'materials consumed' and labour already employed to be counted, but also a proportion of other factory costs. A predetermined costing system will normally be used for this calculation, e.g. motor-cars awaiting spraying will be valued at a certain percentage of the normal production costs of that type of vehicle.

Good layout is extremely important in a manufacturing account, because otherwise, though the overall costs of manufacture may be shown, the breakdown into the component parts of the total costs will not.

A typical manufacturing account might look as follows:

Manufacturing a/c of XYZ Engineers Ltd for the year to 31 December 19–1

		£		£
Raw materials				
Opening stock		42,000	Costs of goods manufactured in 19–1 c/d	228,650
Purchases		85,000		
		127,000		
less Closing stock		39,500		
Cost of materials used		87,500		
Manufacturing wages		81,400		
Manufacturing power		10,750		
Prime cost		179,650		
Factory overheads:				
Depreciation of machinery	15,000			
Machine maintenance	5,260			
Rent/rates	29,000			
Other expenses	9,740	59,000		
		238,650		
Work in progress:				
1 Jan.	25,000			
31 Dec.	35,000	– 10,000		
		£228,650		£228,650

Notes

1 If WIP at the end of the period is less than that at the beginning of the period this will increase costs, unlike in the above example where they are reduced.

Remember that there will be no reference in the manufacturing account to finished goods.

2 In the trading account, cost of goods manufactured will replace purchases, because the manufacturer is making the goods himself. Note that some firms may 'buy in' finished goods for resale, because, for example, their own production capacity may not be great enough to cope with demand.

Trading a/c for the year to 31 December 19–1

		£		£
Opening stock of finished goods		85,000	Sales	402,600
Purchases of finished goods		50,000		
Cost of goods manufactured b/d		228,650		
		363,650		
less Closing stock of finished goods		71,500		
		292,150		
Warehouse wages and expenses		21,600		
Cost of goods sold		313,750		
Gross profit	c/d	88,850		
		£402,600		£402,600

The profit and loss account can be constructed in the usual manner.

Finding a manufacturing 'profit'

Some firms like to attempt to calculate a 'book-keeping profit or loss' for the factory operations of their businesses. They compare the 'factory costs' (in our example, £228,650) with the current market price at which similar goods could be bought. Supposing this was £270,000, then the manufacturing (theoretically) would be £41,350. But obviously the firm has not earned additional profit of this amount. Instead of the cost of goods being debited in trading account, the market price £270,000 is used, thus reducing gross profit by £41,350, to £47,500. This is compensated for by a credit in the profit and loss account for £41,350:

Profit & loss a/c

		£
	Manufacturing profit b/d	41,350
	Gross profit b/d	47,500
		£88,850

A worked example

Examining bodies sometimes introduce variations in the type of questions asked on a particular topic, like the following:

1 A. B. Box Co. Ltd manufactures metal boxes. Currently they have two different contracts to manufacture two different types of boxes, X and Y.

Box X was sold at the factory cost plus 25%.

Box Y was sold at the factory cost plus 10%.

During the year ended 31 March 19–2 the following costs were incurred:

	On box X contract	*On box Y contract*
	£	£
Commencing material stocks 1 April 19–1	7,000	10,500
Direct wages cost	15,000	19,500
Depreciation: plant and machinery	1,500	2,600
Wage costs: plant maintenance	750	1,100
Material purchases	16,150	27,500
Factory rent and other indirect expenses	1,100	2,000
Closing material stocks 31 March 19–2	6,500	9,200

The number of boxes produced during the year was: box *X* 7,000
box *Y* 27,000

Required:

1 Two distinct manufacturing accounts (which may be presented in columnar form) for the year ended 31 March 19–2, one for producing box X and the other for box Y, showing clearly:

(a) Prime cost.

(b) Factory cost of boxes completed.

There was no work in progress.

2 The projected unit selling price for each kind of box.

3 The gross profit for the year ended 31 March 19–2 if 6,000 of box X and 25,000 of box Y had been sold and the stocks remaining were valued at factory cost. (AEB)

Answer

Manufacturing a/c year to 31 March 19–2

1

			X		Y			X	Y
19–1			£		£	19		£	£
1 April	Opening stock of materials		7,000		10,500	31 March	factory cost of boxes transferred to Trading a/c	35,000	54,000
19–2									
31 May	Purchases		16,150		27,500				
			23,150		38,000				
	less Closing stocks		6,500		9,200				
	Materials used		16,650		28,800				
	Direct wages		15,000		19,500				
	Prime cost		31,650		48,300				
	Depreciation P&M	1,500		2,600					
	Maintenance wages	750		1,100					
	Factory rent, etc	1,100	3,350	2,000	5,700				
			£35,000		£54,000			£35,000	£54,000

2 Projected selling prices:

X CP $\frac{35,000}{7,000} = £5$

Profit 25% = £1.25

SP = £6.25

Y CP $\frac{54,000}{27,000} = £2$

Profit 10% = 0.20

SP = £2.20

3 Gross profits:

X 6,000 × £1.25 = £7,500

Y 25,000 × £0.20 = £5,000

As unsold stock is valued at factory cost, all we need to calculate is profit on items sold.

Practice work

MC1 A manufacturing account is drawn up by

A *firms engaged solely in the buying and selling of goods*
B *firms providing personal services*
C *non-trading organisations*
D *firms which make and sell articles.*

MC2 Work in progress at the beginning of the financial year is

A *included in the present year's production cost*
B *not included in the present year's production cost*
C *added to the cost of raw materials*
D *included in the previous year's production cost.*

One or more responses may be correct in the following question.

MC3 Which of the following items, appearing in the manufacturing account of a trader, form part of the prime cost of manufacture?

1 *Direct wages*
2 *Carriage inwards*
3 *Machine repairs.*

2 *J. Smallpiece is the owner of a factory. The following trial balance was extracted from his books on 31 March 19–2:*

	£ 000s	£ 000s
Capital J. Smallpiece 1 April 19–1		50
Loan from T. Smallpiece 1 April 19–1		20
Premises	50	
Machinery and plant at cost	20	
Furniture and fittings at cost	4	
Stocks: Finished goods	6	
Work in progress	*nil*	
Raw materials	5	
Debtors and creditors	8	6
Balance at bank and cash-in-hand	3	
Purchases of raw materials	44	
Sales of finished goods		100
Factory wages (direct)	20	
(indirect)	4	
Office salaries	3	
Office expenses	2	
Rates	4	
Machinery and plant maintenance	2	
Cleaning, etc.	4	
Provision for depreciation		
Machinery and plant		10
Furniture and fittings		3
Drawings	10	
	189	189

The following are to be taken into consideration:

(*a*) Stocks 31 March 19–2:

	£
Raw materials	4,000
Work in progress	1,000
Finished goods	7,000

(*b*) Cleaning and rates are to be charged in the proportion of ¾ to the factory, ¼ to the office.

(*c*) Interest on loan to be 10% per annum.

(*d*) Depreciation of machinery and plant by 10% on cost and furniture and fittings by 25% on cost.

Prepare a manufacturing account, trading account and profit and loss account for the year ended 31 March 19–2 and a balance sheet on that date. (RSA II)

Notes

Factory wages:	Direct . . . Prime cost
	Indirect . . . Factory overheads
Depreciation:	Plant . . . Factory overheads
	Furniture . . . Profit and Loss.

Answers to multiple-choice questions:

MC1 **D**; *MC2* **A**; *MC3* **1/2**.

18 Accounting concepts and conventions; interpretation and analysis of accounts

Accounting statements are used by various parties in addition to the business which has produced them. Thus a set of final accounts will be of interest to shareholders and would-be shareholders, to trade unions on behalf of employees, to the firm's bankers, to a prospective customer who is wondering whether the firm has the resources to tackle a large order, and to journalists specializing in business affairs. Therefore it is important that there is a reasonable degree of objectivity; and that the rules of measurement in the use are known and generally acceptable as applying to accounting records of business firms. These rules are often referred to as 'concepts'.

Concepts of accounting

1 Cost concept and going concern concept

It is convenient to take these together because they are linked. Cost concept means that the basis of valuation for accounting purposes is the cost price; this does not mean that the balance sheet just shows cost price of a particular asset throughout its life but that cost price will be the basis from which reductions are made – for example, depreciation. There may be special cases when the cost price is departed from – one is when the replacement price of stock is lower than cost price.

When accounts are prepared it is normally assumed that the business will be continuing to operate indefinitely. So unless there are special circumstances (e.g. business about to close down), it is not the saleable value of the assets that is taken into account but the cost to the firm. This is called the **going concern concept**. To take a practical example: premises may have been specially designed for a particular business operation, and as far as the accountant is concerned it is assumed that they will continue to be so used.

Business entity concept

This merely means that the business and its owner(s) are treated quite separately; so although Delworthy Stores is just Emma and Jennifer Watson trading under a business name, the accounts reflect transactions from the firm's point of view. If a partner takes £100 out of the business as drawings, it is the firm which gives (credit cash) and the partner (as an individual) who received. Similarly, if Harlow Nurseries Ltd is owned by two shareholders, Lucy and Matthew Abbott, the same principle applies.

3 Money measurement concept

The accounts can only show items which have a money value. To this extent they cannot tell you everything about a business; they cannot take into account personal or human factors like ability of staff, quality of management, and technology changes likely in the future which may materially affect a business (e.g. the invention of the silicon chip made the cheap hand-held calculator a possibility).

4 Realization concept and accruals (matching) concept

Again, these are dealt with together, as they are linked. **Realization concept** means that generally profit is regarded as being earned at the time the goods or services are provided for the customer. So the receipt of an order from a customer is no reason for introducing the profit element on the contract at that stage. Again, bad debts provision is made in the period in which the profit arises – if XYZ appears to be in financial trouble, then an allowance against the profit earned from the transaction should be made in the same accounting period.

Accruals concept was dealt with in detail in Chapter 5. Income relating to a particular period should be counted in that period (whether or not cash has been received). Similarly, expenses must be charged against profits when they arise.

In other words, the question to be put is, How much income would be earned and what expenditure would be incurred if all bills were settled immediately by all concerned and only covered the period in question – no arrears and no prepayments?

Conventions of accounting

A convention can be described as a practice that is generally accepted and applied. It is the way concepts are interpreted. The major accounting conventions that need to be known and understood are the following:

1 Materiality In each organization a decision is made about the level at which transactions will be recorded as assets. There can be no fixed rule about this. A very small builder may regard the purchase of several wheelbarrows as an item to be included in an equipment account; but a large firm of contractors may only count more expensive purchases (say, a concrete mixer) as a balance sheet item – articles like wheelbarrows would be treated as expenses and charged to profit and loss directly.

2 Conservatism Profit is not anticipated even if you feel certain that it will be made in the next accounting period. So unsold stock would not normally be valued at its anticipated selling price.

In general the accountant has tended to be cautious, to underestimate rather than overestimate.

3 Consistency Businesses want to compare the financial results of one year with another. So as far as possible the same methods should be used – there should be consistency in approach. If this is not possible then the change should be clearly indicated; for example, if the method of stock valuation changed from 'average' to FIFO or LIFO (see Chapter 16).

Analysis of final accounts

Many of the people referred to in the introduction to this chapter are likely to be interested in trying to assess the financial results of a business. Just taking the figures and commenting whether they are high or low is misleading and uninformative. For example, consider the following results of two firms both selling electrical goods as wholesalers:

	Firm A	*Firm B*
	£	£
Capital	500,000	5,000,000
Turnover	600,000	3,000,000
Net profit	60,000	150,000

Though firm *B* has made more profit, it cannot be said, purely from the limited information given, that it is more successful than firm *A*. Consider one point: though its capital is ten times that of firm *A*, profit is only two and a half times as much.

There are a number of useful accounting relationships that provide a guide to performance; some of these in any given set of circumstances, will prove helpful in analysis and interpretation. They can generally be expressed as percentages or ratios:

1 Gross profit in relation to sales

Sales £720,000; gross profit £36,000 – as a fraction this is 36/720 (having deleted the same number of noughts in each), *or* 1/20. So the ratio of gross profit to sales is this example is 1:20, or as a percentage it is $^1/_{20} \times 100 = 5\%$. This is the common way of expressing this and many other relationships.

2 Net profit in relation to sales

This is the same basic calculation as in **1** above. An example of the above two relationships:

		Year 1		*Year 2*	*Turnover*
		£		£	*increase*
Turnover		800,000		1,250,000	50%
Gross profit	(25%)	200,000	(20%)	250,000	
Net profit	(10%)	80,000	(8%)	100,000	

Management would want to look closely at the reasons for the falls in profit percentage (shown in parenthesis above). It could be as a result of overtime at higher rates, or additional machine maintenance and repair caused by increased usage of plant.

3 Rate of stock turnover

This was dealt with in Chapter 2. The calculation is either:

Sales (at cost price) ÷ average stock (at cost price), *or*

Sales ÷ average stock (at selling price).

Usually the former is used – answer must be the same, as like is being compared with like.

Note that a comparison between one business and another is valueless unless they are largely identical in size, structure, operation and location and dealing in the same class of goods. For example, consider fish against furniture!

4 Return on capital

Look back at the statistics in the first paragraph of this section (analysis of final accounts). The return on capital is the percentage that net profit bears to capital, i.e.

		Firm A	*Firm B*	
Net profit × 100 / Capital	=	£ 60,000 × 100 / £500,000	£150,000 / £5,000,000	× 100
	=	12%.	=	3%

Note that both calculations have been given for arithmetical purposes rather than for comparison. It would be necessary to know more about the structure of each business before attempting to draw too firm conclusions. It does not follow that firm *a* is four times as efficient, but certainly the owner(s) are getting a much better return on capital. If a limited company is involved, then it is usual to exclude any preference share capital in determining owner's capital (or equity interest). The reason for this is that preference shareholders receive a fixed dividend rate. Consider the following:

	£	
Ordinary share capital	1,000,000	
Preference share capital	100,000	
General reserve	75,000	
Profit & loss balance	25,000	£1,200,000
Net profit for year	£129,000	

Return on capital is $\frac{129,000}{1,100,000} \times 100 = 12\%$ approximately.

For revision, look back at Chapter 15 and note the significance of general reserve and profit and loss balance.

A useful guide to the level of return on capital is to compare it with those obtainable from building societies, banks, the Post Office, etc. However, allowance should be made for possible capital appreciation – your shareholding in XYZ Ltd may increase in value if the company thrives; if it is a public company (Chapter 15), you may be able to sell your shares at a profit.

The following balance sheet will be used to explain the accounting ratios and percentages given in points 5–9 below.

Balance sheet of Delworthy Stores (a partnership)

	£			£
Capital of partners	140,000	Fixed assets		
Balance of profit for year (after drawings)	60,000	Total		149,000
		Current assets		
		Stock	39,000	
		Debtors	20,000	
		Cash at bank	2,500	
		PO investment account	6,500	
			68,000	
		less Current liabilities		
		Creditors	17,000	51,000
	£200,000			£200,000

5 Liquid funds

This means cash-in-hand, cash at bank, or in an investment where cash is obtainable as of right within a short period (say, a maximum of one month). In the above example, total liquid funds amount to £9,000 as PO investment account can be realized quite quickly.

6 Current (or working capital) ratio

You will already know that working capital is the excess of current assets over current liabilities (Chapter 8). Current ratio expresses the relationship mathematically:

$$\frac{\text{Current assets}}{\text{Current liabilities}} \quad \frac{68}{17} = \frac{4}{1} = 4:1.$$

This is a very healthy situation, though the figure is only meaningful if there have been accurate valuations.

7 Acid-test ratio

Because it is difficult to be sure that unsold stock is likely to be sold within a reasonable period, a tougher test is sometimes used which excludes stock:

$$\frac{\text{Current assets } \textit{less} \text{ stock}}{\text{Current liabilities}} \quad \frac{29}{17} = \text{ratio } 1.7:1.$$

The above degree of accuracy (one decimal place) is good enough for this sort of relationship.

8 Average credit period

Selling on credit is the equivalent of lending money without interest. If debtors tend to be slow in settling, then the cash position may worsen materially. It is therefore necessary to watch this carefully.

Assuming that in the case of Delworthy Stores yearly turnover was £145,000 (approximately £12,000 monthly), then the average delay in settling accounts can be expressed mathematically:

$$\frac{\text{Debtors}}{\text{Monthly sales}} \quad \frac{20{,}000}{12{,}000} = 1\tfrac{2}{3} \text{ months} = 50 \text{ days approx.}$$

It would be more accurate to make this calculation several times a year (say, quarterly) because otherwise a distorted picture may be given, e.g. there may have been a drive to collect outstanding accounts near the end of the financial period.

9 Capital employed

There are several accounting meanings of this term, and in an examination any one will be accepted.

(a) Capital employed can be taken to mean the net worth of the business; that is, total assets less total liabilities. This of course is the same as owners' capital; in the present example it is £200,000.

(b) Alternatively, capital employed can be taken to mean total assets less debtors, so in this case it would be: £149,000 + £68,000 – £20,000 = £197,000. The reason for this is that the owners have provided £200,000 and the creditors £17,000 (total £217,000). However, if the creditors are in effect allowing Delworthy Stores to use their funds in the business, then as Delworthy Stores are allowing the debtors to use Delworthy funds in their businesses, £20,000 needs to be deducted from the £217,000 total assets.

Flow of funds

Consider the following summarized balance sheets:

			£
Year 1	Capital 1 Jan. 19–1		100,000
	Profit (*less* Drawings)		30,000
	Capital 31 Dec. 19–1		130,000
	Fixed assets		80,000
	Current assets		
	Cash	15,000	
	Other CAs	55,000	
	less	70,000	
	Creditors	20,000	50,000
			130,000
Year 2	Capital 1 Jan. 19–2		130,000
	Profit (*less* Drawings)		36,000
			166,000
	Fixed assets		90,000
	Current assets		
	Cash	14,000	
	Others	75,000	
		89,000	
	less		
	Creditors	13,000	76,000
			£166,000

Though 'retained' profit in year *2* was £36,000, the business actually had £1,000 less cash compared with year *1*. Here it is easy to see what has happened:

	£
Fixed assets have increased by	10,000
Other current assets have increased by	20,000
Creditors have reduced by	7,000
So net assets have increased by	£37,000

Thus the whole £36,000 profit has been 'used up', and in addition another £1,000 of cash was needed to provide the necessary funds.

Businesses nowadays produce these flow of funds statements to explain the changes in assets and liabilities in the year. Technically the accountant talks about 'sources of funds' and 'application of funds'.

A worked example

The following example with explanatory notes shows the way to tackle this sort of question.

1 The balance sheets of Rhymney Ltd at 31 December 19–1 and 31 December 19–2 were as follows:

		19–1		19–2
		£		£
Share capital		50,000		60,000
Profit and loss account		20,200		23,800
		70,200		83,800
Debentures		—		15,000
Current liabilities		9,220		8,720
		£79,420		£107,520
	£	£	£	£
Fixed assets				
Freehold land and buildings		50,000		75,000
Plant at cost	15,000		15,000	
less Depreciation	6,000		7,500	
		9,000		7,500
		59,000		82,500
Current assets				
Stock	9,200		14,000	
Debtors	7,220		10,000	
Bank	4,000		1,020	
		20,420		25,020
		£79,420		£107,520

NB No dividends were paid in 19–2 and none are proposed. You are required to prepare a flow of funds statement for 19–2. (RSA II)

Notes

Take the balances in the following groups:

1 *Funds become available if* credit balances have increased. Thus there are increases in share capital, in P&L balance ('retained' profits), debentures (a new credit balance). The cash generated by all these is applied somewhere.

Debit balances have decreased. Thus the reduction in cash of £2,980 provides funds as does depreciation – this £1,500 is a charge against profits without any cash being paid out.

2 *Application of these funds*

Debit balances (i.e. assets) – if these have increased, then the differences must have come from the funds sources. Therefore land and buildings, stock, and debtors come into this grouping. Debtors may be troublesome – think of them as 'customers paying us slower'.

Credit balances – similarly, if these have reduced, funds are used. So creditors are £500 less – we are paying them faster than we are buying from them.

Flow of funds statement

Sources of funds	£	£
Increase in share capital	10,000	
Increase in retained profits	3,600	
Issue of debentures	15,000	
Depreciation (reduction in assets)	1,500	
Reduction in bank balance	2,980	33,080
Application of these funds (or activities which require funds):		
Land and buildings	25,000	
Stock	4,800	
Debtors – extension of credit	2,780	
Creditors – prompter settlements	500	£33,080

Practice work

2 The balance sheet of J. Jones at 31 July 19–1 shows the following figures:

	£		£
Capital	30,400	Debtors	4,000
Cash-in-hand	6,000	Provision for bad debts	400
Fixed assets	22,600	Stock of finished goods	10,400
Creditors	4,000	Profit for year	2,600
Accruals	800		
Loan by J. Jones (Senior)	4,800		

You are required to:
(a) Prepare a balance sheet in vertical (narrative) form.
(b) State the amount of working capital.
(c) State the net worth of Jones's business all at 31 July, 19–1.
(RSA I)

Notes

Vertical balance sheet – proceed in the usual way except that the 'left-hand side' (capital, etc.) is shown underneath. Thus:

	£	£
Fixed assets		. . .
Current assets	. . .	
less Current liabilities	. . .	. . .
	Total	£ . . .
represented by		
Capital		. . .
add Net profit		. . .
Loan		. . .
	Total	£ . . .

Note that the £2,000 loan is treated as long-term, so it is a source of funds provided by an 'outsider'. Balance sheets sometimes carry the headings Employment of Funds and Sources of Funds. In our example it is the original capital of the owner plus the profits over the years that he has not withdrawn plus the money from J. Jones (Senior) that has provided the funds to enable the business to acquire the net assets.

3 *Rule a table as indicated below. Show how the following transactions would affect the amount of the net capital and the working capital of a business.*

Indicate in your table an increase by the sign + and a decrease by the sign 6. If there is no effect write the words 'No effect'.

(*a*) £500 was paid to trade creditors.
(*b*) Stock valued at £300 was sold on credit for £375.
(*c*) Furniture and fittings was depreciated by £250.
(*d*) Trade debtors totalling £120 were written off as bad debts.
(*e*) Office furniture valued in the books at £90 was sold for £75.

Item	*Effect on capital*	*Effect on working capital*
(a)		
(b)		
(etc.)		

(RSA I)

Note

It is suggested that, although not demanded by the examiner, the amounts, as well as the plus and minus signs, be inserted.

4 Using the information given in the following balance sheet, answer the questions below:

Balance sheet of Besson Bros Ltd as at 31 December 19–1

	£	£		£	£
Authorized capital			*Fixed assets*		
80,000 £1 ord. shares		80,000	Premises		80,000
20,000 10% preference shares		20,000	Machinery (cost)	60,000	
		£100,000	*less* Depreciation	20,000	
					40,000
					120,000
Issued capital			*Current assets*		
50,000 £1 ord. shares	50,000		Stock	26,250	
20,000 10% preference shares	20,000		Debtors	8,000	
		70,000	Cash	750	
					35,000
Reserves					
General reserve	40,000				
Profit and loss a/c	7,500				
		47,500			
Loan capital					
2,000 £10 Debentures (10%)		20,000			
Current liabilities					
Creditors	16,650				
Bank overdraft	850				
		17,500			
		£155,000			£155,000

(a) What is the value of the total assets?
(b) What is the current ratio?
(c) What is the amount of the proprietor's capital?
(d) What is the quick-asset ratio?
(e) Which item represents a long-term liability?
(f) Could Besson Bros issue any more preference shares? (JMB)

Notes

This should give no trouble. Remember that proprietors' capital means 'shareholders' capital in this case; it is the issued capital that is the operative value, plus reserves.

As you will know, debenture holders are creditors not shareholders (p. 173). Note also that the older-style balance sheet has been employed here with the current liabilities shown with the so-called 'liabilities' side – the term is confusing because shareholders are not creditors in the sense that outside claimants are (refer back to Business entity concept, p.191).

By drawing up a flow of funds statement at the end of 19–2 from the following balance sheets, show how it comes about that, despite making a loss of £2,100 in the year, the business succeeded in increasing its bank balance by £4,500.

19–1		*19–2*	*19–1*			*19–2*
£		£	£			£
36,000	Capital	36,300	15,000	Fixed assets at cost		19,500
4,800	Profit – Loss	2,100	4,500	Additions		8,400
40,800		34,200	19,500			27,900
4,500	Drawings	5,100	3,900	*less* Depreciation to date		5,400
36,300		29,100	15,600			22,500
3,000	Loan from finance company	6,900				
				Current assets		
			15,000	Stock	12,600	
			15,150	Debtors	9,900	
			—	Bank balance	3,000	
			30,150		25,500	
				less Current liabilities		
			4,950	Creditors	12,000	
			1,500	Overdraft	—	
						13,500
			23,700			
£39,300		£36,000	£39,300			£36,000

Notes

1 The sources of funds are: increases in loan and creditors; decreases in stock and debtors; and depreciation of £1,500 (£5,400 *less* £3,900). Total is £20,100.

2 This £20,100 was employed in: acquiring of new fixed assets; increases in balance at bank (£1,500 *plus* £3,000); drawings of

£5,100 (not the difference between 19–1 and 19–2, because this is not an asset account and there is no balance at beginning of the year).

3 If you still find it difficult to see why depreciation is a source of funds, consider what would happen if no depreciation was charged; loss would then be £1,500 less (i.e. £600). Then the £1,500 would be omitted as a source of funds (total would be £18,600) and, similarly, there would be a reduction in the other total. Or consider the following: the £8,400 in 'applications' less the £1,500 in 'funds' as above is the equivalent of £6,900 net in 'applications', which is the difference between the fixed assets balance of £22,500 and £15,600.

5 *The following balance sheets relate to a business run by T. Welldone:*

Balance sheet as at 31 December 19–1

	£			£
Capital	34,000	Fixed assets		20,000
Creditors	2,000	Current assets:		
		Stock	£4,000	
		Debtors	1,000	
		Bank	11,000	
				16,000
	36,000			36,000

Balance sheet as at 31 December 19–2

	£			£
Capital	40,000	Fixed assets		35,000
Loan	5,000	Current assets:		
Creditors	6,000	Stock	£13,000	
		Debtors	2,000	
		Bank	1,000	
				16,000
	51,000			51,000

Mr Welldone considers that he has not done well, as his money in the bank has fallen from £11,000 to £1,000, in spite of the fact that he has borrowed £5,000 and left £6,000 of his profit in the business.

(a) Set out a statement to show Mr Welldone how the money has been spent.

(b) Comment on Mr Welldone's judgement of his success based upon the balance in the bank. (LOND)

Notes

(*a*) This should now give no trouble.

(*b*) Is the business in a better position? Admittedly the fixed assets have increased appreciably, but working capital is less, liquid funds much less. It is the stock increase as well as the fixed assets purchases that have worsened the cash position to such an extent. The increase in stock buying accounts for the sharp increase in creditors. Mr Welldone is probably correct in his assessment but his explanation is inadequate.

Appendix: AEB syllabus 1981–82

The Associated Examination Board have kindly given permission for their new syllabus to be reproduced in full. They have asked that the following statement should be included:

> The following syllabus, which is reprinted with the permission of the Associated Examining Board, applies to the Ordinary Level examination in 1982. Students intending to enter for this O level Accounting syllabus in any subsequent year should first check with the Board that the syllabus details are still current.

Note that from 1982 calculators will be allowed for *Paper 2 only*, and candidates who do use calculators should still show all their workings so that marks may be earned even if there is an arithmetical mistake.

Normally the Board does not allow full question-papers to be reprinted in commercial publications, but on this occasion the author has been given special permission to do so. Some of the questions are also included at various points in the text and are marked (AEB–S).

The Associated Examining Board for the General Certificate of Education

Accounting – Ordinary Level Syllabus 1981–82

Aims of the syllabus

1 To give an understanding of accounting principles and methods.
2 To give an understanding of the usefulness and limitations of accounting.
3 To show the importance of accounting in the communication of financial information.

Objectives of the syllabus

Candidates will be required to demonstrate the following:

(a) a knowledge and understanding of accounting concepts and procedures;
(b) the ability to marshal and classify accounting data;
(c) the ability to communicate accounting information both verbally and numerically;
(d) the ability to synthesize and evaluate accounting information.

Examination structure

There will be two papers. Paper 1: 30% of the total marks; 1 hour 15 minutes. Paper 2: 70% of the total marks; 2 hours 30 minutes. Paper 1 is an objective test of 50 items. Paper 2 is in three sections.

Section A contains two questions based on computations. Both questions are compulsory.

Section B contains questions requiring an answer in continuous prose. Candidates are required to answer one question.

Section C contains two questions based on computations. Candidates are required to answer one question.

Both papers will test knowledge, comprehension, analysis and application. Paper 2 will also test the candidates' ability to use accounting techniques, their manipulative skills, their ability to synthesize knowledge and data supplied and their ability to evaluate accounting information.

Syllabus

1 The role of accounting

Accounting as a means of measurement, interpretation and communication of financial data.

Guidance notes Candidates will be expected to know the functions of accounting and its importance to the working of a business.

They should also be aware of some of the limitations of accounting information so that when they prepare, compare or comment on accounting statements they can appreciate the fact that such information cannot be taken in isolation in view of the fact that, for example, money, the basic unit of measurement, can change in value, government policies may change and firms' objectives may alter.

2 Accounting data

The double-entry book-keeping model. Sources of data on which accounting records are based. The recording of such data.

3 Verification of accounting records

Checks to establish the reliability of accounting records. The effects of errors. Correction of errors.

Guidance notes Candidates should be able to: prepare and comment on a bank reconciliation statement; prepare and understand the purpose of control accounts; prepare a trial balance; correct errors, including the use of suspense accounts; adjust profit or loss for an accounting period following the correction of errors.

Questions will not be set requiring correction of errors in sales and purchases ledger control accounts.

4 Periodic income measurement

The calculation and importance of different costs. The distinctions between (a) *direct and indirect costs* and (b) *fixed and variable costs.*
The distinction between revenue expenditure and capital expenditure.
Matching of costs and revenue.
Methods of valuing stock.
Bad debts and provisions for bad debts.
Provisions for and methods of calculation of depreciation for fixed assets.
Gross and net profit.
Profit as an increase in wealth (net assets).
The preparation of final accounts and balance sheets of sole traders, partnerships and non-commercial organizations.
The preparation and comprehension of the use of forecasted final accounts.

Guidance notes (a) Calculations of prime costs, overhead costs, factory cost including work in progress will be set.

(b) Candidates should be aware that there is a problem when measuring stock – the difference between the cost method and the net realizable value method.

They should also be aware of the methods of valuing stock on the basis of Last In, First Out (LIFO) and First In, First Out (FIFO) and the effect on profit of the application of these. They should also be able to carry out elementary calculations using both methods.

(c) Candidates will be expected to be able to calculate the straight line and the diminishing balance methods of depreciation and be aware of their limitations.

(d) Candidates should be able to prepare and comment on: manufacturing accounts; trading and profit and loss accounts; income and expenditure accounts; balance sheets.

They should be familiar with the different ways such information may be presented including vertical presentations.

(e) Candidates should be able to prepare accounts showing the distribution of profits between partners as agreed and where no agreement exists.

Questions will not be set involving the *calculation* of interest on drawings and interest on current accounts.

5 Incomplete records

The calculation of profits or losses and the preparation of accounting statements from incomplete records.

6 Limited liability companies

The meaning of limited liability. The division of ownership and control.

An introduction to the accounts of limited liability companies.

Guidance notes Candidates will be expected to have an understanding of authorized capital, issued capital, reserves and loan capital. They will be required to prepare simple appropriation accounts and balance sheets.

Candidates will be expected to know the basic differences between the balance sheets of limited liability companies and those of sole traders and partnerships. Knowledge of the accounting requirements of the Companies Acts is not required.

7 The analysis and interpretation of accounting statements

An elementary understanding of:

the interrelationship of cost of goods sold, gross profit, turnover;

fixed expenses, variable expenses;

the relationship between the components of a balance sheet;

the relationship of profit/loss to capital employed and to turnover, working capital, liquidity; rate of stock turnover.

Guidance notes Candidates will be expected to calculate simple relationships and comment on their significance.

The distinction between profitability and liquidity.

Limitations of accounting statements when assessing business performance.

Guidance note Candidates should be made aware of the fact that there are non-measurable items in the firm's assets such as location and quality of staff.

Paper 1; Section 1 (Questions 1–35)

In this section each item consists of a question or an incomplete statement followed by four suggested answers or completions. You are to select the most appropriate answer in each case.

1 *Which of the following concepts distinguishes and separates the business from the owner?*
A *The cost concept* **B** *The dual aspect concept* **C** *The business entity concept* **D** *The money measurement concept.*

2 *A credit balance on a sole trader's capital account is*
A *equal to the cash and bank balances of the business* **B** *the amount the sole trader owes the business* **C** *the difference between the assets and external liabilities of the business* **D** *equal to the value of the fixed assets of the business.*

3 *In the totalling of the purchases day book an error is made and the resulting total is £100 more than it should have been.*
Assuming that no other errors have been made, the effect of this error will be that the balance of the creditors' control account will be
A *£100 less than the net total of creditors' accounts* **B** *equal to the net total of creditors' accounts* **C** *£100 more than the net total of creditors' accounts* **D** *£200 more than the net total of creditors' accounts.*

4 *Which one of the following accounts would be found in the sales ledger?*
A *Sales* **B** *Returns inwards* **C** *E. Owen, a customer* **D** *H. Kean, a supplier.*

5 *A petty cash account has an imprest of £25. Currently the account has a debit balance of £3. How much cash is needed to restore the imprest?*
A *£3* **B** *£22* **C** *£25* **D** *£28.*

6 *A trader purchased goods from a supplier at a cost of £1,000. The terms stated on the invoice are trade discount 10% and cash discount 5% for payment within 7 days.*

If the trader pays within the 7 days period he will send the supplier a cheque for

A *£850* **B** *£855* **C** *£900* **D** *£950.*

7 *The bank column of your cash book shows a credit balance. This would appear in the balance sheet as a*

A *current asset* **B** *long term liability* **C** *current liability* **D** *fixed asset.*

8 *A suspense account can be used as a temporary measure to balance the*

A *trading and profit and loss account* **B** *manufacturing account* **C** *trial balance* **D** *appropriation account.*

9 *The accounting system of a firm of office equipment suppliers includes the use of the usual subsidiary books and three ledgers: sales, purchases and general. If a typewriter were purchased on credit for later resale, the subsidiary book and ledger(s) to be used for recording this transaction should be*

A *journal and general ledger* **B** *journal, general and purchases* **C** *purchases day book and general ledger* **D** *purchases day book, general and purchases ledgers.*

10 *Which one of the following is a 'nominal account'?*

A *Carriage outwards account* **B** *Machinery account* **C** *J. Smith's account* **D** *Drawings account.*

11 *The correct heading for an annual balance sheet is*

A *Balance Sheet as at 31 December* **B** *Balance Sheet for Year Ending 31 December* **C** *Balance Sheet for Period Ending 31 December* **D** *Balance Sheet for Year as at 31 December.*

12 *The amount of a firm's gross profit is calculated in*

A *the profit and loss account* **B** *the trading account* **C** *the balance sheet* **D** *the manufacturing account.*

13 *If a posting is made to the correct class of account and on the correct side, but in the wrong account, it is an error of*

A *omission* **B** *principle* **C** *commission* **D** *compensation.*

14 *A trial balance fails to agree by £40. Which one of the following errors, subsequently discovered, could have caused the disagreement?*

A *A sale of goods, £40, to A. Brown had been debited to B. Brown's account* **B** *A cheque for £20 received from C. Green had been debited to C. Grey's account* **C** *A machine sold for £40 had been credited to the* *sales account* **D** *A payment for rent £40 had been debited to the wages account.*

15 *A credit note received from a supplier would be recorded in*
A *the cash book* **B** *the journal* **C** *the returns inwards book*
D *the returns outwards book.*

16 *A manufacturing account is drawn up by*
A *firms engaged solely in the buying and selling of goods*
B *firms providing personal services* **C** *non-trading organizations*
D *firms which make and sell articles.*

17 *Working capital is described as*
A *fixed assets less current liabilities* **B** *total assets less current liabilities* **C** *current assets less current liabilities* **D** *current assets less capital.*

18 *Given the following details:*

Trade debtors, per trial balance	£10,000
Provision for bad debts	£ 1,000
Provision for discount allowed to debtors	5%

the amount shown as a current asset in the balance sheet is
A *£8,500* **B** *£8,550* **C** *£8,950* **D** *£9,000.*

19 *The cost of goods sold is arrived at by finding the*
A *amount of the purchases less returns* **B** *amount of the sales less returns* **C** *closing stock plus goods purchased* **D** *opening stock plus goods purchased less closing stock.*

20 *Which one of the following would result from a decrease in the provision for bad and doubtful debts?*
A *An increase in gross profit* **B** *A reduction in gross profit*
C *An increase in net profit* **D** *A reduction in net profit.*

21 *A trader prepares balance sheets at the beginning and end of the financial year which show*

1 January 1977	*Capital account £20,000*
31 December 1977	*Capital account £30,000*

During the year he received a legacy of £11,000 which he paid into the business bank account. His drawings for the year amounted to £8,000. His profit for the year is
A *£7,000* **B** *£8,000* **C** *£10,000* **D** *£13,000.*

22 *Using the straight line method, the annual depreciation at 20% for a motor-car which cost £2,000 now valued at £1,200 would be*
A *£160* **B** *£240* **C** *£400* **D** *£800.*

23 *The following information was available for a business in a particular year.*

Rate of turnover	5
Cost of goods sold	£30,000
Sales	£40,000
Closing stock	£ 5,000

By making appropriate use of the information, state which of the following was the opening stock for the business
A *£6,000* **B** *£7,000* **C** *£8,000* **D** *£11,000.*

24 *Which one of the following would increase the working capital of a sports shop?*
A *The purchase on credit of rugby balls* **B** *The receipt of cash from a debtor* **C** *The sale for cash of the delivery van* **D** *Payment by cheque to a creditor.*

25 *During the past year a firm's average stock has been £3,000 at cost, the mark-up on cost price has been 50% and sales have been £13,500.*
The firm's rate of stock turnover during the past year has been
A *4.5* **B** *3.0* **C** *2.25* **D** *1.5.*

26 *Which one of the following items would be classified as capital expenditure?*
A *Withdrawals of cash by the owner for his own use* **B** *Redecoration of existing premises* **C** *Breakdown-lorry purchased by a garage for its own use* **D** *Several cars for resale, purchased by a motor dealer.*

27 *The bank statement shows an overdraft of £300. A creditor has not presented a cheque for £75. When this is presented for payment, the bank balance will be*
A *£375* **B** *£225* **C** *£225 overdrawn* **D** *£375 overdrawn.*

28 *The purchaser of a business pays £15,000 for the business, taking over £12,000 worth of assets and £2,000 worth of liabilities. The value of the goodwill is*
A *£3,000* **B** *£5,000* **C** *£10,000* **D** *£12,000.*

29 *The balance on the accumulated fund of a club can be established at any date by*
A *preparing a balance sheet* **B** *looking only at the bank statement* **C** *preparing an income and expenditure account* **D** *calculating the current balance on the subscription account.*

30 *The following items appear in the balance sheet of a limited company:*

Authorized share capital	
200,000 £1 ordinary shares	*£200,000*
Issued share capital	
150,000 £1 ordinary shares – fully paid	*£150,000*

A dividend of 10% is declared.

The amount shown in the appropriation account as due to the ordinary shareholders for dividends is

A *£15,000* **B** *£20,000* **C** *£30,000* **D** *£35,000.*

31 *In a partnership, the profit and loss appropriation account shows how the net profit will be shared.*

Which one of the following items could also appear on the credit side of that account?

A *Interest on capital* **B** *Partners' capital* **C** *Interest on drawings* **D** *Partners' drawings.*

32 *The appropriation account of a limited company shows*

A *depreciation* **B** *directors' remuneration* **C** *debenture interest* **D** *proposed dividends.*

33 *A company is registered with an authorized capital of £100,000. This means that £100,000 is*

A *the maximum which the company may use for the purchase of fixed capital items* **B** *the minimum amount of working capital permitted before the company starts trading* **C** *the value of shares which a company must issue before starting business* **D** *the maximum amount of capital which a company may raise now by the issue of shares.*

34 *The amount of share capital registered with the Registrar of Companies is known as*

A *fixed capital* **B** *uncalled capital* **C** *authorized capital* **D** *issued capital.*

35 *To prepare the sales ledger accounts, the ledger clerk requires a copy of the*

A *customer's order* **B** *works' requisition* **C** *sales invoice* **D** *dispatch note.*

Paper 1; Section 2 (Questions 36–50)

In this section *one or more* of the options given may be correct. Select your answer by means of the following code:

A if 1, 2 and 3 are all correct
B if 1 and 2 only are correct
C if 1 only is correct
D if 3 only is correct.

Directions Summarized

A	B	C	D
1, 2, 3 all correct	1, 2 only correct	1 only correct	3 only correct

36 *Which of the following items would be included in the current liabilities of a limited company?*
1 *Proposed dividend* **2** *Bank overdraft* **3** *Retained profit.*

37 *Which of the following items appear in the purchases ledger control account?*
1 *Returns outwards* **2** *Cash payments to suppliers* **3** *Discount allowed.*

38 *In a retailer's books, which of the following entries could correctly record the purchase from a trading stamp organization of stamps for issue to customers?*
1 *Credit cash account – debit advertising account* **2** *Credit cash account – debit trading stamps account* **3** *Credit cash account – debit customer's account.*

39 *Which of the following items should be debited to the appropriation account of a limited company?*
1 *A transfer to general reserve* **2** *Debenture interest* **3** *Director's remuneration.*

40 *In the balance sheet of a limited company, which of the following items would it be appropriate to include under the heading 'Ordinary Shareholders' Interest in the Company'?*
1 *General reserve* **2** *Balance on profit and loss account*
3 *Share premium account.*

41 *At the end of a financial period the closing stock of finished goods (i.e. balance brought down) will be shown as a*
1 *current asset in the balance sheet* **2** *debit balance in the ledger account* **3** *credit entry in the profit and loss account.*

42 *Which of the following are books of original entry?*
1 *The cash book* **2** *The journal* **3** *The sales returns book.*

43 *In which of the following circumstances would it be appropriate for a supplier to issue a credit note? When he discovers that*
1 *a recent invoice to his customer had a total which was overstated*
2 *an item was omitted from a recent invoice sent to his customer*
3 *a recent invoice to his customer had been lost in the post.*

44 *Which of the following is/are the reason(s) for preparing a bank reconciliation statement?*
1 *To see if the bank has made any mistakes on the account*
2 *To see if there are any mistakes on the bank account in the books of the business* **3** *To see what cheques have not yet been paid by the bank.*

45 *In a limited company's balance sheet the 'Equity Shareholders' Interest' includes which of the following items?*

1 *Interim dividends paid to ordinary shareholders* **2** *Final dividends paid to preference shareholders* **3** *The nominal value of issued ordinary shares.*

46 *In a sole trader's business, total assets (fixed assets + current assets) less external liabilities equal*
1 *owner's capital* **2** *working capital* **3** *total assets employed.*

47 *Which of the following items, appearing in the manufacturing account of a trader, form part of the prime cost of manufacture?*
1 *Direct wages* **2** *Carriage inwards* **3** *Machine repairs.*

48 *Which of the following items would appear as capital expenditure in the books of a business selling private motor-cars?*
1 *The purchase of a lease of the offices* **2** *Solicitor's fees in preparing the transfer of the lease by the purchaser* **3** *Redecorating the interior of a showroom.*

49 *Which of the following items would appear as current assets in a balance sheet?*
1 *Closing stock* **2** *Cash at bank* **3** *Trade debtors.*

50 *The appropriation account of a limited company will contain details of*
1 *preference share dividend to be paid* **2** *ordinary share dividend to be paid* **3** *debenture interest to be paid.*

Paper 2 (2 hours 30 minutes allowed)

In Section A – answer **both** questions.
In Section B – answer **either** Question 3 **or** Question 4.
In Section C – answer **either** Question 5 **or** Question 6.

Marks are allocated as shown.
Where calculations are not required in a question, you should answer it in the answer book and not on the accounting sheets.
You must show **all** workings.

SECTION A (answer *both* questions)

Question 1 *(17 marks)*
The following balance sheet has been prepared by a sole trader, B. James, with inadequate book-keeping knowledge. He asks your advice.

Balance Sheet
from 1 August 1978 to 31 July 1979

	£		£	£
Drawings	2,160	Creditors	11,054	
Delivery van	3,730	Less debtors	3,720	7,334
Equipment and furniture	3,000			
Buildings	11,500	Capital	20,000	
Stock	5,092	Less loss	600	19,400
Cash	1,252			
	26,734			26,734

You make the following comments with which the trader agrees:

(i) provisions should be made for the depreciation of the delivery van of 20 per cent, equipment and furniture of 5 per cent and a provision for doubtful debts of 5 per cent of the debtors;

(ii) an adjustment is required for the fact that during the financial year the trader drew from stock, goods amounting to £400 for his own use;

(iii) an allowance should be made for expenses due, but unpaid, of £102 at 31 July 1979.

Required:

(a) James's balance sheet as at 31 July 1979 in suitable form, after the necessary adjustments have been made; (10 marks)

(b) an explanation of the significance of making a provision for depreciation on the delivery van, equipment and furniture. (7 marks)

Question 2 (18 marks)

White and Symons are trading in partnership with capitals of £12,000 for White and £6,000 for Symons.

The partners are entitled to interest on capital at 7 per cent per annum and the balance of profits or losses is shared on the basis of 2:1 respectively.

The following additional information is available as at 31 December 1979:

		£
Net profit for the year		6,846
Stock 31 December 1979		7,525
Trade debtors		8,691
Trade creditors		4,120
Drawings White		3,000
Drawings Symons		3,000
Cash and bank		4,896
Current account credit balances		
1 January 1979	White	1,500
	Symons	1,000

The following adjustments had been made before the net profit was calculated:

	£
Distribution expenses in arrears	400
Administrative expenses in advance	60

Required:

(a) for the year ended 31 December 1979:

(i) a profit and loss appropriation account;

(ii) partners' capital accounts;

(iii) partners' current accounts. (10 marks)

(b) an extract of the balance sheet as at 31 December 1979 showing the working capital; (3 marks)

(c) a comment on the significance of the amount of working capital of the partnership. (5 marks)

SECTION B (Answer *either* Question 3 or Question 4. Each question carries 15 marks)
Either

Question 3 (15 marks)

(a) What is meant by the term 'limited liability company'? (3 marks)

(b) What are the advantages and disadvantages of a sole trader compared with:

(i) a partnership

(ii) a limited company (12 marks)

Or

Question 4 (15 marks)

(a) *Name, and describe briefly, three distinct types of shares that a limited company may issue. (6 marks)*

(b) (i) What are the differences between a share and a debenture? (3 marks)

(ii) Why might a company decide to issue debentures rather than shares? (6 marks)

SECTION C (answer *either* Question 5 or Question 6. Each question carries 20 marks)
Either

Question 5 (20 marks)

(a) The following are some of the trading results of a business for the years ended 1978 and 1979:

Trading accounts

	1978	1979		1978	1979
	£	£		£	£
Cost of sales	20,000	24,000	Net sales	30,000	36,000

Profit and loss accounts

Fixed expenses	2,400	2,400			

Variable expenses amount to 10 per cent of net sales for both 1978 and 1979.

Required:

(a) (i) the completed trading and profit and loss accounts for both years; (6 marks)

(ii) assuming that in both years the average stock was £4,000, a calculation of the rate of stock turnover for both years; (6 marks)

(b) a discussion of the importance of the rate of stock turnover to a business. (8 marks)

or

Question 6 (20 marks)

The financial year of a business ended on 30 June 1979, but due to a shortage of staff available for stocktaking this was not completed until the close of business on 5 July 1979 when the value of stock at cost price was £8,342.

You are given the following information for the period 1 to 5 July 1979:

	£
Purchases, all of which were received before 5 July amounted to	725
Sales, all of which were dispatched before 5 July amounted to	1,060

Goods sold on 30 June for £185 were not dispatched until 8 July, but the sale had been entered in the books on 30 June. The percentage of gross profit on all sales is 20 per cent.

Required:

(a) a statement showing the value of the stock at cost price on 30 June 1979; (12 marks)

(b) an explanation of the two methods of valuing stock, Last In, First Out (LIFO) and First In, First Out (FIFO), showing which will produce a higher figure of stock valuation in times of rising stock prices. (8 marks)

Index

For a list of **Pan Study Aids** titles see page two of this book

edited by
S. E. Stiegeler BSc and Glyn Thomas BSc Econ
A Dictionary of Economics and Commerce
£1.50

An authoritative A–Z of the terms used internationally in the overlapping fields of theoretical economics and practical commerce.

A team of expert contributors provides a formal definition of each word or term, followed by an explanation of its underlying concepts and accompanied by appropriate illustrations. Special attention is paid to such new and rapidly expanding subjects as cost-benefit analysis and welfare economics. And the vocabularies of banking, accounting, insurance, stock exchanges, commodity dealing, shipping, transport and commercial law are all included.

Also available

John Daintith
A Dictionary of Physical Sciences £1.95

Stella E. Stiegeler
A Dictionary of Earth Sciences £1.95

E. A. Martin
A Dictionary of Life Sciences £1.95

K. G. Thomson and D. S. Bland
A Guide to Letter Writing £1